I0699031

Life Lessons
A New Love

Liz Hamilton

Liz Hamilton

Copyright © 2025 by Liz Hamilton

All rights reserved v. 1

Liz Hamilton supports the copyright of human authors. Thank you for reading an authorized edition of this book and for complying with the copyright laws by not reproducing, scanning, or distributing any part of it in any form without written permission from the author. You are supporting writers. For more copyright information, please write to lizhamilton@gmail.com.

This is a work of fiction. Names, characters, businesses, places, events, locales and incidents are either a product of the author's imagination or used in a fictitious manner. Any resemblance to actual persons, living or dead, or actual events is purely coincidental.

CONTENT WARNING: The main characters in this book endure an intense attack from their abductors. The female and male protagonist along with their other friends involved will seek counseling to work through their traumatic experience. If this may be triggering for you, please put your mental health first and proceed with caution or skip this story entirely.

Cover Design by Getcovers.

ebook edition ISBN-13: 979-8-9916755-3-6

Paperback ISBN-13: 979-8-9916755-4-3

Dedication

Dedicated to...
I dedicate this to my wonderful husband who has been my biggest supporter in my writing and self-publishing journey.

Contents

Also By

Also By Liz Hamilton:

Making New Friends: A New Beginning (ETC Mystery 1)
Daring to Dream: A New Destiny (ETC Mystery 3)

Prologue

Michelle

Eighteen-year-old Michelle Walters plodded down a hallway in her high school. Her brow pursed in frustration as she stopped at her locker. Michelle glanced to her left and right, and she watched several of her friends holding hands or sneaking a kiss from their boyfriends. Michelle longed to take part in similar activities. The persistent feeling of being left out filled her with a constant ache. She sighed as she pulled out her geometry textbook along with her workbook for chemistry in order to complete her homework for the evening. Because of her brother, she was a wallflower!

"It's not like I have anything else to do for the weekend," she said to herself. After shouldering her heavy backpack, she trudged down the hallway to go outside and wait for her brother, Jeff, to pick her up from school.

"Michelle," she heard her best friend, Jackie, call her name. Michelle stopped and waited for Jackie to catch up with her.

Michelle asked "How was the end of your day?" The two

girls sat together at lunch every day because they only had world history together.

"Good," Jackie answered. "Several of us are going over to Kristi's house tonight. Do you want to come?"

Michelle felt rebellious as she looked at Jackie. "I would love to come. What time?"

Jackie gazed at her for a moment, and she shifted her backpack to her other shoulder. "I'll come pick you up at six," Jackie answered. "Maybe Jeff won't be such a pain in the rear if he knows I am with you." Jackie knew how much her brother controlled her personal life.

"I'm going to tell him to mind his own business and leave me alone," Michelle said as her eyes sparked with excitement from her planned disobedience.

Jackie rolled her eyes. "Those are famous last words, and I've heard them before.. You know Jeff will ask if guys will be there, and he will probably not allow you to come. As much as you claim to stand up to him, you never do it."

Later that evening, Michelle finished putting on her mascara and she looked at herself in the mirror. She had a gift of applying makeup on herself. With so much time spent in her room, she often dealt with boredom. It frustrated her that she never got to go out and show it off to anyone.

As Michelle stepped out of her bedroom, she heard

someone coming up the steps.

"Hey, Muppet," her brother Jeff appeared at the top of the stairs. "Wow! Don't you look nice! Where are you going?"

"Jackie and I are going to Kristi's house to hang out tonight." Michelle said.

Jeff stood with a serious expression until he commented, "What time will you be home?"

"I don't know," Michelle hedged. "Maybe around eleven."

Rubbing his chin, Jeff paused a second time. "Who's going to be there?"

Michelle paused, without looking him in the eye, "Jackie, Kristi, Evelyn, and some other people."

"You're not going if guys will be there. Kristi's parents don't monitor when she has friends over at their house." A firm tone was in Jeff's voice, and Michelle sensed that he would not accept any argument from her.

"Come on, Jeff," Michelle pleaded with him, anyway. "I'm not even sure any guys are coming. And, Kristi's parents are fine. You never let me do anything!"

"It's my job to keep you safe, Muppet. You need to call and find out. If boys will be there, you are not!" Jeff stood with his legs slightly apart and he folded his arms across his chest.

Michelle groaned in annoyance as she stomped back to her room, saying, "I am the only seventeen-year-old on the planet who is not allowed anywhere near boys."

Chuckling, Jeff turned around to go back downstairs as he called out, "You better find me and tell me what you find out. One day, you will thank me for protecting you!"

"I seriously doubt it," she whispered. With tears in her eyes, Michelle trudged back into her room to call Jackie. She knew, deep down, that the evening would not turn out like she hoped and that she wouldn't be going any-where. She tightened her jaw and felt a tightness in her chest as she thought about how unfair her brother was. Ever since her younger years, Michelle's parents gave Jeff authority over her because of their age gap. As she grew, her parents left him to handle all issues involving boys. They were older and both of them had full-time jobs. Her parents felt uncomfortable with handling sensitive issues dealing with boys and sex. However, ever since she became a teenager, Jeff was hellbent on watching her every move.

***

Michelle wiped the tears away as resentment filled her at the thought of her plans being canceled. She sat in the mirror, staring at her reflection. All her life, she obeyed and did what her family asked her to do. Michelle learned early on how to please everyone in her family.

"Maybe just this once, I could do something for my-self," she whispered as she continued gazing at herself. A thought slowly began building until the tears dried up and a sparkle filled her gaze. Immediately, she sat straighter as the idea became larger. "I'm going to sneak out."

Michelle called Jackie to fill her in on what happened with Jeff. "I'm tired of listening to him. It's time for me to show him he can't control everything I do."

"I'll believe that when I see it. But I am curious. What are you going to do?" Jackie asked.

"I'm going to sneak out and you are going to help me."

Jackie released a nervous laugh. "Uh...how am I going to do that?"

Michelle said, "Come over here and I will tell you my plan."

Jackie sounded doubtful, but she told Michelle she was on the way. With her house only four blocks away, so she didn't have far to go. Jackie was the best friend she could count on to be there for her in any situation, and Michelle tried to be the same way with her.

Michelle waited at the front door, peering out the window, when she saw Jackie drive up. Jeff left a while ago, so she thought she could actually pull this off. "Come on." She pulled Jackie up the stairs to her room and shut the door.

Jackie said, "Do I want to really know what your plan is? I'm not sure this is a good idea and I'm afraid it's going to backfire on you."

"Don't worry! Jeff isn't here, and this will be easy." Michelle explained to Jackie how her dad installed a rope inside of the window seat under her window. The seat stored her toys and dolls as a child. Her dad came up with the plan in case of a fire and he installed a rope in all the bedrooms.

"There's no way this will work," Jackie said. "How are

you going to get down from the roof once we are out there?"

"I can climb down the trellis beside the living room window." Michelle's room sat right above the living area of their house and she felt strongly about the two of them using the trellis to climb down.

"Won't your parents see you?" Jackie asked.

"My mom closes the drapes as soon as it gets dark. Since it is November, the drapes are already pulled shut by this time of the night. And my dad is already snoring in his chair."

Jackie nodded, catching on to the idea. "I can go back out the front door and help you climb down. I will tell your mom that I forgot something in my car."

Michelle nodded her head as well. "Okay, that sounds like it might work." She pulled the rope out of the window seat and lifted the window. Michelle thanked her lucky stars that screens were not attached to the windows on the second floor. Her father removed them a few months ago, and he never put them back. When she leaned out and saw the steep slope of the roof, her heart began palpitating. Michelle might not have the guts to do this after all.

"I'm going outside and I will walk around," Jackie said. Michelle nodded, and she waited until she saw Jackie standing below the window.

Michelle pushed both feet out of the window before she moved her torso. Once out there, Michelle remained seated as fear crawled up every part of her body. She thought of how she might slip, fall, and wind up in the hospital. Just as she moved to stand up, she heard a familiar sound. "No, no, no. Not now," she murmured. Her brother's truck appeared and he turned into the driveway.

She heard Jackie and Jeff talking. Eavesdropping on the conversation, she listened as Jackie attempted to detain him from seeing her. Michelle crawled to hoist herself back through the window when she heard Jeff's voice. "Michelle, what are you doing?" He stood beside Jackie. Jackie said nothing to him, but she waited beside him as if she wished to flee.

"Uhh.." Michelle tried to come up with an excuse. "I decided to see the perspective outside while sitting on the roof." Then she mumbled, "The one time I try to sneak out, I get caught."

Jeff gestured at her. "Go inside." He looked at Jackie. "You come in with me." Jackie didn't argue with him and her eyes flashed her apology as she looked up at Michelle.

A few minutes later, with Michelle safely back in her room again, Jeff knocked on the door. "Michelle, let me inside."

Michelle shuffled her feet slightly before opening the door. Her stomach hardened at the sound of his voice.

Jeff moved inside. Jackie remained behind him, but she said nothing. He stood with his feet apart and he folded his arms over his chest. "Tell me the truth."

"This is your fault," Michelle began. "You wouldn't let me go out, so I snuck out to go, anyway. Why are you back when you just left?"

Jeff frowned at her, without speaking, his arms still crossed. Finally, he said, "I came to take you out for ice cream so you will see I'm not a monster. I'm not even sure how to start with this."

"I am," Michelle rolled her eyes. "And, I'm not seven. Ice cream isn't going to cure this problem. I'm going down to talk to mom. You need to give me more freedom and it needs to start now." Michelle rushed down the stairs with Jeff arguing with her and Jackie on her heels.

As predicted, her dad snored in his chair and he didn't even move when they entered the room. Her mother sat with the remote as she watched television. When Michelle asked to speak with her mom, she turned it off. Jeff began to interrupt and Michelle's mom held up her hand. "Let Michelle talk first and then you can have a turn."

Michelle explained how frustrated she felt that Jeff stopped her every weekend from doing anything fun. "Tonight I wanted to hang out with my friends at Kristi's house, but Jeff said no because guys are also going to be there."

"She tried to sneak out her window when I drove up. I'm glad I did. She could have been hurt," Jeff said, thinking his mom would agree with him when he told her.

"The only reason I did that is because you never let me go anywhere." Michelle said.

"Muppet, I'm doing it to keep you safe." Michelle could see that this conversation did nothing to sway Jeff's opinion. "I also know what guys are like at this age. They only want one thing from girls. I don't want anything happening to you, and it's my job to save you from it."

Michelle held up her hand. "You need to stop calling me that. I'm not five years old anymore. And you need to stop trying to save me from bad things happening. Mom, I just wish to be a normal teenager and I want to be able to go to a friend's house."

"Okay." Her mom said. Michelle's whole body froze and her mouth dropped open when her mother agreed with her. "I'm not happy that you were sneaking out. That is never to happen again, but I think I can see why you did it."

Her mom turned to Jeff and used his given name. "Jefferson, we've counted on you to help look out for your sister, but she is almost eighteen now. I see now that we gave you way too much control over her life. From now on, you and I will listen to her and come to a compromise about what is safe for her to do. I appreciate how much you care about her, but it's time for you to let go. She's going to college soon and we need to let her make choices for herself."

Jeff's face looked like a storm cloud, but seeing the look on his mom's face, he only said, "I don't trust any of the guys that will be there tonight. That's why I told her not to go."

"Jeff, I understand why you worry, but you've taken it way too far," Michelle argued. "What's wrong with going and being with my friends at someone's house? Her parents will be there. I know you think they let kids do anything, but it's not true. You know Kristi! She's not wild!"

Michelle's mom intervened. "You make a valid point.

Jeff, it's time to let your sister experience the world. How will she ever learn decisions that are wrong unless she experiences them?" Her mom looked at Michelle, "I'm saying you can go tonight, but you need to be home by ten thirty."

Michelle looked at her watch and saw that it was seven o'clock. She wondered what dream she was in. She bounced several times on her toes. "Really? You're going to let me go?"

"Yes, but if you break curfew, you can count on sitting in your room next weekend." Her mom's face filled with consternation.

"Yes ma'am, I understand." Michelle squealed and hugged her mother tightly. "Thank you, Mom!" She rushed over to Jackie and hugged her. "Let's go before she changes her mind." When she glanced at Jeff, she noticed the unhappiness on his face, but he didn't argue with their mother. Michelle wished she had spoken to her mother sooner.

Ten minutes later, Michelle stepped out of Jackie's car. She followed her friend up the sidewalk to Kristi's house. There were a few cars parked in her driveway and along the street, but it didn't look like too many people.

Kristi opened the door and her face lit up when she saw Michelle. "I'm so glad you could come. How did you convince your brother?"

"She ratted him out to her mom. Her mom listened to her and said she could come." Jackie said. She gave Michelle a side hug. "I've never been so proud of my best friend. She conquered the *general*." Jackie called Jeff that name because of his rigid rules.

Kristi laughed and said, "Come in. We're just getting ready to watch a movie and my dad went to pick up several pizzas."

Emotions that couldn't be described rushed through Michelle at the moment. She walked into Kristi's den and noticed Evelyn, Leslie, and Jennifer. There weren't any guys at the moment, so maybe she could turn off Jeff's voice in her head that he didn't trust any of them. Just as the thought left her mind, the doorbell rang. Kristi opened it to see Derrick, Joey, Matthew, and Aaron walk inside. Of all the guys to show up, they were the calmest and safest. Matthew and Aaron participated in the National Honor Society with Michelle and Evelyn. Derrick's and Joey's families belonged to her church.

As the guys came in and joined them, Michelle felt the smile on her face grow larger from the fact that she participated in the same things her friends got to do on a Friday night. Her lungs expanded with full, deep breaths. "Thanks, Mom," she whispered to herself.

The evening flew by quickly. The group watched two movies and ate pizza and other snacks. Some of the wilder guys who said they would come never showed up. They watched a comedy which had everyone in stitches. The second movie, thriller, had them hiding under blankets. The group waited until Kristi's parents had retired upstairs to watch it. Michelle held a blanket up over her eyes at one point, but she wouldn't trade the terrifying moments for anything in the world. It was wonderful to be a normal teenager watching a scary movie with other teenagers.

***

Danny

Seventeen-year-old Danny Peterson strolled down one hallway in his high school. He was walking toward his locker.

"Hey, man," Tim shouted at him. "Good luck at the game!"

Danny tipped his chin at Tim, but he didn't remove his arm from around the girl, who remained glued to his side. "Thanks, man!" Danny knew it was expected of him, so he pretended like he really cared about Rachel Jameson.

Rachel crooned, "You're going to win the final touchdown! I'm sure of it." She shot a hateful look across the hall at another girl named Mary. Mary dated Danny last year, and her face filled with envy at the sight of Rachel walking with Danny.

He pushed down the irritation rising within him from the squeaky sound of her voice, Danny pulled away to open his locker as he said, "Thanks, Rachel."

Rachel was a forward and pushy girl. Therefore, she pressed herself against him as she pulled him in for a kiss. Danny wanted to groan from the lack of desire that he felt for Rachel. However, she would take it as an invitation.

Mary brushed her shoulder against Danny's as she passed by after leaving her locker. Batting her eyelashes coyly at him, she said, "Hey, Danny. Good luck tonight! Maybe you can save a dance for me!"

Their high school held a dance once a month after one of the football games in the school gym. Danny really didn't want to go, but he believed he had no choice. Being the son of the head coach, as well as the star quarterback of the team, kept him from doing what he really wanted. More than anything, he wanted to go home, take a shower, watch some television, and go to bed.

***

At the end of the fourth quarter, both teams were tied.

"Come on, son," Danny's dad, Colton Peterson, shouted at him from the sidelines. He motioned for Danny to call a timeout.

Danny got the referee's attention, signaling a timeout was needed to strategize their last play. They needed to change the original plan or the other team would wind up with the ball.

Danny's dad nodded at him, and he trusted Danny to decide what play they would execute. Lead settled on Danny's chest as he nodded back. He understood it was his responsibility to execute the play. The familiar tightness in his chest settled in as he puffed out several breaths.

In the center of the huddle, Danny shouted, "Get the ball to me and I'm going to run with it. Got it?" Nobody argued with Danny, and they ended the huddle with their normal countdown before moving into their positions.

His best friend, Brent, passed the football. Danny made a perfect catch. He tucked the ball into his body. He ran like the wind. It was clear to Danny that nobody could catch him due to his exceptional speed.

After scoring the final touchdown securing their win of the game, a crowd surrounded Danny. Many of them offered their congratulations. They were all clamoring for a chance to slap him on the back and give high fives. Deep down, a numbness overcame Danny. The thrill of the win had lost its appeal, and Danny experienced little joy from it. He was overcome with too much fear of making a foolish error and failing everyone. People expected him to play along. With a pretend smile on his face, he moved through the crowd. Danny thanked all the people surrounding him as he moved through the crowd.

Danny walked into the school gymnasium with Rachel clinging to him. Rachel's fingernails dug into his side, and he wanted nothing more than to pull away and tell her to stop. People continued coming up to congratulate him for scoring the final touchdown of the game.

Danny pasted a smile on his face and nodded. He mumbled what everyone expected him to say. He excused himself to Rachel and went to the snack table where his sister Beth stood with his mom. His mother volunteered as a parent chaperone for these events.

Relieved to see his family, he grabbed Beth in a tight embrace and twirled her around.

"Danny, you're making me dizzy," she giggled as he finally set her down. Then he wrapped his mom, Barbara Peterson, in a bear hug.

"I'm so proud of you, son," she whispered. His mom never joined the enormous crowd that swarmed at the end of each game. She waited to have some private time with him to share her pride.

Rachel ran over and said, "Mrs. Peterson, if you will excuse Danny, we need to get out on the dance floor." Her talon-like fingernails latched onto his arm as she pulled him out to the dance floor.

Danny was hesitant to follow Rachel, but he promised himself a half hour of playing his part and then he would head home.

Thirty minutes later, Danny pulled away from Rachel's hooks. He looked at her and said, "Rachel, I'm exhausted. I'm going home. Do you want me to give you a ride, or do you want to stay and catch a ride with someone else?"

"You and I could go to Lookout Point. I promise I can relax you." Rachel scraped her nails down Danny's chest as she looked at him coyly. Danny wanted to grimace, but he kept his facial expressions impassive.

Danny let out a long sigh before he allowed his shoulders to slump. "Perhaps another night, Rachel."

In a whiny tone, Rachel smirked at him. "Fine. I guess I will find someone else to join me at the Point." Her lower lip poked out as if she expected him to give in.

Danny rolled his eyes, and his mouth flattened.

"Rachel, I've had enough of your threats about what you'll do with someone else. Perhaps it is time for us to go our separate ways.

Tears filled Rachel's eyes as she said, "I'm sorry. I didn't mean it."

"I think you did, Rachel." Danny was firm as he said, "We're done."

As Danny walked away from Rachel, his mouth spread in a wide grin and his heart was lighter. It was time to only concentrate on football and end relationships with shallow women.

Vicki

Eighteen-year-old Vicki Robinson slouched on the picture perfect sofa in her mother's living room.

"Sit up!" Anna Robinson glowered at Vicki. "I need you to take this seriously, Victoria."

Vicki's mouth twisted, and she didn't sit up as her mother instructed. "Don't call me Victoria. My name is Vicki."

"Your name is Victoria and I am the one who named you at birth, you ungrateful little harlot. Now, I will not tell you again. You are expected to be at your father's office tomorrow afternoon at four o'clock sharp. It's time for you to begin your apprenticeship and learn what your father and I do."

Her mother planned for Vicki to complete her law degree and join their family practice. Vicki had no desire to follow in the footsteps of the two people who only focused on her as their trophy daughter. Neither of them had ever been to any event she participated in during her youth. Vicki's nanny attended her soccer games and any of her assemblies where she received an award. Her dad never acknowledged her, and her mother only ever addressed her to criticize her lack of perfection. Her attempts to enroll Vicki in dance and to parade her in beauty pageants resulted in failure. One time, Vicki pretended to dance terribly to watch her mother's face, knowing it would disappoint her. Once Vicki entered middle school and entered her teenage years, her mom gave up trying. However, she held fast to the idea that Vicki would one day become a lawyer.

Vicki yawned, and she let her body sag into the couch, knowing her mother hated it. "Sorry I can't. I have a meeting with my probation officer at four tomorrow."

Vicki spoke the truth. In rebellion of her parents' wealth and snobbish attitude toward her, she involved herself with some rather unruly students at her school. She joined in with them when they took part in a vandalism at her high school. The five of them had been drunk, and they raised hell by breaking into the high school to spray paint the gym walls. The group also rolled toilet paper all over the light fixtures and sprayed shaving cream up and down the bleachers. A neighbor down the street had seen the lights turned on and called the police. Vicki and her friends received a community service sentence for the remainder of their senior year. Her father acted as her attorney, and to save himself from shame, he bribed the judge to keep Vicki from jail. He didn't stop the others, including Colin, from serving thirty days in jail. Upon release, they joined Vicki's community service program.

Vicki's mom continued her tirade about her embarrassment that Vicki had to meet with a probation officer and her unforgivable behavior. Vicki ignored her as her mind drifted to Colin. He was the only one who truly cared for her. When the pair grew closer, Vicki finally believed she had someone she could always depend on.

Her eyes softened as she gazed out the back window past her mom. She planned to meet up with Colin later that evening. He was the one she gave her virginity to, knowing that it meant so much more than just sex. Colin shared her sentiment. He had parents on the opposite end. They lived in poverty and struggled with alcohol and drug addiction. Neither of them were sober enough to be aware of Colin's daily actions.

Two hours later, Vicki drove the mustang convertible that her parents had bought her as a bribe, hoping she would do as they wished and focus on becoming a lawyer. That car was sweet, Vicki conceded. Despite her parents' apathy towards her, she appreciated their financial ability to purchase the vehicle.

She pulled into the parking lot of the fast-food restaurant where they always met, and she observed Colin leaning on the side of the building. Good Lord, he was so hot! Her heart fluttered as she sat and watched him. He spotted her at the same time and his smile made her knees weak. Colin sauntered toward her, and Vicki got out of the car to change into the passenger seat. She enjoyed sharing her car with Colin and her heart experienced satisfaction in knowing her parents definitely would not approve.

Colin's hand stopped her as he grabbed her waist and pulled her in for a deep and passionate kiss. Vicki leaned into the kiss and he moaned.

"Hi," she whispered.

"Hey baby," Colin crooned, as she placed the car keys in his hands. They got back into the car and he drove to the cheap motel where he and Vicki often spent time together.

An hour later, she leaned over him and said, "I have to go."

Colin pulled her in for a tender kiss and Vicki's heart melted from his treatment of her. Her hand caressed his bare chest, touching the few hairs in front of his heart. His hands roamed down her back to her rear end, where he squeezed her butt.

Giggling, Vicki said, "No. Seriously, Colin. I need to go."

"Okay," Colin spoke against her mouth. They stood up and began dressing. Vicki drove the small distance and pulled back into the fast-food restaurant. Before he stepped out, Colin leaned over and kissed her one more time. "Friday night?" he asked.

"Yeah," Vicki said. Her heart grew sad when she thought about him going back to the ramshackle home he lived in with his awful parents. "One day, you and I can get a place together," she promised.

"That's what I'm saving for," Colin said. He worked double shifts at the restaurant, which is why Vicki always met him here. His shift had just ended when she came to meet him.

"Bye," Vicki said, softly. "I love you."

"I love you, Vicki," Colin said before he kissed her a last time and stepped out. Colin refused to let Vicki drive him home. He didn't want her to see where he lived. Vicki drove by there once out of curiosity. Her heart burned with anger as she thought of the injustice of her rich parents and how much Colin didn't have compared to her.

August, 1988

Vicki watched her mother drive away. She couldn't believe it! Her parents forced her to come to this stupid school. Her last involvement with the police had driven the two of them to send her away. She fixated on the surrounding buildings as she ground her teeth and dug her nails into her hands. Listlessly, she walked back into the dorm room she had been assigned.

Her roommate, a timid, unintelligent girl, sat on her bed and glanced up at Vicki. Her eyes darted behind Vicki. "Would you like to go to the student center with me? "Her name was Ella. She differed entirely from Vicki.

"Hell, no." Vicki made it look like would lunge at Ella as she growled. Ella shrunk back with tense shoulders. "And if you ever ask me again, you'll be sorry."

Tears filled Ella's eyes, and she rushed to the bathroom. Vicki cackled as Ella slammed the door and locked it. Vicki's laugh lacked the quality of joyous laughter. The girl's fear of her pleased her. If her parents made her come to this stupid school, she would do all she could to make them sorry.

A few weeks later, Vicki found herself summoned to the dean of students' office.

"Thank you for coming, Victoria," the dean said without looking at her. Vicki wanted to give a stare of intimidation, but this guy would not engage. She shrugged and slouched in her seat. When he finally looked at her, she knew that some sort of discipline would soon follow.

Three days before, she had gone joyriding with another girl. The two of them found a gas station that sold alcohol to minors. She and Brandi sped recklessly through town and they stole several street signs. They also knocked over a stop sign. After being caught, she and Brandi spent the night in jail. Her parents refused to come, but they sent money to pay her bail.

The dean's voice brought Vicki out of her daydream. "We believe it is best to move you to a dorm room of your own. Ella Stine's parents do not wish for her to room with you any longer. They do not consider it safe since you have been showing threatening behavior toward her. And considering your recent activities, be advised that you are now on probation with the university. We will not tolerate such activity. It's important that we maintain a working relationship with our community." The dean stared at Vicki for a few moments. She narrowed her eyes and curled her mouth in derision. "I need to hear from you that you understand how serious this is."

Vicki's expression turned detached and unemotional as she said, "Yeah, sure." However, his next words had her sitting up straight.

"You will also begin counseling sessions in our counseling center. I've assigned you to meet with Angela Young. I'm hoping she will help you through whatever you are going through at the moment." The dean's face remained unreadable, but Vicki rolled her eyes and she made sure he saw it. "Victoria, do you understand?"

Vicki frowned at him and said, "My name is Vicki and yeah, I do."

The dean nodded and gestured that their meeting had ended. Vicki stood quickly and sped out the door.

As soon as she walked out, Rhonda Stillman approached her, asking for her help. She promised to pay her if Vicki carried out a job. She knew Rhonda as the girl who went crazy at a school dance.

Vicki was happy to help with the promise of a large sum of money. But Vicki's involvement with Rhonda created more problems. Truthfully, Vicki didn't know that Rhonda's plan involved abducting Hannah. She also didn't know that Rhonda intended to kill her. She probably should have asked more questions before agreeing to get involved.

The police apprehended her, and she then cooperated fully, disclosing Rhonda's plan to separate Hannah from her friends. Telling the police the truth about her participation led to a reduced punishment. However, her parents found a job for her working on campus so that it might help her stay out of trouble. She also served community service hours. This time, the hours were miserable because Colin was not there to serve them with her.

Chapter 1

November 1988, A university in East Texas

Nineteen-year-old Michelle Walters fidgeted on the sofa where she sat. Her counselor, Angela, sat beside her in a chair. Michelle adjusted her short skirt, pulling it closer to her knees. The wide, metallic belt draped over her long, neon pink t-shirt. If she were still at home, Jeff would have voiced his concerns regarding the skirt's length. Michelle thanked her lucky stars for being some distance away from him. His job kept him extremely busy and he couldn't travel up to see Michelle very much. Jeff had absolutely no idea that Michelle shopped with her mom before she moved to college and that she bought it for her to build up a stylish college wardrobe. After speaking up to her mother the year before, her mom became more involved in Michelle's life. Most guys were still scared of asking her out, even though Jeff obeyed what their mother said. But it was nice to act more like an eighteen-year-old teenager in the last few months of her high school career.

"You've told me a lot about your family, but tell me

more about your brother, Jeff," Angela said.

"What would you like to know?" Michelle asked because she was not comfortable talking about her relationship with Jeff.

"How do you see him in your life? Did the two of you have a typical sibling rivalry during your younger years?"

"Umm..." Michelle said. "My brother is nine years older than me."

"That's quite an age gap," Angela said.

"Yeah," Michelle mumbled. "That created the problem."

Angela frowned. "How was his age a problem for you?"

Michelle sighed as she rubbed her hands down the denim of her skirt. "My parents assigned Jeff to look out for me all my life. With their full-time jobs, they believed he could be there for me when they couldn't."

"I'm still not seeing a problem." Angela said.

"The problem became worse in high school. Jeff didn't allow me to date anyone at all. Even at church, when guys would approach me, he shut down all conversations."

"I see." Angela's face remained neutral and relaxed. Michelle pondered her possible response, but her inquiry didn't come across as presumptuous.

Instead, she continued talking. "I love Jeff, and I am so thankful that he is my brother. I could always count on him. He came to all of my dance recitals in my younger years and he didn't miss a choral event at all during high school. I counted on him to be there with my parents."

"Why does your tone sound frustrated when speaking about his care of you?"

"I don't know," Michelle said. Angela said nothing,

which made her uncomfortable. So she blurted out, "I wasn't a normal high school student. I didn't experience normal things because he was so protective of me. When I finally complained to my mom about not having a life of any kind, she began letting me go hang out with friends. She was unaware that he remained a problem in my romantic life. And by that time, guys usually left me alone."

Angela's face remained impassive as she nodded, jotting notes on her notepad. "Was that your first time standing up to Jeff?"

"Yes," Michelle said. "It shocked me when she actually agreed with me."

"How did Jeff continue to hinder your love life?"

"I didn't have many invitations by that point. One time, a friend of mine tried to fix me up with someone who was also in the National Honor Society club that we both took part in." Michelle gazed behind Angela as she remembered her dashed hopes.

"What did Jeff do?" Angela asked.

"He convinced Jackie to tell him about it. I mean, he practically put her through an interview until she cracked and told him about Matthew's interest in me. Our families attended church together, and Jeff cornered Matthew. He persuaded him to stand down and not ask me out." Michelle sighed again. "I came close to going out on my first date ever."

Angela said nothing as she jotted notes on her notepad. She simply said, "That concludes today's session."

Surprise filled Michelle, and she stood up reluctantly.

Now that she was talking about her brother, she wished to continue. "Can I schedule another appointment?"

"Sure, let's get it scheduled on the calendar."

A few moments later, Michelle walked out of the counseling center with an appointment card in her hand. Stepping onto the sidewalk, her eyebrow creased, considering what had been discussed that day. Her feathered hair blew in the wind and she paused for a moment on the sidewalk to slide the card into a front pocket in her backpack. She took the time to add neon pink lip gloss to her lips before continuing to her room. The beginning of her freshman year of college proved traumatizing when her friend and roommate, Hannah Mathis, was abducted by her previous roommate (Rhonda Stillman). Rhonda turned out to be a stalker who plotted revenge on Hannah for believing she had ruined her life. She, Hannah and Jackie were still in counseling as a result. Today was her first time in counseling for just herself.

As she told Angela, Michelle grew up under the radar of her older brother, Jeff. Her parents placed the job of protecting her on his shoulders because of the age gap between them. Both of her parents worked full time, and they expected Jeff to help. They were both older and of a different generation. Neither of her parents felt equipped to handle the changing times of the eighties. They didn't understand rock music and peer pressure to drink alcohol, take drugs, and have sex. Most of Michelle's life had been spent trying to please Jeff and her parents. Since beginning college, she added the responsibility of her roommates, Hannah and Jackie, onto her shoulders. Michelle was overcome with guilt when she considered herself responsible for Hannah's abduction at a basketball game they attended. It took some time, but Michelle came to grips that she was not responsible for what happened that night. Hannah even attempted persuading her to forgive herself as she forgave her earlier.

Michelle questioned Angela's thorough work today, yet recognized this as the reason toward her growth in mental and emotional recovery. She wished the time wasn't up because she actually wanted to sit and talk more. This session passed too quickly.

Still deep in thought, Michelle didn't notice who was walking in her direction until she looked up. Danny Peterson walked toward her with a smile on his face. He came across as the most gorgeous guy that she had ever seen. Michelle couldn't stop the swooning that whipped through her core as he was sauntering her way. His t-shirt and acid wash jeans fit him perfectly and her eyes wished to fixate on his muscular chest. Danny wore a fashionable denim jacket with high-top sneakers. He realized she saw him and he gave a friendly wave, calling out, "Hey Michelle."

Distress filled her, and she pretended not to see him as she spun around and scurried the opposite direction. Michelle wondered what was wrong with her. 'Would it have hurt to wave back and say hello to him?' she whispered to herself as she kicked herself while walking toward her dorm.

***

Disappointment filled Danny as he watched Michelle walk the other direction as if she was trying to avoid him. He was completely puzzled by her reaction to his friendly greeting and his blue eyes creased in frustration. He was attracted to Michelle, but all opportunities to get to know her had been unsuccessful. Their one chance of getting to know each other was an epic failure. He asked her to dance when they went out as a group. As soon as it ended, she ran like a jackrabbit to the bathroom. He tried to determine whether he was the reason for her behavior.

Danny was confident in himself. Sometimes, it became overwhelming because terror filled him. He experienced fear of making mistakes or letting people down. He dealt with anxiety at the idea of disappointing his parents, his grandparents, his sister and even the people in his town.

Danny purposely chose the small university where he attended because there wasn't a football team. His dad tried to guide him to one school, offering him a football scholarship. Danny's mom helped to convince his dad that being closer to home would be a positive thing for all of them. She listened to Danny when he confided in her he was burned out playing football. Her influence on Danny's dad persuaded his change of heart.

Danny believed he wanted to do something involving coaching with his major. He enrolled in the secondary education program at the college, but most of his classes were prerequisites. One of his classes focused on his major. In truth, Danny had doubts about his future plan. His dad encouraged him to follow in his footsteps, and Danny always thought he would, but he didn't have a clear picture or vision of himself as a coach. His senior year offered an opportunity to join a *big brother* program with elementary students in his town. He discovered how much he enjoyed working with younger kids. However, there weren't any full-time coaching jobs for younger kids. Confusion clouded his mind as he contemplated his options. That time of mentoring completely changed his perspective. When he first came to visit the school, he and his mom met with an advisor. After asking the basic questions, the advisor talked to him about secondary education, and Danny immediately agreed. After he got back home and held practice for the younger boys he worked with, he had doubts about his original plan.

Danny's thoughts drifted back to Michelle and her strange reaction. The fact that Michelle always ran the other direction from him was baffling. She looked different from past girlfriends. However, the change in her appearance is what attracted him. She had dark hair and chocolate brown eyes that he got lost in when they spoke together in conversation and there had been very few, in his opinion. She didn't have the willowy body of a cheerleader, but Danny grew to love her shorter stature. He felt captivated by the full curves all over her body. He also loved the sharp and sarcastic words that often came out of her mouth, which showed her intelligence.

His mind was challenged by their two conversations.

Turning back toward his apartment, Danny shoved his hands in his pockets as he walked. He tried to formulate a plan to win Michelle over. Thankful he was friends with Hannah Mathis, Michael Davis' girlfriend ,his hand came up and scratched the back of his head as he created a plan that would require her help. He remembered she knew he liked Michelle. Surely the two of them might figure out how to have a simple conversation with Michelle.

***

Michelle continued to kick herself once back in her dorm room. She didn't handle a simple greeting when Danny called her name.

"Stupid, stupid, stupid." She whispered the words to herself repeatedly. She tried to focus on pages in the textbook for an assignment. However, her mind kept drifting to her feeling of panic when she noticed Danny walking toward her. Fear of what to do overcame her and instead of saying *hello* back to Danny, she simply made a turn and she walked the other direction to her dorm.

Michelle was completely inexperienced with guys. Danny proved to be the best-looking guy she had ever seen, so those insecurities doubled because she couldn't help but feel intimidated around him. Michelle knew other girls noticed him because she observed them smiling at him when they passed their table in the dining hall. Danny joined in sitting at their table with Michael Davis,

Hannah's boyfriend and several other guys. Many of the girls who smiled at Danny were drop-dead gorgeous and Michelle considered herself average, so she thought that she had no chance to compete with any of them. That Danny might be interested in dating her was inconceivable. Put her in a group of girls, and even girls mixed with guys, and she was fine. Anytime she was ever on her own with a guy, she became completely awkward. Most guys where she lived learned to ignore her because they realized her brother would stop any attempt at going on a date.

Michelle's head shook in agreement with her own internal dialogue as she fought to bring her attention back to her textbook. As much as she tried to focus, her study attempt was proving a failure this afternoon. All she could think about was Danny and they way he smiled at her earlier.

The next day was cool. Although East Texas could be warm, it also has fall-like days. The campus of the university was small and easy to get around. Encircled by tall pines and other various trees, the oldest structure was at the summit of a hill. Throughout time, other buildings surrounded it, creating a lovely scenic view at the top of the hill. The town was visible, enhancing the beautiful environment around them.

Danny realized that luck was on his side when he noticed Hannah walking in his direction.

"Hannah," he yelled as he jogged in her direction. A smile came over Hannah's face when she recognized him. He hoped she would help him break the ice with Michelle so that they might become friends and hopefully go on a date. Danny had seen her watch Michelle when he tried to talk with her at dinner and he thought he recognized a spark in Hannah's eye to push her roommate into a relationship.

Hannah stopped and waited for him. "Hey Danny. What are you doing?"

When he reached Hannah, Danny said, "I need your help."

A confused expression came across Hannah's eyes as she said, "Okay, what on earth can I do for you?"

Danny believed if he put himself out there that Hannah would immediately want to play matchmaker for her friend. As he stood beside her, his insides turned over in fear that this plan might not work. His stomach turned over at the thought. Most things came easily to him, including school and sports. What if Michelle really wasn't interested in him?

Danny took a breath and swallowed convulsively. "Look, Hannah. You're friends with Michelle. I have tried and tried getting to know her, but every time I attempt to talk to her, she evades me. I attempted it when we all went out together last month, but she ran away from me after one dance." He was pleased to notice the spark of excitement in Hannah's eyes. Danny continued, "Will you help me in getting to know her better?"

"I will be happy to help," she smiled. "What can I do?" Danny was happy that she wanted to play matchmaker. His only fear was that it might backfire with Michelle. He pushed the thought away as he turned his attention back to Hannah.

"First, can I get your room number? I'm hoping that if I call Michelle that she can't run away from that. It may be easier with a phone call." The idea was shaping into a plan as Danny talked to her despite the churning in his gut. Danny wondered how Michelle would respond to their meddling.

Hannah smiled with excitement. "Our room is 125 and you know how to put the 0 and the 9 in front of it to call, right?"

Danny grinned at her and said, "Yeah, thanks. I also want to ask for your help in getting her to the phone."

Agreeing with him, Hannah was silent for a moment as she gazed into the distance. She touched her chin, and she tilted her head. "I have a plan." She told Danny to call Michelle after dinner that night once they were back in their room. Once Hannah got her on the phone, she and Jackie would go outside and find something to do so that Michelle and Danny might talk privately.

Hannah pointed her finger at Danny. "But you better not hurt her, or you will have to answer to me and Jackie, got it? She is one of my best friends!"

With gentleness in his gaze, Danny said, "I won't hurt her. I promise."

Hannah's eyes softened when she observed the sincerity in his gaze. "I hope it works out with the two of you because I care for you both!" Hannah was happy to see love in other couples because of being in a relationship herself. Danny's brow dipped slightly with the worry that Michelle might not respond positively. As he thought about it, his mouth became dry and his stomach turned again. Just as before, he pushed the fear away.

As Danny walked back toward his place, Michael Davis called Hannah's name. Danny watched her rush toward him, and Michael enveloped her in his arms. He turned his eyes away as they kissed deeply. Danny was happy for his friends, especially after Hannah's kidnapping last month. Danny helped during the horrible abduction by that horrible roommate of hers. Envy filled him and he wanted that for himself. He hoped it might be with Michelle. His attraction to her was something he couldn't explain. He was drawn to her and he sensed a connection the few times they had interacted as a group. Danny believed he detected interest in Michelle's eyes and he desired above all else an opportunity to get to know her. He pushed down the nagging fear of not being what she wanted, he walked back to his apartment.

As he walked, he thought about his inward battle, about what his major would be. Danny really liked Michelle, but he didn't want to lose focus on why he was actually there. He remembered Michael talking about his sessions with Mark, the counselor at the center of campus. Danny stopped and stood on the sidewalk for a moment. He turned and walked toward the counseling center. He would ask if Mark could fit him in on the calendar. Talking to him might give him direction in what to do.

Ten minutes later, he walked out of the center. Mark had been in a session, but Angela, the woman that Hannah and Michelle met with, helped him schedule a meeting with Mark the next day.

***

That evening, Michelle, Jackie and Hannah returned from dinner at the dining hall, and they were each completing homework assignments on their beds. Michelle didn't even lift her head when the phone rang because she thought it was Michael calling for Hannah.

When Hannah said, "Michelle, the phone is for you," Michelle was paralyzed as she wondered who was possibly calling her. Slight fear filled her when she wondered if it might be her brother or parents with an emergency.

Michelle stood up and asked, "Who is it?" She noticed something flash across Hannah's gaze. It was almost as if she was hiding guilt for something she had done. "Hannah..." she continued.

"Don't be mad at me," Hannah began. Jackie had looked up with the same look in her eyes. "It's Danny Peterson. He asked me for our number because he wanted to call and talk to you. He says that he's tried several times, but you run away when he does."

Michelle was numb and at a loss for words as she played with the ends of her hair. She whispered, "What?"

Jackie came over to her, and she nudged her toward

the phone. "Talk to him, Michelle. He's a nice guy."

Pleading filled Hannah's gaze as she said, "Please talk to him." She was still holding the receiver in her hand.

Michelle was between a rock and a hard place. She couldn't flee from him on the phone because if she hung up on him, she would hate herself for being rude. She moved like a robot to the phone, taking the receiver from Hannah. "Be prepared to discuss this," she hissed to her friend.

Hannah's eyes were filled with innocence as she released the phone.

Michelle said, "Hello." As she turned back around, she realized her friends had abandoned her and left the room completely. Michelle rolled her eyes, realizing she had been set up.

"Hey Michelle," Danny's deep voice carried over the line.

Shivers came over her from hearing his voice. Michelle made her voice come across as calm. "Hi, how are you?" Michelle was not a phone talker, and she didn't have many conversations with guys. She experienced complete awkwardness as she played with the phone cord, pulling on the coils as she looked down at the floor.

"I'm sorry if you think Hannah got you involved in this," Danny said in a kind voice. "I asked for her help."

"Why?" she asked automatically, and then she chided herself because she realized that's not what she should have said to this incredible guy.

Danny didn't seem offended or upset. He said, "I enjoyed getting to know you over the past year when we've been out together with friends, but I wanted a chance to get to know you better, one on one."

Michelle couldn't stop the blush that stole over her face and she was glad Danny was not standing there. "Alright, what would you like to hear?"

Danny asked where she was from and about her family. Michelle became more comfortable with the conversation and she told him about her family. She also shared about growing up in southeast Houston. With the phone in her hand, she walked a short distance and sat stiffly on the bed. Michelle set the base of the phone on her bedside table and she continued to play with the cord. Wanting to be polite, she asked, "What about you? Where are you from?"

Danny said, "I'm from a small town right outside of Lufkin. It's called Groverton. My dad is the football coach at the high school and my mom works in the school board office as a secretary."

"I've seen signs for it when I drive from Houston," Michelle commented.

"Yeah, it's tiny. There are only about two thousand people, and we have to drive to larger towns to do anything." Danny said.

Michelle chuckled. "Wow! My high school had over five hundred students in my class alone. At least you don't have to worry about traffic!" she commented sarcastically.

"Very true," Danny commented. Michelle couldn't help but notice that his tone deepened after she laughed at his joke. "Although sometimes there is a line of cars at our two stop lights in the middle of our town."

"Do you have brothers or sisters?" Michelle asked, and she was thankful for the casual tone in her voice.

"My sister Beth is a junior this year. I'm three years older than her." Danny answered. Then he asked, "Do you have brothers or sisters?

"My brother, Jeff, is nine years older than me and sometimes he drives me crazy with his overprotective-ness!" Michelle was shocked with herself for telling that to Danny.

However, he just laughed and said, "Us older brothers have to take care of our little sisters!"

Not wanting to get into the difficult subject of her brother, Michelle changed the subject. "So…" Michelle said. "You said you want to become a coach, but I don't really know anything else about your major and what you really want to do."

Danny cleared his throat He gave a vague answer about liking his classes before he changed the subject back to Michelle.

The two of them talked for another twenty minutes before he said he needed to shower and study for a while before bed. Before he hung up, he asked, "Would you like to meet me at the student center and play ping-pong tomorrow?"

Still slightly nervous, Michelle had enjoyed their con-versation. She appreciated Danny had listened to her and put her at ease. "Okay," she said.

Danny said. "Great. Can we meet around four?"

Michelle agreed with him on the time, and she smiled

as she hung up the phone. As her roommates entered the room, they noticed her expression. While hanging up the phone, she glowered at them and said, "I'm mad at the two of you for meddling and setting me up like that!"

"One day you will thank us," Hannah said in a voice that sounded like a mother talking to a child. Jackie just laughed as she went to take a shower.

Chapter 2

The next morning, Michelle felt breathless when Danny sat beside her at breakfast. He normally sat beside either Alex or Michael. She was unable to halt the blush spreading across her face. She stole a glance at Danny, and she blushed harder as she saw him looking straight at her.

"Is it alright if I sit here?" he asked politely. Michelle found herself speechless, but she nodded her head in agreement.

She looked over and saw Michael and Hannah feeding each other bacon and eggs, totally wrapped up in each other at the moment. Envy stole over her as she cast a sidelong glance at Danny again, and she found him gazing at her with a gentle smile.

"Did you have a good night?" he asked.

Michelle realized that talking with him on the phone last night helped to break the ice. She understood little about conversing with guys, but she no longer felt like she a need to run away from him every time he tried talking to her. In her mind, that showed progress. However, she heard Jeff's voice telling her to always be careful with boys. *We can just be friends,* she told herself.

With a soft smile, she said, "Yes, I studied for a little while before taking a shower and going to bed. How about you?" She became shy as she looked into his blue eyes, but she found herself captivated by them.

"I finished a paper that is due tomorrow. Tonight I have to revise it before I have to turn it in tomorrow." Danny said, and he averted his gaze.

Michelle knew of his desire to go into education and that he wanted to be a football coach and follow in his dad's footsteps. Last night, when she asked him to share more, Michelle felt he did not give her a straightforward answer. However, she wasn't comfortable pressing the topic.

"Nothing feels better than finishing a paper!" she agreed. Michelle smiled and her entire face lit up. Danny seemed speechless for a microsecond and she foolishly wondered if it had to do with her smile.

When breakfast ended, Danny offered to walk with Michelle on the way to his first class, and she surprised herself again by agreeing.

They talked as they walked together, and she couldn't help but notice as his arm brushed against hers. Butterflies fluttered in her stomach from the slight touch and she fixated on on his extremely well developed biceps as they bulged under the sleeves of this shirt.

They paused and Danny said, "I need to leave you here so that I can walk that way to my first class." He pointed to the left, where the sidewalk intersected.

"Thank you for walking with me," Michelle said, glancing down shyly at her feet.

Danny touched her arm, and her eyes lifted to his. He said, "I've enjoyed this morning and talking to you last night."

"Me too," the words came out as a whisper from her mouth.

"Are you still meeting me at four in the student center?" Danny's blue-eyed gaze mesmerized her for a split second.

"Yes," she answered. A smile came across his face, and he reached down to take her hand in his as he squeezed it.

"See you this afternoon," he commented softly before he lifted her hand to his lips.

A gasp flew out of Michelle's mouth as his soft lips touched the back of her hand, leaving her speechless again as he turned and walked to class.

***

Danny didn't stop smiling every time he thought of Michelle. She finally opened up to him and he wanted to celebrate it as a victory. The night before when they talked on the phone, his heart pounded with elation when she laughed and teased with him. When she smiled a few moments ago, his heart felt like it would stop because it illuminated her entire face. He was counting the hours until they would play ping-pong together that afternoon.

Danny grew up with two loving parents who showed

what a good marriage should look like. He dated many girls, but none of them were relationships that had substance like his parents did. Most of the girls who acted interested in him were not doing it for the right reasons. They just wanted to date him because he led the football team.

Danny's leadership on the team added extreme pressure. His dad didn't intentionally ask him to give more than the other players on the football team, but Danny always felt like he needed to be the leader when he would have loved to sit and follow someone else's guidance. Nobody ever saw him when he didn't feel up to any of the challenges. Danny hid his clenched jaw or his tightened fists. Many times, he would have an anxiety headache after the game, but he made sure not to show that he was in pain. He frowned as he thought about how lost he felt for his major and what he really wanted to do. Shame filled him because he couldn't give Michelle an honest answer when she asked.

It had been wonderful to start fresh here at college, where his background and family history were unknown to others. He was on the basketball team, but no one expected him to have the answers for how to win every game. Danny relaxed and enjoyed playing with his friends.

Bringing his thoughts back to the present, he experienced a connection to Michelle, and he wondered if she was the woman for him. Danny wanted to go slow with her so that she didn't get frightened away from him again. He was more than willing to pursue it as far as she would allow him to, and a grin came to his mouth as he remembered the gasp when he kissed her hand. It revealed the connection that he also felt.

Danny straightened his face as he focused on his professor, even though he looked forward to seeing her that afternoon. Danny listened to the lesson. His stomach turned as his thoughts turned to his original plan of becoming a high school coach. He believed he had a gift of working with younger boys, but he wasn't sure exactly how to apply that gift. The seven-and eight-year-old boys he worked with his senior year clung to him, soaking up the attention of a starting player for the football team. Not every boy had a dad like him, and he wanted to make a difference for someone else. Danny counted the hours until his meeting with Mark. He also counted the hours until his date with Michelle. Both of these distractions continued filling his mind to where he could not listen or focus.

Thankfully, his class ended, so Danny grabbed a quick bite at the snack bar in the student center and he ate it on his way to the counseling center. When he walked in, Mark was standing behind the desk.

"Danny," Mark said. "It's great to see you. How have you been?"

Danny shuffled his feet, and he looked down at them. "I'm doing okay, but some advice would be helpful."

"Let's head back to my office," Mark said, and he held out his arm for Danny to lead the way. Once seated, Danny occupied a couch while Mark sat in a chair to his left. Mark said, "Tell me what's on your mind."

Danny huffed out a breath. "I'm having a hard time with what I'm supposed to be doing here."

"Here, as in school?" Mark asked.

"Yes. I always thought I would become a coach like my dad, but I just don't sense it's my calling.

"I want to back up some so that I can get a clear understanding. I should have started with these questions. Tell me about your family." Mark opened his pen and held it as he waited for Danny to begin.

I'm from Groverton, which is only an hour from here. My dad is the head football coach. We lived there all my life. My mom works in the school district's main office. She's in the human resources department. I have a younger sister named Beth. She's sixteen and a junior in high school." Danny became more at ease telling his story. He was proud of his family and where he came from.

Danny shared about his family's ranch and his grandparents, who also lived on the land. Discussing family came easily. He frowned slightly, wondering why Mark was asking about all of this instead of answering his question about what his major should be.

Mark remained quiet as he jotted notes from what Danny had said. After a few minutes, he looked up. "Tell me about your dad as the head coach. Did you love it or hate it?"

"I loved it," Danny said. "As a child, I always felt so proud when I saw him standing on the sidelines of the football field. I would hang out down there as much as he would allow when I was younger. When I turned eleven,

I worked as a towel boy."

Mark smiled. "It sounds like you and your dad have a good relationship."

"We do," Danny nodded. "I love my mom and Beth, too."

"So tell me why you don't believe you are on the right path with your education." Mark said.

Danny stayed quiet for a moment. He sat, rubbing his hands up and down his jeans as he stared off behind Mark's head.

Mark said, "Danny, do you have guilt? Are you afraid to think about what you really want?"

Mark stood as Danny remained silent. Danny realized he thought the session was over. "My dad always talked about me becoming a coach and I loved the idea during my childhood. It took a lot to convince him to let me come here where I didn't have to play football."

"Were you burned out on playing?" Mark asked.

Danny nodded again. "It got to where I didn't enjoy it anymore. I rejoiced when the football season ended."

"Why do you think you felt that way?" Mark asked again.

"I really am not sure." Danny's fingers tapped restlessly on the side of the couch and his other fingers drummed on his leg.

"I think that will be all for today." Mark stood a second time. Shocked that the hour had passed, Danny couldn't believe how quickly the time flew by.

Before Mark walked to the door, he handed Danny a spiral notebook. "I want you to take this and write any thoughts that come to your mind. I also want you to write about why you became so burned out playing football for your dad. When you come back for the next session, we can talk about what you wrote."

Danny shook Mark's offered hand. "Thank you. I appreciate the time with you."

The two of them walked out to the front, where Danny scheduled a session for Friday. He had a lighter schedule on Fridays. He had a full schedule on Tuesdays and Thursdays, including basketball practice each night.

***

That afternoon, Michelle walked to the student center after some good natured teasing from both of her roommates. The night before, she had talked to Jackie while Hannah took a shower. Jackie understood how hard high school had been for her with her brother's constant hovering. Jackie encouraged Michelle. "Just be yourself with him because I think he genuinely likes you." Then, as Jackie hugged her, Michelle felt silly as tears welled up in her eyes. The idea of getting emotional over a guy made her wonder if it was worth it.

She walked into the student center, which consisted of an upper and lower level. The upper level comprised the dining room and a snack bar where students purchased snacks. Couches were placed beside it where students studied near the snack bar. If students bought cups of coffee, there was a receptacle with a dishpan on the top to return used cups after students finished. The dining hall was also located on the second floor.

The lower level housed the bookstore where students books, school paraphernalia, and other supplies for classes were purchased. The other part of the bottom level comprised a larger sitting area with three groups of couches. Pool and ping-pong tables, as well as an equipment window, could be found at the opposite end of the bottom floor. Vending machines were also in that part if students wanted immediate refreshments. Michelle spotted Danny sitting on one couch, chatting with another guy from the basketball team. As soon as he saw her, he stood and made a beeline toward her.

"Hey," he said with one of his easy going smiles.

Michelle remembered Jackie's advice to be herself. She said, "Hi," softly as she got lost in his blue eyes.

"Are you ready?" Danny asked as he gestured to one of the ping-pong tables. Michelle nodded, and he walked to the small equipment window to request two paddles and a ball. His hands in his pockets, shoulders stiff made Michelle wonder about his nervousness, then she dismissed the idea. He gave the impression of someone comfortable with themselves. She figured his years of playing football scored him many dates with many girls.

Once the two of them began playing, Michelle loosened up even more. It helped that she grew up playing with her brother. She learned to be competitive and fight for her own victories. Of course, Danny excelled because he was so athletic. He won a game and then she won the second one.

Danny smiled as if he enjoyed her competitiveness, and he asked, "Are you up for a third match?"

In her snarky way, she narrowed her eyes and commented, "Bring it on!" Danny laughed as he served the ball over the net. He wound up winning the third match, but she fought hard until the end and he complimented her.

By the time they finished their last game, it was time for dinner. Danny suggested they walk up together, and she agreed. When they got their food, Danny put his tray beside hers, just as he had that morning. He pulled out her chair for her to sit down. Overwhelmed by the gesture, she blushed as she dropped into the waiting chair.

Both of her roommates sent her pointed looks, showing her they noticed his treatment of her. She sent them the stink eye as a warning not to say a word. Even though they didn't, she couldn't miss the teasing in their eyes. As she and Danny continued talking, Jackie wagged her eyebrows up and down several times, causing her to blush again.

When Danny got up to refill his drink, she muttered to her friends, "Will the two of you please stop?"

"What?" Hannah teased. "Can't I smile at my friend?"

She and Jackie both laughed as Michelle threw them a withering frown. "Okay, but Danny is going to see, so please stop!"

Hannah and Jackie laughed again. At that moment, Michael reached for Hannah's hand, and watching them interlace their fingers filled Michelle with a wanting of her own. Then he leaned over, kissed her softly, and he whispered softly into her ear, causing her to smile and flush. Michelle wondered what it would be like to love someone that much as she caught the sparkle of Hannah's promise ring on her left hand. It seemed impossible to her. Even as she got to know Danny, she heard Jeff's voice in her ear. She doubted that this could amount to anything.

After dinner, Danny pulled out her chair again. Michelle wondered if he had gotten coaching from Michael because he always did that for Hannah.

"Thank you," Michelle commented as she looked up at him. His gaze froze on hers and the moment filled with electricity as they stared into each other's eyes.

He swallowed, and his voice deepened. "You're welcome. Are you ready to go?" Then he held out his hand, and she waited a few seconds before taking it. She had never held a guy's hand before, and she found she liked the warmth of his large hand covering her small one. Of course, her blush took over her face again. She also willed her hand not to become sweaty because of her nerves.

"Can I walk you back?" he asked, and Michelle blushed again, wishing she had some kind of switch in order to turn it off when he asked her questions.

She smiled again as she answered him. "Yes, I'd like that."

As they walked hand in hand, Danny asked, "I wanted to ask you if you would like to go out with me on Friday night."

Michelle was unable to stop herself as she blurted out, "You want to go out with me?"

"Yeah, why wouldn't I?" He observed as he gazed down at her with a look of disbelief.

Michelle felt she needed to be honest as she blew out

a nervous breath before she said, "Look, Danny, I haven't ever dated in my life. Not once. I never even went to homecoming or prom. I just wanted to tell you in case it makes you change your mind. My older brother liked to scare off anyone who might have been interested in me at home. You look like someone who could date any girl he wants, so I might not be the right person for you to ask."

Danny's mouth fell open, and he raised his eyebrows as he paused for a moment before he answered. "Well, he's not here now, and I don't care about that. Michelle, I want to keep getting to know you. That is, if you are interested."

With sarcasm Michelle said, "I wonder why you are still interested after you heard me say all of that, but I've enjoyed becoming acquainted with you. I just need you to be patient with me because I'm not very experienced with any of this."

Stopping in the middle of the sidewalk, Danny let go of her hand as he put his hands on her shoulders so that she would look up at him. His voice sounded encouraging. "I can be patient with you. But Michelle, I think you are beautiful and funny. I have loved talking with you for the last two days and I am still very interested." Michelle's stomach clenched and she bit her bottom lip as she glanced at Danny's hands on her shoulders. The charge of electricity returned as she felt the burning of his hands into her skin.

Michelle moved back slightly, increasing her personal space for a few seconds before she answered. Her voice sounded breathless, like she had been running two miles. As much as she wanted to say yes, she heard her brother's voice in her ear. "I have a hard time believing that, and I don't feel ready for a date with you. However, I will hang out with you as friends."

***

Danny hunched his shoulders as he slowly wandered back to his apartment, not paying attention to where his surroundings. He stumbled mid stride as he trudged along. With his hands stuffed in his pockets, Danny pressed his lips tightly. He realized he would need to take things slower after hearing Michelle's story about her years of high school. Unbelief filled him that her brother blocked any guy from even asking Michelle on a date and he shook his head as he thought about it. Maybe it would be a good idea for them to become better friends until she trusted his intentions to be honorable.

He sat beside Michelle every day that week, and he got into the wonderful habit of pulling out her chair. His heart felt like it shrank when Michelle told him she would only hang out as friends. Danny realized he would need to take things slower after hearing Michelle talk about the fact that she had never gone out, even to a prom or homecoming.

Danny and Michelle sat together in the student center many afternoons or they enjoyed challenging each other in the game of ping-pong. He built a friendship with her to ensure she perceived his intentions toward her as honorable. Not normally strong in sports, Michelle surprised herself when she beat Danny and he absolutely loved it. When they played, it seemed she felt no threat from spending time with him. They were simply friends. He noticed she didn't blush when they competed against each other.

Along with sitting beside her, Danny also walked her to the dorm every evening, and he got in the habit of hugging her goodbye or squeezing her hand. With all he was doing to reassure her, his own insides turned upside down. The struggle with what he should focus on filled him with an anguish he had never experienced before. Often, Danny struggled to fall asleep when he went to bed. It was impossible for him to turn off his mind. The ongoing thoughts were overwhelming.

***

After Danny dropped her off that evening after supper, Michelle found her heart melting even more over his gentle manners toward her. Deep down, she believed that if he asked her out again, she would tell him yes. Then her thoughts felt like they were on a seesaw. Her heartbeat became erratic as she thought about how terrifying the thought was.

Hannah talked to Michelle the night before telling her that no other guy had ever used those kinds of manners with her before, not until she started dating Michael.

"Enjoy it," Hannah said. "He must be a special guy and I think he finds you special as well." Again, Michelle found herself tearing up just as she had done with Jackie and she wanted to laugh at herself for acting so foolish. Hannah continued, "I think you need to put him out of his misery and go on a date with him."

Michelle questioned whether her relationship with Danny could compare to Hannah and Michael's. Hannah was much more confident in her interactions with Michael. Michelle still struggled with feeling awkward, even though she knew her friendship with Danny became stronger. The thought of a date with him filled her veins with ice, and she just didn't know if she could accept an invitation from him.

Chapter 3

Two weeks passed. Danny experienced success in his developing friendship with Michelle. She didn't realize it, but her facial expressions revealed so much to him. Every time he pulled out a chair for her or complimented how she looked, Danny noticed raw interest in her eyes as she blushed and looked flustered by his attention. He noticed hesitancy as well and he became more determined than ever to prove himself to her.

Danny planned to execute the next phase of his plan. In order to do that, he needed Hannah's help again since she enjoyed playing matchmaker for them. He decided to include Jackie since their friendship had lasted many years. His adrenaline spiked and his heart raced at the idea of not measuring up or being good enough to convince Michelle to accept a date with him.

Danny talked to Michael the night before, so his friend wouldn't be suspicious of him making a move on Hannah or anything. Michael supported his idea.

Danny sat on a bench outside of the counseling center until Hannah walked out from her latest session with

Angela.

"Danny," she smiled. "What are you doing?"

Danny grinned at her and said, "I need your help again. You initiated my first conversation with Michelle. I've laid the groundwork for friendship before making a move because she told me she wasn't ready for an actual date. But the time has come for me to try asking her again, and I want you to help with it.

"What's your plan?" Hannah grinned widely in return.

"I'm thinking of a large gesture so that she can't say no." Danny took a breath as he continued, "Tomorrow night, I need you to get her to basketball practice. Can you do that?"

"Absolutely," Hannah answered as Danny explained how he hoped to sweep Michelle off of her feet.

***

Tuesday evening, Hannah had no problem convincing Michelle to come with her and Jackie to watch basketball practice. It developed into a habit during their first few months of college. After not going to any because of the trauma of Hannah's abduction, Hannah, Jackie and Michelle were back to attending them again.

Hannah caught Danny's attention. She gave him a subtle nod.

Michelle's eyes widened, and she bit her lip as she noticed none of the guys were sweaty from warming up. As she puzzled over the current events, music came over the speakers in the gym.

Michael stepped forward in his basketball uniform and he started singing. Seeing him gazing at Hannah, Michelle breathed a sigh of relief. *This is for Hannah* she thought to herself. Michael crooned the words to a popular love song. Michelle frowned. This wasn't the most romantic proposal if that was what Michael was doing.

"What on earth is happening?" she asked as a movement to the side attracted her attention. Suddenly, a flush crept up her neck and Michelle clutched her stomach. Her mouth dropped as Danny sprinted across the floor holding the middle of a banner and sweat broke out on her brow. She began blinking rapidly and part of her wished to sink into the bleachers.

Alex and James held the other end. All of them were in their basketball gear, but their focus was not on the game at the moment. The words on the sign read, 'Michelle Walters, will you go on a date with me?'

Michelle's eyes narrowed as she glanced at Hannah and commented, "That handwriting looks very familiar."

"What are you talking about?" Hannah said with wide eyes as Jackie was grinning in a ridiculous way. Both Danny and Hannah told her ahead of time so she could help if needed.

"Hannah," Michelle argued, "that handwriting does not belong to a guy!"

Softening her voice, Hannah said, "Come on, Michelle. Danny wants so badly to go out with you. Give him a chance."

Michelle gazed back at Danny, and she noticed his

flushed face along with his sheepish smile. She hadn't seen him nervous before. Tears sprang to her eyes, and she blinked rapidly to get them to go away. She rolled her eyes and shook her head at her erratic emotions. Michelle finally said, "Yes, I will go out with you." She wiped the lone tear away on her cheek.

Michelle felt like the sun was even brighter as Danny beamed at her. He dropped his part of the banner, causing it to sag as he raced up the bleachers and enveloped Michelle in a hug. When he pulled back, he said, "Thank you, Michelle. If you wait for me, I will walk you back to the dorm after practice. We can talk about the details." Then, taking both of her hands in his, he leaned down and placed a gentle kiss on her cheek, leaving her without words once again. Jackie and Hannah were beside her squealing with delight.

Instead of watching the guys scrimmage each other, Michelle's heart pounded from what had happened. She actually agreed to go on a date with Danny Peterson! Her eyes gazed toward the court, but she couldn't help but wonder if she was crazy. The rest of practice was spent in mental torture.

***

Danny walked over to Michelle after practice ended. Hannah left with Michael, and Jackie rode back to the dorm with them. Holding the door open for her, she stepped out, and they walked quietly side by side.

Danny felt elated from her acceptance of his invitation. He reached for Michelle's hand and he clasped it lightly in his.

He swallowed as he glanced over at Michelle and noticed her looking down at her shoes.

"Michelle," he said softly, "are you sure you're ready for this? I don't want you to feel pressured if you're still not sure about it." Danny felt his heart beating out of his chest, terrified she might cancel on him.

"I know," Michelle said. She stared straight ahead.

"Will you look at me?" Danny asked gently. When Michelle looked at him, his heart dipped and there was a tingling in his chest when he saw the look in her eyes. He said, "Please talk to me about what you're thinking."

Michelle wanted to kick herself when the tears filled her eyes again. Then, she muttered, "Nobody has ever treated me like you do. I don't have any experience, but you are such a gentleman with me. It overwhelms me because I'm not sure how to react."

"Michelle," Danny stopped and placed his hands on her shoulders. "I really like you. Yes, I dated in high school, but I didn't ever feel about them the way I feel about you."

"Why me?" Michelle whispered.

"Why not you?" Danny said. Stepping closer, he pulled her toward him as he said, "I know you don't have experience, but you are so beautiful to me. I want to date you. I want you to trust me that this feels real."

Nodding her head, Michelle whispered, "I have a hard time believing that, but I will try to take you at your word. But I need you to be patient with me. I was finally getting used to us being friends, but now everything is changing."

"I will be as patient as you need me to be," Danny said.

They walked for a few more minutes in silence. Almost to the dorm, Danny said, "Is Friday night okay?"

Michelle nodded.

"Great. Michael suggested we go to the same restaurant where he and Hannah had their first date. Is that okay with you?"

Michelle smiled shyly at him. "It sounds wonderful."

Danny's face lit up at her words. "Great. See you at breakfast tomorrow." Then he leaned down and gave her another gentle kiss on the cheek.

As if in reflex, her hand floated up to where his lips touched her cheek as he whispered good night. Danny walked away toward his apartment before she could answer him.

✳✳✳

Friday morning, Michelle scheduled a counseling session with Angela after her class. She confided in Angela about Danny's invitation to go out on a date with her.

Angela's eyes sparkled as she said, "Congratulations!"

"I don't know what I'm doing," Michelle murmured as she looked at her hands.

"Michelle, look at me," Angela said. "There isn't a right way or a wrong way of dating. You don't need to memorize a rulebook."

Tears filled her eyes again, and Michelle groaned. "I just

don't want to mess up on my first date."

Angela touched her hand. "Just be yourself. That's all Danny wants from you."

"Okay, but I'm terrified of being a huge disappointment to him." Michelle whispered.

After a few more words of encouragement, Angela leaned forward. "I'm proud of you for stepping out of your comfort zone. I can't wait to hear all about it. I wanted to talk more about your relationship with Jeff, but maybe we ought to focus on you today."

"What do you mean?" Michelle asked.

Angela leaned forward slightly. "I believe you are scared, but let's think about why. Michelle, do you trust yourself when it comes to making decisions such as dating?"

"I don't know," Michelle whispered. "I guess I don't know how to trust myself."

"Let's think about what you do like and what you don't like." Angela said.

"What do you mean?"

"What are your interests outside of school and going on this date?" Angela asked.

"I love to read," Michelle said. "I participated in choir in school, so I guess I like to sing. I just don't like to do it in front of anyone but myself. I love hanging out with my roommates."

"That's a good start," Angela said. "I think you need to write down other things that interest you before going on this date. This might build confidence so that you can be yourself when you go out with Danny."

"I don't really like sports other than basketball. I do like watching Danny's games. Other sports have never interested me, either in person or on television." Michelle continued as though Angela hadn't spoken.

"This is a great start, but I want you to write down as many other things as you can think of. Then, you must reread it before going out. Learning who you are and what you care about will help you to focus on just being yourself. Honestly, I think every young person ought to do this before dating anyone seriously." Angela said.

Michelle nodded as her mind continued turning with multiple thoughts. She couldn't wait to get back to her room and continue writing her list of likes and dislikes.

***

As Michelle walked out of her session with Angela, she noticed Vicki Robinson sitting in the lobby. She slouched low on the couch and looked out the window. Her gaze showed intensity and she didn't blink. When her eyes landed on Michelle, she narrowed her eyes and sneered, "Well, if it isn't Miss Goody Two Shoes! I prayed I would never have to lay my eyes on you again."

Michelle didn't say a word as Angela spoke up, "Vicki, maybe you should come on back." She walked to the door, ready to open it, when she glanced back.

Standing and moving toward Angela, Vicki muttered, "It's your fault that I'm having to do these stupid sessions. It's also your fault that I'm on probation."

Michelle looked at her evenly. "I'm sorry you feel that way."

"Just keep away from me," Vicki snarled and she bared

her teeth at Michelle. "You and both of your stupid room-mates." Twisting her face in a hateful way, she said, "Maybe that stupid girl should have died!" When she noticed the pain and anger on Michelle's face, her own expression took on a gaze of satisfaction as Angela barked, "Vicki, that's enough! Let's go!"

Michelle blinked back tears as she walked out and headed back to the dorm. She had come so far in dealing with the emotional trauma from Hannah's abduction. Vicki's nasty words brought it all back in a snap. On the way to her room, she practiced the breathing exercises she learned as she recognized the pain. "It wasn't your fault," she whispered repeatedly.

Danny strolled into the counseling center and he recognized Angela behind the desk. He told her his name and she said Mark would be out for him shortly.

Danny set the spiral notebook on his lap. He struggled in learning how to express his feelings. His dad was someone who always told him to shake it off and toughen up. He knew his dad believed it was important to toughen him up in preparation for football.

He forgot about the assignment until the night before. Right before bed, he opened the notebook and sat there. Danny was unsure of what to write. His hand remained frozen as he frowned at the blank page. Why had he gotten so burned out on football? Once he wrote one sentence, the rest flowed out. His eyes widened as he reread the page of words.

"Danny," Mark walked toward him. "How are you?"

"I'm doing well." Danny stood and shook Mark's hand.

"Let's head back to my office."

The two of them sat in the same positions as the first session. Danny stared down at the spiral notebook, hesitant to start. When he glanced up, he noticed an open and kind expression on Mark's face.

Mark had been patiently waiting for him. He smiled. "Were you able to write any thoughts?"

Danny nodded, opened the notebook, and he handed it over to Mark. His fingers tapped on his thighs and the similar tightening of his chest filled him. He couldn't tell what Mark was thinking. A moment later, Mark looked up. "Danny, this is great."

"Really?"

"You expressed honesty in your words on the page. I'm starting to see why football lost its passion for you. This gives me some great background information on you." Mark said.

"And how will it help me?"

"Let me ask a few more questions. What are feelings you have experienced during your eighteen years of life? What do you prioritize your thoughts around?" Mark asked.

"Feelings? I'm not sure what you mean."

"You mentioned a great relationship with your family. Because of that, I think you battle with devotion to your parents and sister. Am I right?"

Danny frowned as he thought about it. "Yes, I can agree that's true."

"Danny, this is normal for most people. You are the older brother always desiring to please your parents and take care of your sister. Your parents probably asked you to watch out for her. Am I right?" Mark's eyes sparkled.

"Yes."

"Also being the oldest, I'm sure it was expected to get decent grades and live responsibly. Is that correct?"

"How is that different from any other kid?" Danny asked.

"It's not. But I think you have learned to place way too much pressure on yourself. I don't think anyone in your family meant for it to happen, but Danny I perceive you don't want to ever let anyone down." Mark's eyes danced with passion with his words.

Danny shook his head as he gazed into the distance. "I wanted to be that way for my family. It was my duty."

"Yes, that is true. But you learned to expect perfection from yourself. You didn't want to ever make mistakes. I believe that you have developed anxiety over the fears you have of failing yourself and your family." Mark said.

"Anxiety? Like something that might need medication?" Danny shook his head adamantly. "I don't think so. I don't have anxiety." "Danny, it's possible to manage anxiety without medication. It can involve learning how to change your thinking. It might involve steps to release the tremendous pressure you put on yourself." Mark's voice softened.

Danny continued shaking his head as he stood up. "I

need to go. This is too much for me to deal with right now." Danny got five steps out the door before he did an about face and he walked back into the room and sat on the edge of the couch.

Mark observed him, but he remained silent.

"I don't want to be someone who has anxiety. That will make people not like me and think I'm crazy." Danny moaned as he looked at the carpet while still sitting on the edge of his seat.

"Danny." Mark said his name and nothing else.

Danny looked at him.

"Anxiety is not a bad thing anymore. People all over the place worry and place pressure on themselves." Mark stopped as he reached under the side table for a cassette tape. "I want you to listen to this tape. It is a psychologist who teaches about anxiety and worry. I agree maybe we should table the rest of this session. Take some time to listen to this and you can schedule another meeting when you are ready to talk further about it." Danny took the tape from Mark's hand and he studied the cover with the title and the doctor's name.

"Okay." He stood up again and Mark opened the door. "Can I go ahead and schedule another time with you?"

"Sure, but if you feel you can't make it, you can cancel it."

"Thanks, Mark." Danny's mind swam. He felt so dizzy that his fingers and toes were tingling and he wondered if he might pass out. Danny pocketed the card from Mark, thankful that it was for the following week. He ambled toward his apartment, wondering how his feet were even carrying him.

***

Friday afternoon, Michelle fidgeted and jumped all day in her classes. Normally, her focus was perfect, but today her mind zoned out elsewhere. Her class load was not too difficult, other than a quiz. Having studied for two weeks, she exceeded it with an A. Unfortunately, when she tried taking notes in her other class, she couldn't pay attention and missed a lot of pertinent information. Michelle was tempted to slap herself in the head to see if it would help her listen like she needed to.

Michelle also struggled with what to wear as she finally made it back to her dorm. Indecision filled her as she stood in front of her closet, not able to choose anything. It all seemed to be a ridiculous choice for her. Never having gone on a date before, she tried to remember what Hannah wore on her first date with Michael. Michelle had picked out her outfit, but she couldn't recall what she loaned her.

As she began getting ready, she saw her hands shaking uncontrollably, and she was terrified she might poke herself in the eye with a mascara wand or an eyeliner stick.

Hannah walked past her as she tried to make her trembling hand apply blush in the proper place and not all over her face. Jackie was at the library completing research for a term paper.

"Michelle, what's wrong?" Hannah gently took the brush from her hand. "Why are you so nervous?"

Michelle released a shaky laugh. "I'm sorry. I've just never done this before. I mean, I've never gone on a date."

"But you and Danny danced when we all went out together last year." Her friend applied blush as she commented.

"Hannah, that was with a large group. And, I thought we were dancing as friends. Terror filled me at the thought of stepping on his feet!" Michelle breathed. "Tonight, he and I are the only ones and I don't want to mess anything up!"

Hannah chuckled. "I remember how nervous I felt on my first date with Michael. Once we went out, the experience was absolutely wonderful and my nerves went away. Yours will, too. Danny seems to really like you, so I think you can relax and just be yourself."

Michelle muttered something intelligible under her breath. "That's exactly what Angela said, but I'm not even sure how to do that! I can't even pick out anything to wear!"

As soon as the words came out of her mouth, the phone rang, causing her to shriek loudly. Michelle squealed, "He's early."

Hannah stepped to answer the phone, and she held it out. "It's not Danny. I think it's your brother."

"Crap," Michelle breathed. She knew if Jeff were here that he would have not allowed this date. She began breathing heavily, wondering if this entire night was a bad idea.

She took the phone as her brother said, "I haven't heard from you in a few days, so I wanted to call and see how it's going."

"Great!" Michelle said. "I'm having so much fun hanging out with friends and I have straight A's in my classes at the moment."

They talked for ten minutes and Michelle didn't dare utter a word about her date because she wouldn't put it past Jeff to drive up there this very night.

"Call Mom and Dad soon," he reminded her before he said goodbye.

After promising she would, they hung up the phone. Hannah guided her back over to finish her makeup. As she did, Michelle looked at her friend and said, "If Jeff ever calls and I'm not here, you can't tell him I'm going on dates with Danny. Okay?" She hadn't really explained about her brother to Hannah other than to talk about his overprotectiveness.

"Why?" Hannah asked with a bewildered expression.

"I haven't ever told you this before, but he always kept guys from even asking me out when I was still in high school. Guys didn't even approach me, much less ask me on a date. They felt intimidated by him." Michelle felt frustration as she looked at her friend. "It's why I've never been on a date before."

"Enough said," Hannah said. "You can count on me not to say a thing! Now, I'm going to help you get you dressed and then I'll help you finish your hair." She went to her closet and chose a tight acid-washed denim skirt along with a bright blue button-down blouse.

"Try this on," she said.

Michelle felt doubtful that it would flatter her because her shape differed from her friend's. After she put it on, she walked out of the bathroom as Hannah breathed in sharply.

"Oh, Michelle," she said. "That looks fabulous on you!"

Glancing in the mirror, Michelle's jaw dropped at seeing how nice it looked on her. "Thank you, Hannah."

Her roommate put finishing touches in her hair. When her phone rang again, she jumped. Thankfully, it was Michael. Hannah was staying over at his place for the night. Picking up her bag, she hugged Michelle and said, "Have a fabulous time!"

Michelle said, "Thank you," but it was to herself because Hannah left.

The third time the phone rang that evening, Danny told her of his arrival in the lobby.

Michelle rubbed her damp hands on her skirt, picked up her purse, and walked out to meet him.

Chapter 4

"Wow!" the word gushed out of Danny's mouth. His gaze swept up and down in a respectful manner. "You look fantastic!"

"Thank you," Michelle said, as her heart quickened at his compliment. Hannah did a beautiful job curling her shoulder-length hair. She glanced down at the blue, gauzy blouse and she felt thankful her friend shared her clothes with her. She just about fainted when she looked at Danny because he looked wonderful in a black-button down shirt and jeans. Again, her eyes zoomed in on his biceps and how the shirt spread across his muscular chest.

"Are you ready?" he asked with a gentle smile.

"Yes," Michelle replied.

Danny held out his hand, and Michelle panicked because her hands were sweaty. Her nerves went haywire at the thought of touching him. Directly meeting his gaze, she said, "I'm nervous and my hands are sweaty."

Danny kept his hand out. "I'm nervous, too. I don't care." He enfolded her hand in his and led her out to his truck.

Snorting in an unladylike manner, Michelle mumbled, "I have a hard time believing you're nervous. It sounds like you dated all the time in high school."

Danny stopped beside his car, leaned closer, and placed his hands on her shoulders. With a serious expression, he looked into her eyes and he said, "None of the girls I dated were anything special. And they only dated me because I was the quarterback of the football team. They didn't even care about me as a person. Trust me, I felt terrified that you wouldn't ever agree to go out with me."

Captivated by his gorgeous blue eyes, Michelle was speechless. She missed her hand in his as his hands burned deeply into her shoulders. She just nodded her head as he moved to open the passenger door to help her into his truck.

As soon as he started the truck, he said, "Are you still okay with the steak place we talked about?" Danny looked as if he wanted to reach for Michelle's hand again but he placed his hand on the gearshift instead.

Michelle smiled at him and, in her snarky manner, she said, "Hey, I'm from Houston, Texas, so something is wrong with me if I don't like steak!"

Danny laughed with Michelle. "I think steak should be a required food for anyone who lives in this state!" He turned on the radio, which was playing popular eighties music.

Michelle relaxed as she laughed at his joke and she started moving her head with the beat of the song. It made her happy to glance over and see Danny bobbing his head to the song as well. The teasing broke the ice, and she found her nerves easing as the two of them talked about school and their classes on the drive to the restaurant.

Danny pulled into a parking space, and Michelle moved to open her door, but Danny stopped her. "Wait, I want to come around for you."

Her heart fluttered nervously, and a tightness in her chest appeared with a flourish. Michelle nodded her head, blowing out a breath. Once he helped her out, he took her hand in his again and they walked into the restaurant. As they strolled, Michelle wondered if Danny sensed the spark when their hands touched. She mentally shook her head, thinking it was her because this was her first date ever with a guy.

They were shown to a booth after Danny told them he made a reservation. Both of them took a moment to study the menu until the server came and took their drink orders. The silence caused Michelle to fumble with her hands and she pulled on the ends of her hair, wondering if she should say anything. However, she wasn't sure what to talk about. Knowing that they both wanted steaks, they placed their orders instead.

Danny smiled at Michelle across the table. "Thanks for coming out with me tonight."

"I'm having a good time," she said with indecision in her eyes.

"But..." Danny said, encouraging her to speak what was on her mind.

Looking into his eyes, she was truthful. "I'm so nervous. I'm afraid I'm going to do something totally stupid like spill my drink or drop my fork."

Danny reached across the table for her hand and he intertwined their fingers together before he said, "You are doing fine. I want you to relax and enjoy your first date. I'm honored to be the person getting to experience it with you."

Michelle blushed and she blinked back moisture in her eyes. "Thank you for being patient with me. I'm having a good time."

"I'm glad and me too," Danny agreed, keeping her gaze as he raised her hand to his lips, kissing the back of it. Then he placed it on his heart before he continued, "If you feel my racing heart, you can see how nervous I am with you."

Michelle wanted to cool herself from the sensation of his lips on her fingers, but she refrained. She sensed perspiration beginning. Despite her overwhelming emotions, she stayed silent. However, her eyes widened at the rapid beating of his heart.

Even though one hand held hers, he put his other arm on the back of the booth and asked, "How was your exam today?" They talked about it at breakfast that morning.

"I got an A," she replied. "This class is important to my major, so I need to stay focused on it and not fall behind."

"I'm happy for you," Danny answered. "You must be super smart to be a business major, having to take all of those math courses."

"I definitely have to study, so I don't know that I'm a

genius or anything. But thank you." Michelle smiled at him.

They continued chatting until the server brought their salad and bread. Michelle asked more about his family and the small town where he grew up. They found they shared similar interests. They both enjoyed listening to country music as well as eighties music. Surprisingly, Danny also enjoyed reading, but he was more of a non-fiction reader.

To Michelle, the dinner passed by quickly. She felt like they had just gotten there and she was surprised that they sat and talked for two hours. Astonished to see that the time was nine-thirty on her watch, Danny helped her out of the booth and they walked outside. In his gentle-manly manner, he opened her truck door again before walking around to drive them back to the school.

All too soon, he pulled up and Michelle waited this time until he moved around the truck to open her door.

Danny continued to hold her hand as he asked, "Would you like to sit on the swing for a while? I've had a great time and I'm not ready for it to end."

Overwhelmed by the same sensation, Michelle nod-ded her head. Danny squeezed her hand, and he walked them over to the swing. He sat at a respectable distance from her, and he put his arm up around the back of the swing. Flutters filled Michelle's heart at the action and her voice was breathless as they discussed their hopes and dreams after college.

Like Hannah, Danny hoped to become a teacher. Michelle was aware he desired to be a coach like his dad, but he also talked about hoping to make a difference in younger kids' lives. However, the conversation was vague before he moved the questions back to her. Michelle got the idea that he really didn't wish to talk about his plan for the future. Since she didn't know him that well, she shifted to talking about herself. She shared her dream of owning her own business, not quite sure what that would entail. Danny's eyes shone admiration as he intently listened to every word.

After an hour longer, Danny said, "I guess I should go."

They stood and walked to the front of the dorm and nerves flew through Michelle again, as she was uncertain what to do.

"Michelle," he whispered in a low voice and she looked up at him with wide eyes. Her mouth was dry and she felt faint. "Thank you. I've had a great time."

"Me too. Thanks for asking me." Michelle said as she attempted to smile up at him. She wondered if her mouth was twisted and looked funny.

Danny asked, "Would you like to see a movie with me tomorrow night?"

"Yes," Michelle whispered as her heart began pounding in anticipation.

Danny leaned down and kissed Michelle's cheek. It soon became a habit he enjoyed throughout their building friendship. "Good night.

Michelle felt slightly let down as she whispered a reply to him and walked into her room. Truthfully, she desired a proper kiss from him. Even though she did not know how to kiss anyone, Michelle believed she was ready for more than holding hands and kisses on the cheek. "It's your own fault," she mumbled to herself as she unlocked her door and walked inside.

***

Thankful that she had little to do on Saturday morning, Michelle allowed herself to sleep later than normal. Jackie occupied the bathroom at the moment, and Hannah stayed over with Michael the previous night.

When Jackie walked out and noticed Michelle's eyes open, she smiled. "Well, how did it go? Did you have a fabulous time on your first date?"

"Yes, it turned out wonderful." Michelle spoke in a soft and dreamy voice as she sat up. Then she shook her head at herself, pondering the fact that she sounded like a lovesick schoolgirl. "The restaurant was really nice, and we spent four hours talking together."

Jackie dipped her head to study Michelle's face as she joined her on her bed. "What are you not telling me?"

Michelle sighed. "I'm surprised to admit this, but I was disappointed."

"You just said it was wonderful. What are you disappointed about?"

"Danny only kissed me on the cheek."

Jackie snorted. "You wanted to make out with him, right?" Michelle glared at her and she laughed in glee.

"I told him to be patient with me and to take things slow," Michelle said. "But now I want more than that."

"It sounds to me like you're going to have to talk to Danny and give him a signal that you are ready for more." Jackie said.

"We're going to a movie tonight," Michelle said.

"That's perfect!" Jackie said. "It will be dark and you can snuggle against him. That should show him you're ready to do more than hold hands."

The idea filled Michelle with terror. Her hands began shaking as she remembered a movie theater as a place her friends would talk about making out instead of enjoying a movie. The idea terrified her since she had never done it before. Michelle reminded herself of Danny's gentlemanly nature. It wasn't her feeling that he wished for her to be uncomfortable. Michelle remembered Jeff and how he would not like her going to a movie with Danny at all. She heard his voice telling her he only wanted one thing. Michelle felt conflicted about what to do. Maybe she should halt the relationship and just be done with it.

***

That evening, when Danny called her to let her know of his arrival, Michelle was ready. Hannah shared another top with her and this time, she put it on with jeans. The top featured a button-down design, shoulder pads, and the color was bright blue. Looking in the mirror, it pleased her to see how it flattered her extra curves in her figure. Michelle paid little attention to how she looked in high school as she never dressed for a boy Now it seemed to be all she cared about.

When she walked out to the lobby, Danny stood by the window. When he turned and noticed Michelle, it still overwhelmed her at how his eyes always lit up, making her heart flutter.

"Hi," she said, smiling up at him. He stood taller than her, at six-foot-two.

Danny took her hand in his and he lifted it to his lips while keeping his eyes on her. "You look wonderful," he said.

"Thank you. So do you." She tried not to swoon at his jeans and polo shirt. The shirt looked to be the same color blue as his eyes and it showed off his muscled chest.

He kept her hand in his as they walked out to his truck. His manners in opening her side of the truck door never got old. Sometimes it seemed to her that she was another person and it was all a dream. He came across as one of the best looking guys she had ever met and he treated her like a princess! She never felt that way in her life, even though she had never dated before. Again, the constant fear of Jeff's reaction remained in the back of her mind.

The drive took about thirty minutes because they had to drive to a nearby town. The small town where they went to college didn't have a movie theater. Danny pulled into the pizza restaurant next to the theater and Michelle knew to wait for him to come around and open her door. He kept her hand in his as they walked inside.

They shared a supreme pizza and breadsticks; their conversation felt natural, like lifelong friends. Michelle sometimes felt dizzy from the degree to which she was developing feelings for Danny. Many football players were stuck up jerks at her high school, but he was one of the kindest people she had ever met.

While talking, they moved to Danny's classes and what he thought about them. The more he shared, the more Michelle realized he struggled with knowing his major. It remained too soon in their relationship to say anything, but she was noticing Danny had little focus. As he had been doing, Danny quickly moved off of the topic. Her brow furrowed slightly because her high school years were consumed by thoughts of her future. Michelle took advantage of the Friday nights at home to study and put all of herself into her schoolwork. What she had learned about Danny came across as the opposite of her. He wasn't a poor student. She knew he made decent grades. She just didn't see a drive to push himself toward his future. The doubts from Jeff came to mind, but she shoved them away.

After dinner, Danny paid for the movie, buying a soda for Michelle since she was full from eating. Once he bought their drinks, they walked into the darkened theater and Michelle's gut filled with an uneasy feeling. As if he read her mind, Danny put his arm behind her seat, and he whispered, "I won't do anything else if you aren't comfortable. You can trust me to be a gentleman with you."

Michelle believed him, and she leaned her head against his shoulder, before. "Thank you. I do trust you."

Danny tightened his arm slightly as he pulled her closer

against him and he breathed out a sigh of contentment. A few minutes later, the movie began, and they became lost in the plot. A sad scene occurred at one point. The protagonist witnessed her father's death, and Michelle's tears flowed uncontrollably. As attentive as Danny was, he pulled her closer and rested his head on top of hers in comfort. Michelle turned her head to where she looked up at him because of how tender he was with her.

His eyes bored into hers, and she leaned up to kiss him softly on the mouth. Danny couldn't help but gasp. Once the initial shock wore off, he cradled her face and placed a second kiss on her mouth. It was soft, and Michelle was overwhelmed by the softness of Danny's lips.

Michelle sighed in contentment as he pulled her close to his side once again. Once the movie concluded, a sense of weightlessness came over Michelle as they walked to Danny's truck. She had her first kiss, and she kissed Danny!

Chapter 5

The thirty-minute drive flew by as Danny guided his truck back toward the school. Then they returned to her dorm. After he helped her out of his truck, Danny squeezed Michelle's hand and said, "I know you wanted to take things slow because you haven't dated. But I think you're ready for the next step. Am I right?"

Shyness overcame Michelle, but she nodded. "Yes."

Danny's serious gaze held Michelle captive. He asked, "Can I kiss you good night?" As he asked, his own heart flip-flopped again as uncertainty filled him. He was petrified of moving too fast.

Michelle froze, and she began breathing harder. "I don't know if I did it right in the movie or if I am any good at it. But, I would like that."

One of Danny's hands caressed one cheek. "I'm not complaining at all about your kiss during the movie. Do you trust me to kiss you now?"

Michelle's eyes filled with longing as her gaze moved to his lips, and she nodded again.

Danny moved slowly, and he cradled her face for the

second time that night. As his lips touched hers in a tender and loving kiss, his entire being filled with warmth. The excitement he had been experiencing intensified as his lips met Michelle's. As he deepened their kiss, Danny sensed a connection deeper than anything he'd ever experienced before. Michelle was like a breath of fresh air and his heart pounded at the softness of her lips. Danny desperately wanted to deepen it even more, but he refrained because he didn't want to push her too fast.

When Danny pulled back slightly, she breathed, "Wow!" Her head was spinning, and she appeared as if she might pass out. She gazed at nothing as if dreaming.

Danny laughed with her. "Wow." Truthfully, he wasn't sure how to slow down his own erratic heartbeat. He kissed her twice more, not wanting it to end. However, he made himself pull back, and he smiled gently at her. "I promise you that you are not bad at this," he whispered. His lips moved to her forehead as he held her close for a few more seconds.

Michelle's eyes remained closed as she breathed, "I really liked that." She leaned in against him.

Danny laughed again as she opened her eyes and looked at him in wonder. "Me too," he said, running his hands down her arms to clasp her fingers.

He was happy to see desire in her eyes, as if she wanted another kiss from him.

Danny beamed. "I will see you at breakfast on Monday." He leaned down and tipped Michelle's chin so he could gaze into her eyes. Gently, he placed one more kiss on her cheek as he squeezed her other hand. "Good night."

***

Monday morning, Michelle was thrilled to see Danny waiting for her with Michael. Michael always waited for Hannah before going into the dining hall, and Michelle's heart leapt from seeing Danny's eyes light up as he pulled her into a gentle hug and whispered, "Good morning." When Danny kissed her the other night, she found herself unable to breathe from the sensation of his lips touching hers. It seemed as if butterfly wings were flapping within her, and she experienced the sensation of lightning bolts zig-zagging through her.

"Morning," she whispered against his rock-hard chest. Embarrassed from wanting more, she pulled back and blew out a breath. He caused her to experience sensations completely new to her, but she enjoyed it. A small nagging sensation was in the back of her mind of how her brother would react to her dating. She wondered if she shouldn't welcome Danny's touch this much.

Danny tilted her chin up. His eyes reflected understanding as he softly said, "I want more, too." Her heart was overwhelmed, because it seemed like he knew exactly what she was thinking. Danny placed his hand over her heart. "Do you feel that?" Michelle nodded. Relief filled her as she felt the pounding in his heart. She worried he could hear hers and it was nice to hear similar feelings within him.

Danny clasped his fingers with hers as they followed Hannah and Michael inside. Normally she noticed their constant public displays, but she didn't pay attention this morning. Her mind and heart remained in conflict with one another during breakfast. Thankfully, Jackie had already walked in ahead of them.

***

Two weeks flew by quickly, with the same routine each day, and Michelle fell deeper for Danny. Every emotion seemed new, and she often wasn't sure how to process her feelings. Excitement, nervousness, and anticipation of seeing him again filled her. Her heart skipped when she saw him waiting for her at breakfast, and warmth filled her every evening as he walked her back to her dorm. Michelle felt cherished every time he walked her to class or held out a chair for her. She wondered if she should even feel these sensations at all. What if he was just trying to get her to sleep with him? It's what Jeff talked about and Michelle had a hard time seeing past his words. However, when she was with Danny, she had a hard time believing the words Jeff preached to her all of her life. Danny didn't come across as an arrogant man who was trying to get what he wanted from her. When they talked, he came across as the most genuine guy Michelle had the privilege of knowing. She was growing weary of the confusing thoughts running repeatedly inside her head.

She called her parents on Saturday, and she evaded talking about going on a date with them. Michelle knew her mom would love to hear about it. She knew Jeff would find out, and she wanted to enjoy this experience without his meddling. Wishing she could remind him that she was old enough, Michelle knew the minute she told him, she would fall back into the cycle of pleasing him again. Michelle had confided a little to Angela about her relationship with Jeff. But maybe she needed to ask her for advice on how to confront his constant protection of her from people of a different sex. If only she didn't feel inept in every word she spoke to Danny and every decision she made as their dating relationship continued building.

Vicki walked into the dining hall when she spotted Michelle with Danny and all her other little friends. Anger rushed through Vicki as memories of the past two months came rushing back to her. She thought Rhonda would be a friend to hang out with, but she used her because of her poor reputation. When Rhonda told her she would pay her cash if Vicki helped her out, Vicki jumped at the chance by creating a diversion in the gym so that Rhonda's plan would happen. Vicki's fake emergency gave Rhonda time to block the doors so that they wouldn't be followed. Rhonda was arrested, and she received no money at all.

Hannah's stupid roommates, Michelle and Jackie, detained her until the police got there and arrested her. Michael had also been a jerk to Vicki about it when he yelled at her for allowing Rhonda to escape outside with his mousey girlfriend. Vicki hadn't meant to blurt out that she wished Hannah had died in the counseling center the other day, but she allowed her rage to get the best of her when she saw Michelle. The words spewed forth before she checked herself.

Vicki might be attractive if she wanted to be. Her mom wanted her to appear a certain way and Vicki did all that she could to rebel against it when she became a teenager. She dressed in a grungy manner on purpose. Immediately after arrival at this terrible college, she had her hair cut short. When Vicki still lived at home, her mom experienced embarrassment because of the friends she spent time with from her hometown. Vicki found great joy in that small feat. What her parents didn't realize: such people existed everywhere, even at this stupid college. Her mind drifted to Colin, the love of her life. She had spoken to him a week ago, and she missed him beyond words. It seemed like half of her was missing. Before they hung up, she promised to find her way back home to him.

Vicki got her food and went to sit at the corner table with a girl named Brandi, who also earned a negative reputation. People ignored them and pretended they weren't there in the corner where they sat. Either that or they considered the two miscreants to be invisible. Michelle glanced in her direction and her mouth flattened as she noticed Vicki walk by with fury in her eyes.

Brandi wore short, dark hair. She wore a loose tee shirt, and she had a chain belt around her cargo pants. The two of them fell into trouble when they first got to college, when they bought beer at a convenience store and drove recklessly through the small town.

Brandi looked at her, tipped her chin as a way of saying hello, and said, "You interested in making some money?"

Vicki popped a spoonful of cereal in her mouth as her eyes perked. "What do you have in mind?"

Danny felt overwhelmed by his strong feelings for Michelle after the little time he had spent with her. When he wasn't with her, he missed her as he sat in his classes and completed homework assignments, longing to see her again.

Some football players struggled with schoolwork and understanding everything they were taught. It presented no problem for Danny. Other than hard classes such as calculus or chemistry, he was average in intelligence and he had maintained A's and B's in high school.

Sometimes he put way too much pressure on himself to balance his schoolwork, along with being a football star. His driven nature led his team to two state championships in his last two years of high school. After winning the year before, Danny realized he couldn't let his team down his senior year. He shook his head and remembered how much his teachers loved him because of his dad's leadership and his mom working in the school district's office. The few times he failed exams or papers, he blamed himself for not trying hard enough, even though he was often stretched thin. Danny didn't stop to realize that his anxiety stemmed from his drive for perfection. Danny frowned at himself as he recalled the meeting with Mark. He listened to the tape as he went for a drive after their session to think. Just as Mark said, the person talking made it sound like anxiety was a normal reaction. Danny wondered what his teachers would think about him now. He loved playing basketball with his buddies, but it remained a struggle for him to ponder about what he wanted to do when he graduated. His heart skipped a beat at the fear of disappointing everyone.

He and Michelle met most afternoons for a game or two of ping-pong before dinner. Sometimes Hannah and Michael joined them. Other times, it was just the two of them, and Danny learned that he never wanted their time together to end.

When he called his parents last Sunday, he shared about their date and how much he liked her. His parents were wonderful, and they always supported him. His mom opened an invitation for Danny to invite her to their home with him one weekend so that they might meet her. They couldn't visit his college in the fall because of football season and Friday night games.

At that moment, Danny headed to the student center to meet her, and he quickened his step in his excitement to see her again. He found Michelle's inexperience enchanting, and he felt thrilled with the knowledge that he was the one waking her up to new feelings. The desire he noticed in her eyes for him made his chest swell with pride, and he vowed to himself that he would never disappoint her. His chest tightened and his breaths increased in speed as he thought about letting her down.

Danny opened the door to the student center. He spotted Michelle sitting on a couch with a textbook on her lap. As he walked in her direction, she glanced up and her eyes lit up when she saw him.

"Hey beautiful," he said, loving how it made her blush.

Michelle dipped her head, and she shuffled her books before standing. "Hi," she said, and she placed the textbook in her backpack. Danny observed her ears turning red. It was an endearing trait to him.

As soon as she straightened, he gently shouldered her backpack before pulling her to a secluded corner of the student center, and into his arms. After dropping both of their bags, he tugged her closer with the intention of hugging her. Danny looked into her eyes and it seem he was unable to stop himself. He leaned close, capturing her lips in his for a gentle kiss. He hadn't anticipated her enthusiastic response to the kiss. Danny groaned, wrapped one hand around her waist, and he ran his fingers of his other hand through her hair as he tilted their heads to deepen the kiss. He relished in hearing her gasp. Michelle froze slightly as he urged her to open her mouth. His tongue found its way inside and he felt her zing of shock from it. However, a tiny moan escaped her and Danny wondered if she knew she had made the small noise. Because of that, he extended the kiss a few more seconds before pulling back.

Michelle opened her eyes with a dazed expression. "Wow!"

Pleased with himself for bringing that expression to her face, he chuckled, pushed the hair away from her forehead and kissed her gently one more time. "You are intoxicating, Michelle Walters. I apologize if I startled you, but I couldn't help myself.

She still didn't speak, but she only stared at him. "I think I can say the same about you, that you are also exciting!"

Danny hugged her gently as he chuckled again at her comment. He learned that he really liked her sarcasm.

After playing for another half hour, they joined their friends for dinner. Michelle was learning to be open to him, holding her hand while they ate. Danny felt grateful because he always wanted to touch her. Progress had been made when she no longer blushed as he reached for her fingers to clasp them with his.

His daily habit involved walking her back to her dorm and pulling her into the shadows for a goodnight kiss. She returned his kisses with fervor and he deepened the kiss to invade her mouth again. As he did, an underlying fear of pushing too fast and too hard filled his gut. He sensed hesitation in her. He wasn't exactly sure why, but it was there.

With his forehead pressed against hers, he said, "Don't forget we are going out tomorrow. Are you still okay with that?'

"I am," she whispered against his cheek. Then she

pulled back to look at him when she asked, "What are your plans for the evening?"

"Would you like to get pizza and go to another movie?" Danny's thumb caressed her cheek as his blue eyes remained fastened on hers.

She smiled up at him. "That sounds wonderful." Her eyes filled with regret when she continued, "I need to go inside because I have two exams tomorrow and I need to review the material."

"I have two tests tomorrow, so I need to go as well." Danny kissed her once more before he stepped back. "I will see you in the morning. Good night, beautiful!" He didn't miss her intake of breath as he said the word for the second time that night. However, the night hid any blush in her cheeks.

"Good night," she whispered, and she turned to walk inside.

***

Michelle found she loved when Danny kissed her. It became a wonderful and new experience and she mastered returning his kisses with fervor. Sometimes disquiet filled her because she felt uncertain in what she was doing. In her heart, she desired a book or manual to guide her on dating.

In Michelle's mind, kissing constituted an integral part of dating guys. She remembered the public displays of affection that she had observed in high school. Therefore, she allowed Danny to lead with his gentle kisses. Beneath those thoughts lay the fear of pushing herself too fast. Danny knew what to do, but Michelle lacked experience spending time with a guy. However, she continued responding to Danny because she didn't want to disappoint him. And she truly enjoyed kissing him. Deep down, Michelle longed for a knowledge of how to proceed. It was something she was even afraid of talking to Hannah about.

Jeff's face came to mind and the expression he used when he defended his protectiveness to their mother. She remembered his words, "I know what guys are like at this age. They only want one thing from girls. I want nothing happening to you and it's my job to protect you from it." Michelle's mind warred with itself and sometimes she had difficulty completing a task. It was unheard of for her because she could always zoom in on her schoolwork with single-minded focus. Ever since her relationship with Danny had begun, that focus had become less consistent. She frowned slightly, rubbing a hand through her hair as she walked to her dorm.

***

Danny feared he was moving too fast with Michelle, but she brought out a desire in him he couldn't seem to quench. Along with wanting to be with her was the pressure he put on himself. Danny wanted to be a knight in shining armor to Michelle because he understood she knew little about men. Determined to be all that she needed made his shoulders hunch up nearer to his ears as he coached himself in how to do it. The constant nagging sensation to slow things down and move slower burned within him, but Danny ignored it.

He wanted to invite her to his place, but he had doubts about her readiness. Perhaps he should speak to Hannah about it again to assess Michelle's feelings regarding their time together.

Danny nodded to himself as he walked back to his apartment. His plan was to talk to her in the next few days. He believed she would be at the apartment complex between now and then so that Michelle wouldn't find out.

Chapter 6

Michelle walked into a conference room in the library when she overheard talking in the room beside hers. The door propped open and she stepped to move on when she recognized one of the voices as Vicki's. She couldn't help but pause because she felt certain that Vicki was not studying. There was another voice but she didn't recognize it.

The other girl said, "This shouldn't be too hard. The girl and her family are loaded! I know for a fact she has expensive jewelry along with plenty of money."

Vicki replied, "Okay, so what's your plan?" Her voice didn't sound like she was sold on the idea that Brandi was presenting.

"We need to work out a plan to learn her schedule so we know when she comes and when she goes. Once we figure out when she isn't in her apartment, we can strategize about how to pull this off." the other girl said. "I've been trailing her for a few days and I've learned her apartment is across the street from the school. Her daddy is so loaded that she could live without a roommate, but she is rooming with her best friend from her hometown."

"Brandi, how is that going to work? I'm not sure we can pull off breaking into an apartment. If her daddy's that rich, it might have an alarm system or something." Doubt laced Vicki's voice.

"Stop questioning me!" Brandi snapped. "Just be ready for your times of watching and following."

Vicki said. "Alright. How do you know she's so wealthy?"

"I told you I've already been watching. She used to go to basketball games and one time I sat behind her and heard her brag about it! Apparently her daddy gives her anything she wants!" Brandi's voice was filled with impatience and she spoke to Vicki like she was an idiot. Brandi had no idea that Vicki's parents were also wealthy, but Vicki didn't plan on sharing the information.

Michelle heard the chairs scraping against the carpet and she hurried to the next empty study room. She hoped they didn't hear the door open in the study room beside them. Michelle winced when the hinges squeaked. She quickly spread out her textbook and notes on the project that she was working on.

However, she couldn't concentrate on the work. Michelle felt distracted by what she had overheard. Vicki and her friend were planning a burglary! Not knowing who their target would be, she couldn't do anything. If she reported it to authorities, there wasn't much that she could tell them. She decided she needed to follow Vicki. The knowledge that she still attended counseling meetings, Vicki decided the next time she noticed her in the center that she would wait over to the side of the building until she left.

***

The door squeaked. "What was that?" Brandi twisted her head in surprise.

Suspiciously, Vicki crept to the corner of the room and peeked around. "Bitch," she mouthed to herself when she spotted Michelle inside.

"What do you see?" Brandi whispered, more persistent this time.

Turning back to Brandi, Vicki schooled her snarling face. "Just another girl studying. We shouldn't have left the door open."

"Shut up!" Brandi whispered. "I wonder if she overheard us." Brandi's tone turned hard, as if she wanted to do something to Michelle.

As much as the temptation to rough Michelle up filled her, Vicki had never assaulted someone before. Most of her indiscretions were indirect attacks, like shoplifting or painting graffiti on a building.

Brandi's eyes narrowed as she peered around and noticed Michelle sitting in the room studying. It appeared as if Brandi wanted to confront Michelle. Vicki said, "Not a good idea. If you do something now and get in trouble, you can kiss your plan goodbye."

The other girl's narrowed and angry gaze landed on Vicki, and she smirked at her. "You were stupid to say my name because she probably heard it!" She slung her bag across her body and stalked out of the room they were using.

Vicki considered what she should do if Michelle had overheard the conversation. She just couldn't get away from that girl who thought she was so self-righteous! Vicki opted to lie low for a few days, and she would let Brandi start her crazy plan without her. She needed to come up with some excuse why it was necessary to wait.

***

Danny trudged toward his session with Mark. His emotions bounced all over the place. He dreaded the upcoming conversation about anxiety, but he longed to hear more. Could it be possible for him to work through these feelings? Was it why he struggled with knowing his plan?

When he stepped into the counseling center, Mark was sitting behind the desk. His greeting was short before he led Danny back to his office.

"Last session ended on a rough note." Mark's tone was matter of fact, and Danny nodded.

Mark paused. "Did you listen to the tape I gave you?"

Danny nodded again. "It matched exactly to your words."

"What thoughts are passing through your brain?" Mark asked.

"Man, it scares me to death. But, if I truly have anxiety, I want to learn to get past it."

Mark leaned forward. "You will. Your acceptance of it that I am seeing today is a great start."

"Thanks." Danny wiped his sweaty palms on his jeans.

"Let's take it a step further today. I think small steps in the right direction are the best ones for you." Mark said, and Danny nodded again.

"There are four things I want you to do. One of them is exercise. Playing basketball is great, but maybe hiking or jogging could be added to it on days when you aren't practicing with your team."

Danny appeared to be thinking about it. "That sounds simple. I can do that."

"Great. Number two, I want you to focus on your diet and what you eat. Make sure that your three meals include healthy fruits and vegetables." Mark smiled. "Being eighteen, there's no way to completely cut out junk food. But, learn how to balance it with healthier food."

Danny's eyes filled with determination. "I can do that, too."

Mark paused before his next question. "Do you sleep well?"

Danny paused. "Most of the time. Sometimes I wake up in the night when I have a big test. I used to wake up on Fridays a lot."

"The pressure of winning those football games, right?" Mark asked.

"Yes." Danny's eyes grew large as he realized how he agonized over making sure he won.

"I want you to keep a journal of how you sleep each day. I'm going to give you a chart to fill in so that you can keep track. I think it's important that you get seven to eight hours of sleep every night as much as you can. When the semester ends and finals are upon you, that might become difficult. We can work through it at that time." Mark said.

"Is that all?" Danny asked.

Mark nodded. "I think it is for now. I would like for you to write your thoughts in your journal, but I don't want you to stress yourself out over it. The point is not to add more anxiety to your life." Mark's smile turned teasing and Danny chuckled. "Just write when you have five or ten minutes, like a diary."

Danny's face screwed up. "A diary, like a girl?"

"Diaries don't have to just be for females." Mark smiled. "We won't call it a diary. It can just be your journal."

"Okay," Danny's mouth scrunched tighter when he realized the hour had passed so quickly. He relaxed it as Mark handed him another tape.

"Keep listening and learning more about anxiety. If you have a chance to find material at the library, you can read about it as well."

"Thank you." This time, Danny held out his hand and Mark shook it.

After scheduling his next appointment, Danny walked outside. It felt as if a load had been lifted from his chest. He repeated the things he needed to do in his mind. *Exercise, diet, sleep, learn* he thought out loud to himself.

***

Friday night arrived and Michelle sat in Danny's truck as he drove them to the next town.

"Instead of pizza, do you want to go to a place that serves really good burgers?" Danny asked.

Michelle smiled at him, with her hand clasped in his. "Hamburgers are the second most important food in Texas. I would love to go for a burger."

Danny laughed at her joke as he lifted her hand to his lips and kissed her fingertips. Michelle shivered from the gesture.

The restaurant that Danny suggested was new and the burgers were fabulous. Michelle and Danny both ordered medium-well burgers and fries. The burgers were extremely large and freshly made, not anything like fast food hamburgers. Michelle couldn't eat another bite, so once they got to the movie, she turned down the offer of popcorn or candy. Danny bought them drinks before they found their seats.

This time the movie was a comedy. Michelle loved snuggling against Danny's side as they laughed together.

Halfway through the movie, she looked into Danny's eyes. His eyes stared into hers, and she was the one who leaned up to kiss him. For some reason, dark movie theaters drove Michelle to become more intimate. After gasping in surprise, one hand cradled her face as Danny leaned into her kiss. She realized he was letting her decide how deep to take it. Surprisingly, she extended the kiss, and it was satisfyingly long. When she pulled back, Danny whispered, "Baby, I love you."

Michelle pulled back with a sharp intake of breath. Her eyes darkened as she whispered, "What did you just say?" Panic filled her thoughts and she wanted to run away.

"Let's talk about it after the movie ends. I don't want to interfere with others who are watching." Danny whispered, but he took her hand. He intertwined their fingers and placed her hand in his lap.

At that point, Michelle heard nothing of the movie anymore. Overwhelmed from hearing him say those words, she wasn't sure whether to be ecstatic or petrified.

Thirty minutes later, the movie ended. They walked silently, hand in hand, to Danny's truck. However, he didn't move to start it. Instead, he leaned against the driver's side door. "I'm sorry if I shocked you, Michelle. I don't want to pressure you into anything you aren't ready for." His expression looked crestfallen.

Michelle's heart broke at seeing it. "I just don't know what to do with your words." Michelle moved her gaze straight ahead. Her voice came out as whisper soft.

"What do you mean by that?" Danny questioned in a soft voice.

Completely humiliated, when her voice started shaking, she said, "Nobody other than my family has ever said those words to me. I've come a long way with you by going out on dates and kissing. I feel okay with all of what you and I have been doing. I just hope you won't be mad if I can't say those words back right away."

"Michelle, look at me," Danny implored with a gentle gaze. "Please." He put his hand on her arm, as if he was afraid to touch her anywhere else.

Michelle finally glanced at him. "I'm so sorry if this was not the right time." He gazed down at his own hands. "I can't stop thinking about you, and I want to be with you all the time. When we aren't together, I miss you so much that all I do is think about you. I can promise you I have not said these words to any other girl because I've never felt this way before for anyone else." He glanced up and observed her studying him.

With wide eyes, her voice turned to a whisper. "I did not know you felt all of that for me."

Danny reached for her hand. "Baby, why wouldn't any guy feel that way about you? You don't know how beautiful you are, do you?" His eyes turned a cobalt blue as they sparked with fire.

With unbelief in her eyes, Michelle shook her head without speaking. "I told you I have never done this, so it's all new to me."

"Come here," he requested. "Please."

Michelle allowed him to pull her against his chest, and she heard the pounding of his heart. She moved her eyes up to his again in wonder. She shook her head. "You are incredibly good-looking, and you carry yourself with such confidence. It's hard for me to believe that your heart desires me so much."

Danny cradled her face in his hands and he said, "My heart has never raced like this for anybody else. I can promise you that."

Michelle worked to stop the tears from welling up in her eyes as she blinked rapidly, hoping they would disappear. "Can you be patient with me if I don't say it back to you right away?"

With her face still in his hands, Danny murmured, "I told you because I couldn't hold back anymore. It wasn't so that you would say it back. I know we are still in the early stages of our relationship, so I expect nothing from you." A tear leaked out of her right eye and rolled down her face as he reached to wipe it away. She nodded, and he continued, "Will it bother you if I keep saying it to you?"

Speechless, she shook her head. "You can say it again. I enjoyed hearing it."

"I'm glad." Danny's eyes were tender as his gaze held hers. "Can I kiss you?"

Michelle reached up and kissed him first.

***

Deep down was the fear that Danny was moving too quickly. He didn't mean to blurt out his love for her, but the words just flew out of him before he could stop himself. He kicked himself for pushing Michelle too fast, and his heart ached at seeing her terrified expression. As he reached for her hand, he was ecstatic when she didn't pull away. When she reached to kiss him first, Danny considered it progress even though Michelle's face was pale. Not able to contain himself any longer, he pulled her as closely as possible and he deepened their kiss.

He was relieved when he heard a sharp inhale from her as he urged her to open her mouth. When she did, his tongue explored inside of her mouth and he felt a positive rush of euphoria. Once Danny pulled back, his mouth moved to the side of her neck. Michelle breathed in pleasure as his lips trailed down it and over to her ear. When she pushed herself as close as the console would allow, he saw it as acceptance. He was thrilled she was clinging to him instead of holding onto the door handle of his truck like she had been moments before. His mouth found hers again. His hands caressed up her neck and through her hair. His kisses turned feathery before he finally pulled away.

"Oh my," she whispered with a far-off look on her face. "That was extraordinary!"

"Yeah," he agreed as he pressed his forehead against hers. Then he pulled back and touched her cheek as he repeated, "I love you, Michelle Walters."

"You keep kissing me like that. I may say it sooner than you think!" she exclaimed with glazed eyes.

Danny couldn't help but laugh as he pulled her against him for a hug. "I need to get you back because it's getting late." Holding her closely against him felt so right.

Michelle looked at her watch to check the time. She surprised herself when she said, "It's only nine."

Elated by her words, Danny kissed the side of her head. "Would you like to come to my place for a little while?"

Even though she hadn't said it back to him, he was happy to see warmth in her eyes as she smiled into his. "Yes, I would."

He wasn't about to turn down her offer for more time. The fear of letting her down filled his gut, but he desired to be completely honest with her.Deep down, the anxiety reared its head because Danny was terrified she would be overwhelmed by his strong feelings for her. He feared that his anxiety would be difficult to overcome as he wanted to make himself be what Michelle needed. All of Mark's words flew out of his head as he started his truck and drove to his place.

***

As soon as Danny pulled up to his apartment, he parked and walked around to open Michelle's door. She was familiar with the apartment complex because Hannah's boyfriend, Michael, lived next door with Michael's room-mate, Alex.

When Danny unlocked his front door, she walked into a very similar layout. However, the kitchen was positioned on the opposite side as well as the door into the living room.

It looked very much like a guy's apartment. There were a few dishes piled in the sink and a pair of shoes was sit-ting in the living room on the floor. When she glanced into a bedroom, she looked away quickly in embarrassment. She saw an unmade bed and clothes scattered on the floor. Michael's apartment was extremely neat because he couldn't stand when things were not tidied up and put back in their place. Michelle knew it not to be typical behavior for a guy and she wasn't surprised because her own brother was a total slob. As she thought about Jeff, it reminded her she needed to call and talk to him. Michelle hadn't spoken to him in a couple of weeks and the worry about not telling him about Danny filled her mind. Also, the doubts of what she was doing with Danny was always an underlying feeling, but she always pushed it down.

"Sorry, I didn't know you were coming over or I would have cleaned up a bit." Danny said as he looked around sheepishly.

His voice brought Michelle back to the present and the fact that she was standing in his apartment. "Don't worry about it," Michelle said. "I understand because my brother is even messier than this! I've tried to help him over the years but I haven't made any progress with him!"

Danny chuckled. "Do you want to sit down and watch television?" He gestured to a very large television. Then he continued. "My roommate, James, is out tonight but I'm not sure where he is or when he will be back."

Michelle smiled as she sat on the couch. "I'd like that."

"Are you thirsty?" he asked and she shook her head no.

He grabbed a remote control and sat beside her on the couch. After finding a familiar sitcom, he put the remote down on the coffee table and stretched his arm behind Michelle on the back of the couch. As they watched, she found herself leaning against his shoulder again. His declaration of love exhausted her and she found comfort from his embrace. She loved it when she felt his arm tighten protectively around her.

At one point, she lifted her head and gazed up at

Danny. He glanced down at her and noticed undisguised longing in her eyes. Danny must have taken it as an invitation, and he pulled her closer. He bent down, touching his lips to hers. Danny moved his lips over hers and he let out a gasp when he heard her exhale loudly. He moaned and deepened the kiss as she pressed herself closer to him. As she leaned toward him, one hand caressed her back up to her neck while the other one ran through her beautiful soft brown hair.

Somehow, when Danny uttered that he loved her earlier, Michelle's desire for him rose double-time. Michelle kissed him back with a passion she didn't realize that she had as their tongues rhythmically moved in and out of each other's mouths. She whimpered softly when his lips left hers to travel to her cheek and down the side of her neck. The touch of his lips on her sensitive neck touched something deep down inside of her and she heard a groan come out of her own mouth. Michelle almost sat up, wondering where the sound had come from.

Danny's lips found hers again, filling her with delirium as his tongue traced the seam of her lips. She opened for him again as the idea of kissing became something she thoroughly enjoyed. Michelle pushed all thoughts of Jeff and what he would think from her mind as she was swept up in Danny's kiss.

When Danny pulled back, they were struggling to catch their breath as his hands continued their hypnotic movements. His fingers were magic and they ignited a spark in her as she found herself wanting more.

Danny whispered against her ear. "Kissing you is magical."

"Mmm," Michelle replied, and she reached up to kiss his lips again. Slightly terrified, but filled with a renewed desire, she whispered, "Can we do more?"

Danny pulled back to look into her eyes. "Are you sure you're ready for that?"

Michelle caressed his cheek and smiled. "I know I haven't said the '*I love you*' words back to you, but I care deeply about you. I trust you to care for me and I am ready to try other things, but only with you." She shoved her fears and worries to the back of her mind.

Danny's gaze turned liquid. "Baby, thank you." He cradled her cheeks and stared into her eyes. "I will take care of you and you can tell me when you are ready to stop. I don't know when James will be home and I don't want you to be embarrassed if he comes in, so are you comfortable moving to my room?"

Eyes filled with anxiety and excitement, Michelle trembled. "I have absolutely no experience in knowing what to do next. But yes, I would rather he not catch us out here."

Danny caught her off guard when he stood, detaining her with his hand. He reached down and picked her up in his arms as if she was as light as a feather.

"Danny, what are you doing?" she squealed as she flung her arms around his neck. "I'm too heavy for you to do this!"

Danny paused before carrying her to his room and he looked at her. "Are you kidding me? I love your figure. There is nothing heavy about you at all!"

Michelle had no idea how to argue with him so she

nodded her head and laid it on his shoulder.

Chapter 7

Once Danny placed Michelle on his bed, he closed his door and locked it before sitting beside her. "I promise to take this as slow as you want, and I am going to make sure you are completely comfortable with all that we do. Do you want to sit up or lie down?"

Michelle's response was to lie back on his bed with invitation in her eyes. His eyes sparked with renewed desire as he gazed at her laying on his bed. She looked absolutely perfect with her hair fanned out around her on the pillow. When his hand traveled up her neck, he loved the silky skin underneath her hair.

"You're beautiful," he said as he stroked her cheek again before laying down beside her. Danny propped his head on his hand so that he could watch her. His hand trailed down to the hem of her shirt and he stopped. Staring at Michelle, he whispered, "Yes?"

Michelle took his hand, put it under her top, and he thought he might lose his mind. Gently, he trailed his hand up her belly, reveling at the feel of her soft skin. Her eyes closed from the pleasure of his fingers as they stopped under her bra.

Her eyes opened at his hesitation. "Touch me," she whispered. Danny believed he really would lose his mind at that moment as his finger dipped into her bra. He explored her softness with his finger.

He laid down beside her and said, "You can touch me, too."

She looked adorable as she pursed her mouth in indecision. Then she placed a hand on his chest, trailing it down to the bottom of his polo shirt. Michelle felt his taut muscles beneath it, and she let out a noise of wonder before she placed her hand under his shirt. Her fingers trailed up his slim waist to his chest, and Danny closed his eyes in pleasure.

His hand dipped into her bra cup and cradled one breast. His large palm cupped it, squeezed and caressed it. She moaned, saying, "Oh my." Danny watched the pleasure that his hand was giving her. It made him feel like he was on top of the world because he knew he was the first person who had ever touched her in this way. He gave himself a stern warning to be the perfect man for her as his fingers caressed her nipple, causing her to whisper a second time, "Oh my!" All of his training on anxiety went out the window at the moment.

Danny leaned in and captured her lips in his as his hand trailed to the other breast and his finger found that nipple. As he caressed it, Michelle whimpered against his mouth, giving him the perfect opportunity to invade it with his tongue.

Her hands were driving him mad under his shirt as

they traveled over his pectoral muscles and his own nipples puckered from her palms on them. His mouth traveled down her neck to her chest, and he moved her top down a little lower to kiss her collarbone. Michelle gasped in pleasure for a second time. Impatiently, she sat up, pulled her shirt over her head, and threw it on the floor.

"So beautiful," he whispered as he gazed at her cleavage. He kissed her again as he moved his hand back to her breast. "Oh my god," Danny moaned, caressing the top of the breast that was protruding from her bra cup as his hand pushed her bra cup down. He peppered kisses all over it before he took her nipple into his mouth, causing her body to buck up from the mattress. Michelle moaned loudly. He kissed and suckled her nipple to where it was hard as a rock. His hand moved to her other breast, and he pushed the bra cup down on that side, gazing at her other breast. He took both hands and pressed her breasts together as he leaned down to kiss them in the middle and his tongue dipped into the cleavage. Michelle lay panting and writhing under him.

Danny sat up to remove his own shirt because he needed her hands everywhere. He gazed down at her, his hand caressed her neck. His fingers trailed back down to her breasts as she watched him through heavy-lidded eyes. Danny lay down beside her again and reached around her back to unclasp her bra and he tossed it onto the floor. When her breasts were completely unencumbered, he moaned as his fingers and his mouth learned them. He loved learning what pleased her, as his tongue ran circles around her nipples.

Michelle whimpered again, crying, "Danny, it's so amazing. Please don't stop!"

However, Danny hesitated to go any further until they talked about it first. "Do you want more, or would you like to stop?" He moved his hands off of her breasts, afraid of what he might do next without her permission.

Michelle's eyes filled with yearning, but she asked, "What did you have in mind?"

"Do you want to keep touching as we are? Or are you willing to go south of our belly buttons?" Danny's voice growled as he felt his erection against his jeans.

Trepidation momentarily filled her gaze, but he could tell that her desire drove her to make the next decision. "We can touch down there, but can we wait to go all the way?"

He cradled her face a second time. Danny pulled her against him as they laid facing each other. "Baby, I want you to be completely comfortable with what we are do-ing. Yes, we can wait. How about if we just unbutton and unzip? Will that be far enough?"

Michelle nodded her head without speaking as his hands trailed away from her breast and down her belly, stopping at the button on her jeans. Gently, he released the button and his finger stroked the soft skin under-neath, above the seam of her underwear and around the top of her thighs, causing her to rise off the bed again.

He took her hand and moved it down his belly to his jeans. Michelle followed his lead and released his button. She caressed him just as he had done to her while looking her fill at his stomach. Michelle's eyes widened at the bulge peeking through his underwear.

Danny pulled Michelle close and kissed her deeply as one hand traveled inside her panties and over one of her buttocks, causing her to tighten it in pleasure from his caresses. She followed him by putting her own hand down his underwear as his mouth traced its way down her neck, her chest, and back to her breasts.

When her hand traced his butt cheek, a breath whooshed out from his mouth. "That feels good."

Michelle's hand stilled, eyes closed in pleasure from his mouth on her breasts. His hand moved around to the front of her jeans and dipped into her panties. His fingers caressed her mound and dipping lower. Michelle yelped out in pleasure as one finger traced front to back, circling her opening. "Danny," she cried as her eyes closed in ecstasy. She pressed her face against his neck and he felt like he was the king of her mountain as he continued touching her.

"Keep touching me," he whispered. Her hand dipped into the front of his underwear and she was amazed at the hard length of him that was almost protruding out of his pants. Her fingers traced it from the top down to his balls, causing him to groan. Patiently, he took her hand and showed her how to grip him and squeeze. She gasped when her finger felt the drop of moisture escape from the top.

Michelle pulled back with a wild look in her eyes. "I'm ready to take my pants off."

Danny groaned again, and he helped her remove her

jeans and her underwear. Gasping, he gazed at how beautiful she was lying on his bed, completely naked. "My turn," he growled, and she helped him just as he did with her. Danny knew it was all new for her as he lay beside her. His eyes darkened as she gazed at all of him. Danny couldn't help but moan as she took one finger, and she traced around him again before gripping him as he showed her and squeezing.

Not able to contain himself, his hand moved between her legs and it traced her again before dipping slightly inside. Michelle cried out and completely lifted off the bed from the sensations washing over her.

"Do you like that?" he whispered, amazed at how beautiful she was as he watched her.

"Oh, yes," she whispered back, and he took that finger and pushed all the way inside of her, causing her to cry, "Danny!"

When he moved two fingers inside of her, he pumped them until her felt her spasm in pleasure. Danny was proud of himself for bringing her to her very first orgasm. With quick, shallow breaths, she pulsed against his fingers. He continued caressing her and whispering his love until her climax subsided.

"Can I do the same thing to you?" she whispered, and she grasped him again.

Danny had a hard time uttering anything from the feel of her hand on him, but he guided her hand, showing her how to make him come, just as she did. It didn't take her long to figure out how to pump him while her other hand caressed his balls.

"Oh my," he groaned. "That's it!" He shivered with eyes closed as he rode out his orgasm.

Danny pulled Michelle against him and he kissed her forehead. "What did you think? How was it?"

"I never knew how special it could be! And we haven't even gone all the way yet!" He pulled Michelle tighter against him.

"We can take our time. I will wait for you to tell me when you're ready for more." He kissed her head as his hand stroked her bare back. "I love you, Michelle." He turned her face toward his and he kissed her softly.

Michelle smiled up at him. She was on an emotional high from this experience. "I know I already said this, but I don't think it will take much longer until I can tell you the same thing! Thank you for being patient with me and teaching me!"

"You figured it out pretty quickly," he joked as they lay there, holding one another. "I probably should drive you back before it gets too late."

She nodded in wonder realizing that he was right. Michelle studied anatomy in biology, and her mother had the basic *talk* with her. However, she had never seen a man's entire body before tonight. As soon as he showed her how to please him, Michelle was filled with wonder at seeing the liquid pulsate out of him and she was proud of herself for learning how to bring him the same pleasure.

They got dressed before he drove her back to the dorm. He kissed her softly and whispered his love a final time before Michelle floated inside to her room.

***

The next morning, Michelle called her brother, Jeff.

"Hey Jeff," she said after he answered his phone. He lived in an apartment near to his parents' house and he worked as an electrician. His hours were long and he was often deployed when there was ever a hurricane or other natural disaster.

"Where were you?" Jeff asked. The fact that he asked so bluntly filled Michelle with dread of his knowing about her dates with Danny.

Michelle's eyebrow dipped, as dread filled her. "What are you talking about?" she asked. She already predicted that he would not be open to hearing about her dating someone.

Jeff's voice was choppy. "I called last night and Jackie said you were out. She said she would tell you to call me when you got back."

Michelle scrambled for a suitable answer. "Umm...I was out with friends."

"Jackie's your best friend. How come she wasn't with you?" Suspicion laced Jeff's tone.

Michelle's gut burned. She answered impatiently. "Jefferson, we aren't joined by the hips. Even though we are best friends, sometimes we do separate things!"

There was a pause. "Michelle, what's really going on? Tell me the truth."

"Jeff!" Michelle rolled her eyes in exasperation. "That is the truth!"

Not wanting to continue arguing, Jeff replied, "Okay, okay. Muppet, I just worry about you."

Michelle rolled her eyes again when he called her his pet name. It made her feel five years old again every time he used it. "I'm almost twenty, Jeff. I can take care of myself now."

Thankfully, the conversation moved to a safer topic, and Michelle caught him up on all that was going on with her classes.

Chapter 8

Just as Michelle hung up the phone, she heard the door open to her room and Jackie walked inside.

"Hey!" she exclaimed. "Thanks for covering for me with Jeff last night!"

Jackie looked at her. "No problem." Then she moved into the bathroom and shut the door.

Michelle's eyebrow dipped and her stomach clenched. She wondered about her best friend's attitude toward her. Thankfully, Hannah stayed the night at Michael's and the thought crossed Michelle's mind that they should do something together, just the two of them.

When the bathroom door opened, Michelle said, "Do you want to go get some ice cream?"

"Not really," Jackie mumbled, avoiding her gaze and grabbing a textbook. Jackie sat on her bed and opened it to begin reading.

"Jackie," Michelle said as she tensed her shoulders as she realized she had been too focused on Danny. "What's wrong?"

Jackie looked at her. It made Michelle feel as if she had

been slapped. "It's been days since I've seen you, and now you want me to tell you what's wrong?" Her voice rose in volume.

Sighing, Michelle realized her words were true. She was totally caught up in her relationship with Danny that her best friend had taken a back seat. "I'm sorry, Jackie. I guess I've been ignoring you. It wasn't on purpose."

Jackie's eyes softened as she said, "I'm happy that you like Danny so much. I just miss you. It's like you have a new best friend because I never see you anymore, not even at meals."

Michelle's heart broke upon hearing the words. Her eyes closed in agony. She could sense the tears behind her closed lids. Michelle opened her eyes, and she moved to sit on Jackie's bed. "You and I became best friends when we were eleven. Nobody else can fill that role except you. I've been a lousy friend and I'm really sorry. I haven't juggled a boyfriend and my best friend before. Danny and I dating has been a whole new adventure."

"I understand." Jackie replied, as her eyes softened more. "If Jeff had let you go out with guys at home, you would probably be better at this."

Michelle looked down. "Danny told me he loved me last night."

Jackie's eyes lit up with joy. "That's amazing."

"Do you want to get some ice cream and I will tell you about it? You can catch me up on everything with you." Michelle's eyes were filled with pleading. "Please?"

Jackie chuckled. "Sure, let's go. Studying can wait a while." She closed the book and placed it on her bed.

The two of them spent the next two hours talking and catching up. Jackie teased Michelle when she shared about getting to what they considered *third base* the night before. It was their own code of intimacy in dating, although Michelle had not used their code until now.

"I'm worried about Jeff, though," she said as she drove them back. "He sounded like he didn't believe me, even though what I told him was a deception. It's impossible not to feel guilt because I've never lied to him before. Ugh! If only he wasn't so involved in every moment of my life!"

Jackie shook her head. "Michelle, you've got to force him out of your life. You're almost twenty years old! It's time for him to allow you to have a life!"

"That's easier said than done," Michelle said. They were silent until Jackie spoke up.

"Umm...I need to tell you something and I don't want you to tell my parents, okay?" Jackie whispered.

Curiosity filled Michelle's eyes, and she glanced over at Jackie. "You can tell me anything. What is it?"

After staying silent for a few more minutes, Jackie was looking in her lap when she said, "I'm gay."

Michelle said nothing for a moment. "Okay. Were you afraid to tell me that?"

"A little," Jackie said. "It's not something most people accept easily."

"Jackie, look at me," Michelle said, and Jackie raised her head to gaze at her friend. "Deep down, I've always known you probably were because you never dated guys in high school. And you didn't have a big brother to get in your way and stop you!"

Amazement filled Jackie's eyes. "So it won't bother you? You know that you and Hannah can trust me, right?"

Michelle laughed out loud. "You don't need to worry about a thing with me or Hannah! Tell her soon because she will be fine with it! But, I'm curious. Why did you tell me today?"

"I've been getting to know a girl who's on the team with me. We're getting acquainted, and she told me she's also gay," Jackie said.

They were back at the school, so Michelle squealed as she parked the car. Then she reached over and hugged Jackie. "I'm so happy for you! I want you to share more about it!"

Jackie shared about how they met at basketball practice. Michelle went to Jackie's high school games, but her college ones hadn't started yet. "Her name is Jennifer."

"Jackie and Jennifer," Michelle said. "It sounds meant to be! Please tell me I can meet her soon!"

"We haven't gone out or anything. But sure, she can join us at dinner one night so that you can meet her." Unease filled Jackie's gaze as she continued, "I'm just not sure if everyone else will be as open as you are."

"They will have to be!" Michelle declared. "But you won't ever find out if you don't give them a chance. I think they will be more open-minded than you realize."

Michelle wondered if she should tell Jackie what she overheard in the library, but she stayed quiet until she could do a little more sleuthing first to determine Vicki was up to. Deep down, she knew her friend would also advise her to back off.

***

Michelle's heart leapt at the sight of Danny on Monday morning during breakfast. He traveled home on Saturday to watch his sister perform in a dance competition with her high school team, and Danny promised not to miss it. They spoke on the phone the night before and her heart palpitated when the phone rang, as well as from the warmth of his voice. Intimacy with a guy was something she never experienced, and she liked it. She liked it a lot!

As Danny took her hand, he pulled her to the side of the dining room before he put his arms around her. "Good morning." Then he kissed her deeply.

When he finally released her, Michelle caught her breath. "Good morning. Wow!"

Danny rained kisses down her face. "I missed you during my time away."

"You were only gone one night!" Michelle giggled, but shivers ran down her spine from his mouth on her neck as she tilted it to give him better access.

When he pulled back, the love evident in Danny's gaze warmed her heart. He caressed her cheek. "I get it, but you're irresistible! And I need to catch up on what happened during my time away."

"Not much. I hung out with Jackie and Hannah, along with studying," she said as he entwined their fingers before they walked into breakfast.

Michelle made sure they took a seat next to Jackie. She shared her Saturday experience with Danny when he called, and he understood. Danny even said, "Jackie is right. I'm glad we are focused on each other, but we can't forget about our friends."

As they sat beside their friends, he took her hand in his and asked, "Would you like to come home with me in two weeks? I've been bragging about you to my family, and they want to meet you."

Michelle was hesitant before answering because the idea of meeting his family felt daunting. Deep down, she wanted to, so she answered him, "I'd like that." The normal annoying voice of Jeff intruded that she didn't need to move so fast with Danny. Her brow dipped as she wondered they were pushing too fast for Michelle to meet his family.

Danny leaned toward her for another tender kiss as he said, "Great."

***

After her first class ended, Michelle walked to the counseling center to set up her next appointment. She had gotten behind on sessions and she found that she missed talking to Angela. The guilt she experienced over lying to her brother had not eased any, and she wanted to ask her about it. Angela was standing at the desk and her face lit up when she noticed Michelle enter. They set aside a time the following day since Michelle had a lighter workload on Tuesdays and Thursdays.

As Michelle turned to leave, she recognized Vicki walking out with one of the other counselors that she didn't know. She wanted to pump her fist in victory. Instead, Michelle quickly exited and shielded herself behind a bush to wait for Vicki to come out.

A few seconds later, Vicki exited and walked her direction, so Michelle ducked down not wanting to be seen. Michelle allowed Vicki get some distance ahead of her, she trailed behind her and ducked behind trees when it looked like she might be glancing back at her. Later, her dismay grew when Vicki only visited a bookstore, made a purchase, and returned to the dorm.

"Maybe I need to follow the other girl," Michelle whispered to herself. She just wasn't sure what the other girl (Brandi) looked like. She made a plan to watch where Vicki sat at dinner, she went back to her own room to complete some homework. Deep down, Michelle understood she didn't need to become involved in this situation. Vicki proved untrustworthy, and it clearly showed Brandi shared that trait. Anger filled her as she thought about Jeff. *To hell with him,* Michelle surmised. *He wasn't here, and she knew what she was doing.*

***

Vicki snickered, considering how that foolish girl was shadowing her. She believed herself discreet, but Vicki had experience in following people and Michelle lacked expertise! It cinched her original idea of lying low for a while since she would probably try to follow her again. Part of her even wondered if she should sit with Brandi at meals. If she didn't, she would be sitting by herself and that would also be conspicuous.

That afternoon, she suffered through a call from her mother. Although, the term *mother* could loosely apply to the woman who had given birth to her. All her life, Vicki believed she was just a trophy daughter and not someone her mother or father really cared about.

"Darling, we love you," Anna Robinson said robotically. "But you need to behave like we've raised you. Someone as affluent as you need to remember that you live by different standards as middle-income families. Don't let us down."

Vicki's lip curled in disgust at her mother's syrupy words and it made her more determined to do the opposite. "Sure, Mom," she mumbled in the deeper pitch, knowing her mother hated it. She had always been taught to call her *mother*.

"Stop speaking to me like that!" her mom snarled before going back to her false voice. "Call us soon, sweetie."

***

At dinner, Michelle watched Vicki come out of the food line. She turned her head to notice her walk to a table in a back corner of the dining hall. Vicki sat at a table next to another girl. She decided it must be Brandi and

Michelle wondered about her. She was completely inattentive with the conversation happening around her.

"Michelle, are you okay?" Danny asked. He had been talking, and she was distracted by looking over at Vicki's table.

Michelle shook her head to focus on her friends. "Uh... yeah. Sorry, I saw that girl, Vicki. Remember her from that horrible night last spring?"

Danny took her hand. "That's a night I will never forget. Why were you watching her?"

"Oh, I was surprised she still went to school here. I thought she transferred. Sorry for getting distracted." she replied as Jackie glanced over at her curiously. She knew her friend saw through her ridiculous comment. Danny simply squeezed her hand before turning back to continue his conversation with Michael and Alex.

After taking a walk with Danny and more kissing, Michelle finally came back into her room. Danny had turned her into a sex fiend because she found herself wanting to go all the way with him. All of a sudden, she had become insatiable and what they did wasn't enough! She decided that she would tell him she was ready for it on their next date.

"What was that tonight?" Jackie asked as soon as she walked inside.

"What?" she commented.

Jackie stood and walked over to her. "Why were you watching Vicki? What are you up to?"

"I have no idea what you're talking about." Michelle answered evasively.

Jackie narrowed her eyes and studied at Michelle and said, "I think you do." Then she gave her a hard stare, "Michelle..."

"Okay, okay," Michelle answered, rolling her eyes at her friend. "Last week, I overheard her and another girl in the library. It sounded like they were planning some kind of burglary." Hannah was just walking in the door and she heard the tail end of the conversation.

Both Jackie and Hannah moved closer and they yelled, "What?! What are you talking about?!"

Michelle explained the conversation she eavesdropped on and her plan to follow Vicki and her friend. Both of her friends' eyes widened, and they both said, "You are not following her by yourself!" "Are you crazy?"

"I don't want anything bad happening to anyone else because of that crazy girl!" Michelle remarked.

"Then go to the police and tell them what you overheard." Jackie exclaimed. "Michelle, I don't want anything happening to you! Don't you remember last month?!"

Hannah nodded her head in agreement and shuddered. "That girl is bad news, Michelle. She was willing to take money from Rhonda as a part of her scheme to kidnap me."

When Michelle threw up her hands in exasperation, she said, "Of course I remember! I'm still in counseling over it, but what am I supposed to tell the police? I won't know what to say until I know more."

"Well, you're not doing it alone!" Hannah said firmly. Jackie nodded her head in agreement.

Michelle groaned. "Fine! I won't follow her unless the

two of you know about it. Are you happy now?"

She could tell that her friends were not happy about it, but they let it go because the phone rang. Michelle had never been so happy to have Michael call Hannah because it meant their conversation could be put on hold.

Chapter 9

The next morning, Danny kissed Michelle passion-ately. "Would you want to go on a double date with Hannah and Michael on Friday?"

Michelle swallowed her disappointment at wanting time to tell him she was ready to go all the way. Instead, she smiled up at him. "That sounds wonderful!"

Danny yanked her against him for another thorough kiss.

Michelle stopped to inhale oxygen, and she gasped. "What was that for?"

"You were so beautiful the way you were looking at me and it made me crazy!" Danny growled into her ear. Michelle chuckled, but he was giving her goosebumps as he nuzzled her ear and her neck, so she couldn't form a response.

Reluctantly, Danny pulled away. When he entwined their fingers, he tugged her closely against him as they walked into the dining hall.

Michelle felt as if she was glowing from his gentle treatment of her. She was truly beginning to feel like she was beautiful to him. The nagging feeling that was becoming a constant sensation these days whispered he was saying those words to get to her. What if Jeff was right all along? She was having headaches from the conflicting emotions pinging through her.

***

Michelle and Angela walked back to her office carrying on an easygoing conversation.

Once they were seated, Angela said, "Today, I want us to talk more about your family. You mentioned your brother the other day. Would you like to tell me more about him?"

Michelle nodded. "Yes, he's five years older than me."

"How would you describe your relationship?" Angela asked.

"We are close." Michelle said. "My parents were older when they had both of us and they taught Jeff to look out for me in case anything ever happened to either of them."

Angela nodded as she recorded notes in her notebook. "What was that like growing up? How do you feel about him having authority over you now?"

Michelle stiffened, and she fidgeted, uncomfortable with the question. "It seemed normal to me when we were kids. I knew his job was looking after me. I love him and I know he cares about me, but sometimes he can drive me crazy."

"Drive you crazy, how?" Angela asked.

As Michelle looked down at her hands. "I never dated in high school because he was so overprotective and he scared off any guys who wanted to ask me out."

Angela's face showed little emotion, but her voice softened. "How did that make you feel?"

"Frustrated!" Michelle said. "I wasn't normal as a teenager. All of my friends had social lives and enjoyed going out on dates, but he foiled any chances I had of going out with anyone, even guys who went to our church!"

"Did your parents know he did that?" Angela said.

Michelle shook her head. "Not really. I know they loved us, but they were not very involved in my life other than hearing about each day and making sure my grades were good. I think they were relieved to leave the more sensitive issues to Jeff."

"Are you and Jeff still close? Is he someone you feel you can confide in?" Angela asked.

The question brought out an enormous sigh from Michelle. "I love him and I share with him about most things. However, I've been dating someone, and he doesn't know about it because I know he would come up here and try to stop it. Ever since I stood up to him last year, I feel as if there is a gap between us."

Angela nodded and remained quiet for a moment before she commented again. "Have you ever talked to Jeff about backing off and giving you more space? I know you spoke with your mom with him there, but maybe the two of you should sit down and talk through your feelings."

"Not really," Michelle said.

Softly, Angela asked, "You're a people pleaser, aren't you?"

Michelle repeated Angela's question with a question. "What do you mean?"

"You're afraid to speak up to Jeff and tell him how you feel about his interfering with dating relationships because you're afraid to hurt his feelings." Angela dipped her head slightly as she gazed at Michelle. "I've struck a nerve, haven't I?"

Refusing to make eye contact, Michelle spoke softly. "Yes. I don't want to hurt him because he has always taken care of me."

"Michelle, look at me," Angela said. When Michelle glanced up at her, she said, "It's okay for you to want a life of your own. Your brother needs to allow you to explore during these college years. You are over eighteen, so you can decide for yourself if you want to see someone. But you need to talk to him and tell him how you feel."

Anguish filled Michelle's gaze, and she nodded. "I guess I can try talking to him about it. I like Danny, the guy I'm dating. He is so polite and caring with me. I want Jeff to see that."

"Maybe Jeff will surprise you and like him just as you hope. But you won't know until you talk to him." Angela smiled gently.

Hard as it was to discuss her relationship with Jeff, Michelle felt better after the session ended. She needed to find a good time to sit down with Jeff and tell him how she felt.

***

As soon as Michelle walked out of the counseling center, she glanced around and her heart dropped when she recognized Brandi walking down the sidewalk toward the dorm. Michelle followed her, and she told herself that she might be on the way to her own room.

However, Brandi's gaze darted around herself as if she wondered if she was being watched. Michelle darted behind a large bush so that she wouldn't catch her watching. She also noticed that Brandi wasn't wearing a backpack of any kind, like she was coming back from a class. A small bag was strapped across her torso as she walked into the dorm. Michelle felt like it was a sign to keep following her. She stayed ten paces behind her. Thankfully, if she saw her, her excuse was that she was going back to her own room. Just as she was about to walk in the door, she heard a voice behind her.

"Hey, baby," Danny said. Michelle grabbed her stomach as she yelped. His eyebrows dipped, and he took her hand. "Are you okay?"

Michelle said, "Yes, I was just lost in thought and you startled me. I finished my counseling session with Angela and she gave me a lot to think about." She was proud of herself for covering up what she was doing, but her heart sank because she lost sight of Brandi. Her fear was that she might break into someone's room and she needed proof of it. Michelle also felt guilty for not telling Danny the truth.

Thankfully, Danny seemed to accept her explanation as he pulled her into a hug. Resting her face against his chest, Michelle was so thankful that he had dated her, even though her plan to follow Brandi fell through. She pulled back. "Did you need something?"

"Oh," he said. "I know this is spur of the moment, but I have a couple of hours free, and I wanted to see if you had time to get an ice cream."

"Sure," Michelle said. "Can you wait while I drop off my backpack?"

When Danny assured her he would wait, she walked down the hall to her room. Deep in thought, she didn't notice Brandi until she was walking toward her from wherever she was coming. She didn't say a word to Michelle, but a look of recognition came over her face. Michelle said nothing either, but the look on Brandi's face sent shivers of fear down her spine. Thinking quickly, she darted down another hallway, making a rectangle to get back to her own room in case Brandi followed her. With the hallway now empty, she darted down it and unlocked her door. Then she shut it and bolted it. Brandi was someone that did not need to know where she lived. A few minutes later, after putting her backpack away, she opened her door. Michelle glanced into the hallway and saw it was empty. She stepped out and walked to the lobby to meet Danny.

***

Thursday evening, Michelle, Jackie, and Hannah went to watch basketball practice because Michael and Danny were on the team. Hannah had been filled in on what was going on with Jackie and just as Michelle told her, she was fine with it. Jackie promised they could meet her soon, but they didn't realize it would be tonight.

As they sat down, Michelle noticed a lovely blond girl walking their way. Jackie stood while clearing her throat. She glanced at Hannah and Michelle before she said, "I want to introduce you to Jennifer Franks."

Michelle wanted to yell with excitement about meeting this girl, but she knew it would make Jackie mad if she reacted that way. Standing up, she shook Jennifer's hand. "It's nice to meet you."

Hannah introduced herself, and she also refrained from gushing or teasing. Her eyes were dancing. "Would you like to join us?" She gestured toward the spot where Jackie had been sitting.

With a shy smile, Jennifer said, "It's nice to meet both of you." As she sat down, Jennifer continued by saying, "Jackie has told me so much about both of you."

Michelle wanted to be snarky in her response. However, she refrained. "We've also heard about you." And she left it at that as she watched Jackie's expression because her friend eyes showed fear of Michelle sharing more. It was easy to see why Jackie liked Jennifer. She fit right into their circle.

The four girls talked and visited, getting to know each other better as they watched the guys split into two teams for a scrimmage. The negative was that Michael and Danny were on opposite teams from each other, so Hannah and Michelle were rooting for opposite sides. However, they handled it by laughing and teasing each other when either Michael or Danny scored.

After practice ended, Jackie and Jennifer excused themselves to walk to the student center. Michelle and Hannah waited for Danny and Michael. When the guys walked over to them, Michael grabbed Hannah, making her giggle as he planted a sweaty kiss on her mouth. "Ew," she laughed, but she didn't push him away.

Danny was kinder and wiped his hands on his towel before taking Michelle's hand and kissing it instead of her mouth. "Thanks for coming," he whispered.

Michelle didn't disguise her desire for him, and she whispered, "You looked amazing out there." Michelle laughed when she saw Danny's gaze change to a smoky one, and she knew he was restraining himself from pulling her into his arms to kiss her. After watching him wipe his face with his towel, Michelle put him out of his misery when she reached up, and touched her lips to his. Danny moaned in approval as he deepened the kiss before pulling back.

Waving goodbye to both of them, Michelle and Hannah walked back to their room. As they did, Michelle knew she wanted to speak to Danny about going all the way with him. The doubts were quiet at the moment as certainty filled her.

***

Friday night, Danny and Michael came to the dorm to pick up Michelle and Hannah. They had invited Jackie to come along with them, but Jackie had plans with Jennifer.

Hannah made a beeline for Michael as soon as she walked into the lobby. He embraced her, kissing her thoroughly while Danny did the same thing to Michelle. Unnerved from being included in the intimate action, Michelle felt sparks zinging all over her body. She also remembered that they could get in trouble for such public displays, so she pulled back without wanting to.

After the guys opened their doors for Hannah and Michelle, Michael began driving. The original plan was to go eat pizza and see a movie.

However, Hannah spoke up. "Michael and I were talking, and we wanted to do something different. What if we go to that sports bar we went to last year?"

Michelle's fingers were intertwined with Danny's and she nodded in agreement. "That's fine with me. What about you?" She began having heart palpitations from the way he was looking at her.

Danny didn't remove his gaze from hers as he kissed the fingers on her hand. He remarked. "A chance to dance with my girl? I'm all for it."

Michelle was distracted from Danny and his kisses on her fingers. Her insides felt squishy from the softness of his lips.

Michael kissed Hannah's hand. "It's settled, then."

It took thirty minutes to get to the restaurant, and Michael found a parking spot. After the guys helped them out, Hannah wrapped her arms around Michael's waist. He kissed her in an inappropriate manner before they walked toward the entrance. Danny stopped Michelle as he pushed her against the car to kiss her again. When she pulled back with questioning in her eyes, he said, "I'm warming up for later."

Michelle chuckled at his words zings shot through her, and she couldn't help but agree with him. She anticipated the evening because it was the first time she danced with someone on a date. Last year, when they all came here, Danny asked her to dance. However, she didn't enjoy it because she was so nervous about stepping on his feet and she didn't enjoy it. She bit her lip as she struggled with the possibility of stepping on Danny's feet tonight.

Michael and Hannah had already given their names for a waiting list. There was a ten-minute delay, and they spent the time waiting outside in the cool, fall air. Both Michael and Danny had their arms wrapped around the girls from behind. Michelle's heart was skipping several beats again as he nuzzled her ear. It was a heady emotion to think about how she was in a relationship with some-one and on a double date with one of her best friends.

A few minutes later, they were shown to their table. When they came as a group the last time, they ordered wings and fries to share.

Michelle and Hannah decided they were in the mood

for a burger. Michael and Danny split a large order of wings.

Chapter 10

After the server brought their drinks, the four of them walked out to the dance floor. The upbeat song ended and a slow one began. Danny attempted to pull Michelle close to him. Michael and Hannah were already locked in an embrace, and it would take the jaws of life to pry them apart.

With wide eyes, Michelle looked up at Danny. "I'm not experienced at dancing. I don't want to step all over you."

Danny cradled her face. "Baby, it's me. You don't have to worry about that because I love you and I don't care."

Lost in his eyes, she nodded as he pulled her close against him and they began swaying together. Just as he said, she realized she had nothing to worry about because he was holding her so tightly that she was actually steady in her movements.

She listened as Danny took in deep breaths next to her ear, "Mmm...this is just what I needed tonight! It feels wonderful to hold you."

"Uh huh," Michelle mumbled. She was caught up in the heady sensation as she listened to his heartbeat and smelled the spicy scent of his aftershave. Michelle was short enough that she moved her nose into the hollow of his neck and took a deep breath of her own. She felt as much as heard Danny's soft moan.

Then he whispered, "You are making me crazy with your lips and your nose right now."

She looked up at him and her senses heightened from how he was gazing at her. "Do you want me to pull back?"

"Maybe slightly." He answered honestly. "The feeling your lips on my neck makes me want to do inappropriate things to you right now." His smile was gentle, but Michelle recognized the smoldering desire in his eyes.

A smile came to Michelle's eyes, along with a devilish gleam. "Hmm...maybe I need to do it again." She soon regretted her words when Danny's eyes darkened and his hands went under her shirt, one finger tracing her under her breast on the outside of her bra.

Her breath hitched as that one finger traced circles, making her dizzy. "Oh my," she whispered. Michelle closed her eyes. The breath she was holding whooshed out of her from his touch.

Michael and Hannah walked past them, saying that their food had arrived, interrupting the moment. Reluctantly, they separated, and Michelle missed his closeness as they fell into step with Hannah and Michael. The feelings inside of Michelle cinched her decision that she was ready to go all the way with Danny. It also helped her to realize that she was totally in love with him. She wished they could be by themselves so that she could tell him. Instead, she forced herself to focus and enjoy the time with friends.

The four of them laughed and joked together, enjoying a night together away from the stress of school. Hannah and Michelle talked about Jackie's new love interest with the guys. Jackie had given them permission to tell them, and they thought it was great. Michael and Danny talked about basketball practice. Games would start up in another week. Michelle was distracted with thoughts of Vicki. Determined to find out what she and Brandi had planned, she pondered ways she could detect what was actually going on.

"Michelle," she heard Danny's voice.

Michelle glanced around. "What?"

Hannah's look was filled with questions as Danny repeated his question. "Do you want to go on a double date with them after the first game? They suggested pizza."

"Absolutely, yes," Michelle smiled, ignoring Hannah's eyes on her. Her friend's questioning eyes narrowed, and she tried to disregard it.

Thankfully, another slow song came on, causing Michael to tug Hannah back out to the dance floor. Danny held out his hand for Michelle. However, he maneuvered them into a darkened corner before pulling her close again. He moved one hand up to her neck and ran his fingers through her hair. Danny stared deeply into her eyes as they swayed together.

Michelle realized she couldn't hold back any longer. She gazed at him. "I love you."

Danny stopped and his hand gripped the back of Michelle's neck and his gaze turned molten. "What did you say?"

As she realized how much it meant to him, her own heart sang that she was finally telling him. Michelle placed a hand on his heart and, with tears in her eyes, she whispered, "I love you, Danny Peterson."

Danny whispered, "Oh, baby." He glanced around and pulled her deeper into the shadows, where people wouldn't see him kiss her. Danny tilted her head and touched her lips with his, showing her how much he loved her in his kiss. He invaded her mouth, demanding submission with his tongue. Danny lengthened the kiss as long as possible. Finally, he pulled away so that they could catch their breath. Danny continued to caress her hair. "I love you, too!" His eyes were shiny, almost as if he had tears in them.

He peppered kisses all over her face and neck as they went back to swaying to the music that was playing. Michelle tried to think coherently, but she was failing miserably. "I have something else I want to tell you." The way she kept gasping for breath, she wasn't sure if he actually heard her.

Danny spoke against her neck. "I'm listening."

Tiny pulses of pleasure rippled through her. "I'm ready for more."

Her words caught Danny's attention, and he pulled back to ask, "What do you mean 'ready for more?'"

Michelle chuckled at his expression. "I'm ready to go all the way with you."

For the second time that night, Danny paused and stared at her. He placed his hands on her shoulders and dipped to speak closer to her ear. "Michelle, are you sure? I'm not trying to pressure you."

"Danny," she voiced. "I just told you I love you, and I meant it. Danny, I love you so much! I am happy to say I do not feel pressured. And I want this because I love you."

Unable to control himself, Danny pushed Michelle up against the wall that they were closest to and he laid a kiss on her she would never forget. His hands found their way under her shirt again and his fingers coasted over her bare stomach. Michelle couldn't breathe and she couldn't think because of what his hands were doing. When he was finished, he pulled them back out from the wall and began swaying again. All doubts were pushed from her mind as she relished in his kisses.

They finally left a while later. None of them were old enough to drink, and they didn't take part in drinking alcohol like many of their friends were doing. Danny and Michael joked and teased one another, and the girls laughed with them. Michelle told Hannah her declaration to Danny when they took a restroom break, and Hannah squealed and hugged her tight. "I knew you two would be together!" she gushed as Michelle laughed with a flushed face.

Once they arrived at the dorm, Danny said, "I'm sure the two of you want some time alone, so Michelle can drive me back later."

Michael and Hannah didn't argue because they were probably hoping for the same thing. Michelle ran inside to get her bag before she drove them to Danny's apartment. As she waited, she saw that Michael's car was already parked. "Wow! That was quick," Danny noticed her smirk as his own heart skipped in anticipation.

Danny opened her car door, and he took both of her hands in his. He pulled her hand to his lips, and he kissed each finger gently while watching Michelle's reaction. Her legs looked like they would give out. However, she followed behind Danny as he tugged her inside.

As he shut the door and locked it, Michelle asked, "Is James here tonight?"

"No, he went home this weekend." Danny's voice deepened with each word, and tingles raced down her spine.

"Okay," she whispered, and her heartbeat increased. Danny shut and locked his door before he strolled toward her. He came close enough that his nose was touching hers. However, before he even tried to kiss her, he questioned her one more time, "Are you sure that you are ready for this?"

"Oh my word, yes," Michelle breathed. In a split second, his mouth was on hers.

Even though he was excited, Danny took his time kissing her, remembering to be gentle. Michelle went limp with pleasure from how his tongue was moving across the seam of her lips. Danny heard a moan come from somewhere within her, and he felt a joy that he was able to bring a noise like that from her.

His eyes were dark with passion as he pulled back and

mumbled, "Come here." His arms lifted her feet off of the floor and he wrapped her legs around his waist while his mouth found hers again. This time, his kiss took everything from her as he demanded her total submission with his lips. Danny walked into his room with Michelle in his arms.

Michelle slid down his front as his fingers were making feathery touches on her back. He kissed her again, deepening it as he worshiped her lips in adoration. Her lips parted and his tongue invaded to play with hers. Needing to catch her breath, Michelle pulled back as far as Danny would allow and she attempted to lift her top because he was touching her everywhere.

He detained her with his hand and whispered, "Let me." As he raised her top, his fingers grazed every spot where the shirt lifted and she trembled from his gentle touches. Danny knew this was her first time with a man, so he made himself move slowly and lovingly. Overwhelmed by the tremendous pressure he was putting on himself, he almost stopped and said they needed to wait a while longer. But after pulling off her shirt and gazing at her in the satiny black bra, he knew he didn't want to do that. He groaned at the sight of her standing there so beautifully.

She whispered, "Will you show me what to do?"

He chuckled. "You've already been doing it. I am so aroused by you, Michelle."

He moved to stand behind her, and she gasped as his mouth found the nape of her neck, pushing her hair to the side. Then he whispered, "I will do all that I can to make this a wonderful experience for you." As he said the words, he kissed her neck and shoulder as she inhaled in pleasure.

Danny startled her when he lifted her in his arms and lay her on his bed. Then, sitting beside her, he took a finger and traced it down her neck and over her upper torso. He reached behind her and unhooked her bra and dragged the straps down until there was nothing holding it in place and it fell to the side.

"Oh, you're so beautiful," he whispered as he cradled her breasts with both hands, until her nipples tightened in his palms.

"Oh my god," Michelle breathed with closed eyes as both of his forefingers pinched her nipples and pulled them to tight buds. Danny laid beside her. He continued fingering one breast as he leaned to put his mouth on her other one. "Oh my," she cried from the sensation of both his fingers and his mouth.

Danny wanted to protest when she pulled back, and it took him a moment to realize that Michelle was attempting to remove his shirt.

He mumbled, "All clothes need to come off now."

They made quick work of taking off the rest of their clothes and Michelle laid back down on Danny's bed. As he gazed at her, she became self-conscious of how she looked. She lifted her hands and tried to conceal herself.

Danny grasped her hands, gently clasping her fingers with his. "You don't need to hide your beauty from me."

"I know I'm not a model," Michelle whispered back, as one of his fingers touched her lips to keep her from saying any more.

He laid down beside her and kissed her passionately before saying, "No, you're better. You are the one who makes me react like this, Michelle. I only want you." His hands continued to do wonderful things to her breasts.

Michelle was writhing from pleasure and she immediately turned the tables on him by caressing her hands down his chest, to his stomach and touching him. She gripped him with her hand as he showed her the last time. She was watching his eyes closely as her hands roamed his body. This time, the fidgeting and moaning was coming from Danny. Michelle moved down toward his legs, and she licked his shaft. She continued stroking it as he bucked off the bed in pleasure. "That's amazing," he groaned as her tongue continued to lick him.

He suddenly flipped over, pinning her underneath him. "I don't want to come too soon for your first time." His mouth went back to her breasts, paying careful attention to her nipples, and Michelle gasped and moaned in response.

One hand went back to playing with a breast as the other slipped between her legs, stroking her front to back as she breathed out, "Danny!" His cock was hardening even more from watching her pleasure from his fingers as he slipped one inside and pumped it. She was wiggling and whimpering as he added a second finger. He touched her at the exact spot, and Michelle came apart as wave after wave of pleasure rippled through her very essence.

"I thought you wanted to wait," she whispered.

Patiently, he explained how it was much harder for him

to come twice. But she could orgasm more than once. He looked at her and said, "Are you ready? I'm going to get a condom."

"Oh my word, yes!" she whispered with her eyes half closed.

"This will hurt at first, but it shouldn't last long. I promise to be gentle." Danny gave her a soft kiss after telling her.

With amazed eyes, Michelle watched him pull a condom out of his nightstand, and he opened it. "Help me slide it on," he whispered. His own eyes closed as she pushed it all the way down his shaft.

He moved between her legs and said, "Tell me if it hurts too much and I will stop."

Michelle nodded without speaking as she felt him resting against her opening. When he pushed in slightly, she was extremely tight and she winced. He knew it was from the pain. "Breathe," he suggested. When she took a breath, he pushed in about halfway. She took another deep breath and let her legs fall further open until Danny pushed all the way inside of her.

"Are you okay?" he whispered with a look of concern. Michelle nodded.

Danny watched the pleasure on her face, and it eased his fear of hurting her. He pulled out to thrust inside again. "Oh," she moaned as her eyes closed in ecstasy. Groaning himself in the pleasure of her tightness, he pulled out and began moving faster. However, he didn't want to push too hard, as his thrusts were gentle with the exact right pressure. Both of them began moaning the other's name as Michelle pulled her legs back further to increase the pleasure. Danny's eyes began rolling in the back of his head, but he made himself hold on as long as he could to bring her to climax. It took little time before she was crying out and saying, "It feels so good! Don't stop!" Watching her reach her second orgasm was one of the best experiences of his life. As soon as she was finished, his own burst forth, and he groaned loudly before collapsing on top of her and burying his face in her neck. He heard her struggling to catch a breath, and he finally moved to the side to dispose of the condom. Danny pulled her against him. "How was it?"

Michelle looked at him with tears in her eyes. "It was the most wonderful experience of my life!"

Danny pulled her tightly against his chest. "Yes, I agree." Then he pulled back so he could kiss her tenderly and said, "You made it my most wonderful experience!"

Michelle touched his face. "Thank you for teaching me. I love you so much!"

Danny felt his own tears as he kissed her again. "I love you, too! It means so much to hear you say those words!"

"I'm exhausted," Michelle confessed.

He peppered her face with kisses. "You will probably be sore."

She closed her eyes and cuddled against his chest. They both dozed off.

At one point, Danny mumbled in a sleepy voice, "Do you want to go back tonight?"

"No," she answered. She was completely comfortable in his arms and she knew James would not be back until

Sunday. "But I need to call and tell Jackie that I'm staying the night."

Chapter 11

The next morning, after one more time togeth-er in Danny's bed, Michelle drove herself back to her room. The experience was magical, something she couldn't describe to anyone. It was the truest form of intimacy that she could share with a man, and she knew beyond the shadow of the doubt that she was in love with him. As Danny warned her the night before, Michelle felt tenderness. However, she wouldn't have traded this moment with him for anything else in her life.

She finally understood why Hannah missed Michael all the time. Part of her wanted to stay with Danny the rest of the weekend, but she had a project to work on and an exam to study for. She knew if she stayed there, she would be distracted by him. The emotions she felt for Danny were deeper than she could describe. She wondered if this was the reason Jeff warned her off for so many years. However, she refused to give into her misgivings. She flinched as she remembered she needed to speak with Jeff about their relationship. As she thought about her brother, she remembered her worry that he might call while she was with Danny. After the adrenaline spike from the fear, it took her a while to fall asleep after she called Jackie to tell her she was staying with Danny for the night. She snuggled against him and listened to his even breaths, but it was many more minutes before she succumbed to sleep herself.

After working on homework, Michelle planned to call her brother and her folks. She hoped she could speak honestly with Jeff about her relationship with Danny. She wanted more than anything for him to understand and give them his blessing.

When she called his apartment a while later, after speaking to her folks, she announced, "Jefferson, I'm dating a guy. I'm telling you I really like him and I want to see where our relationship goes. I'm nineteen years old and I think I am old enough to decide this myself."

The line was quiet. Because of the silence, Michelle understood how the conversation would go. She rolled her eyes, and she knew his lack of speaking was not his approval, but his disapproval. "Michelle, this is the first guy you've ever gone out with. What has he done to get in your head to think it's an actual relationship? Guys in high school and college say anything to get what they want!"

"Jeff, you're not listening to me!" she said as her volume increased. "He is a wonderful guy, and he treats me so well. He opens my car door every time we go somewhere, and he checks with me on anything we do to make sure I am okay! Why do you have to be so difficult about this topic?"

"Muppet, I know you don't like what I'm about to say,

but I'm trying to look out for your best interests! This guy will distract you from your classes, and you may not finish at the top, like you planned." Jeff said. "I'm on my way up there!"

Michelle growled as burning filled her gut. She shouted, "Stop calling me Muppet! You won't even listen to what I have to say so this conversation is over! And, if you come, I won't be here! Don't expect to hear from me again! " She slammed down the phone so hard, she heard a ding. Tears began falling down her face and she covered her face with her hands as she sobbed for several minutes.

Michelle wished she could talk to Angela, but her plan was to go by the center first thing Monday morning. She didn't want to tell Danny what Jeff said, but he knew she was calling to talk to him. She hadn't shared as deeply as she should, explaining how her brother reacted with any romantic opportunities. Danny was not completely educated on Jeff and his reactions. This coming weekend was when she was going with Danny to visit his home. A slight terror filled her that Danny might break up with her over this. Since they were still getting to know each other, Jeff's attitude might become a deal-breaker. Deep down, her heart ached because Jeff was refusing to listen to her and the thought of losing Danny was more than she could bear.

***

On Monday, Michelle walked out of the bookstore and she noticed Vicki walking across the university commons. She was on the way to her session with Angela, and she was early. Michelle decided to watch where Vicki was going without giving herself away. Vicki knew she was in counseling, so if she accused Michelle of following her, she would say she was on her way to the counseling center.

Michelle pulled one of her textbooks out of the bag from the bookstore to appear as if she was reading and not paying attention to where she was going.

Instead of going straight to where the counselor center was, two streets away, Vicki turned to the right toward a set of apartment buildings across from the main building in the center of the campus.

Michelle stopped to think before following Vicki any further because this was in the opposite direction of her destination. She darted behind the oldest building on the campus, Bennett Hall, and she watched as Vicki checked behind herself before crossing the street. Michelle darted behind another building. As she moved around to the back side of it, she peered around the other side of it. Disappointment filled her to see Vicki was gone.

Damn it, she exclaimed to herself. She leaned against the wall before she checked her watch, and turned back toward the counseling center. As she walked, she wondered if she knew anyone who lived in that complex. There was a girl in one of her business classes that lived in the large apartment complex. Michelle decided to ask her on Wednesday when she saw her in class.

She turned the other direction, walking to her session, deep in thought. Deep down was the thought of following Vicki as a rebellion against her brother and his ridiculous hold on her. The idea made her stumble, and she rubbed her eyes in disbelief. She was still angry with him so maybe she was trying to prove to herself as well as him she could handle her own life.

***

Angela waited in the lobby when Michelle entered the building. Her face lit up with a smile. "Hello, my friend. I'm glad to see you. Are you ready for our session?"

Michelle smiled back. She, Jackie, and Hannah discussed how they loved to talk to Angela. The three of them agreed she would be someone they would be friends with if she wasn't their therapist.

Angela shut the door, and Michelle sat down with a sigh on the couch. With a concerned look, Angela said, "Is something wrong?"

Michelle looked at Angela before she sighed again. "I tried talking to Jeff."

"I'm guessing from the sound of your voice it didn't go well," Angela said.

Michelle groaned. "That's the understatement of the

year! He wouldn't even listen to me!" She spent the next few minutes explaining how she began the conversation with her brother and how it ended when she hung up on him.

"Michelle, I'm not condoning ending a conversation in anger. You should always try to talk out your feelings to resolve issues. However, I think it was a good thing that you hung up on Jeff. Perhaps it got his attention." Angela was matter of fact as she said it.

"He told me he was coming up here, and I told him I would be out of town. We aren't going until this weekend, but I didn't tell him that," Michelle said. Then she shared Danny's invitation to visit his family.

Angela nodded her head, "That's a good thing, too! Did you tell him where you were going?"

"No," Michelle replied. "And I told Danny that I love him. Angela, I believe this is real."

Angela nodded, and she smiled in encouragement. "I'm proud of you for putting yourself out there and getting out of your comfort zone. This is the time in your life where you can learn who you truly are and focus on the goals in your life. Falling in love is a wonderful goal for you."

"You don't think I'm too inexperienced?" Michelle asked.

"The only way for you to become experienced is to actually 'jump in and swim.' Otherwise, you will never know what might be out there in terms of romantic relationships. I believe this is a great environment because our university is smaller than others and more sheltered.

Trust me when I tell you that you are smart and have a strong sense of right and wrong." Angela smiled.

"Okay, so how do I handle Jeff? I wouldn't put it past him to drive up here today and find out where Danny lives." Michelle's shoulders were filled with tension as she vented her frustration. The headache she experienced with her worrying returned with a vengeance.

"What if you spoke to your parents about it? Do you think they would listen and talk to him concerning this?" Angela asked.

"I guess I can try," Michelle said.

"Try talking to them and see how it goes," Angela suggested. "If that doesn't work, then write him a letter and mail it to him. It will be difficult for him to ignore your words when they are written on paper. Reading your perspective might open his eyes."

Angela gave a few more suggestions of thoughts and feelings that she could record when writing her letter to Jeff. As always, Michelle was disappointed when their time was up for the day. After scheduling her next appointment, she stepped outside. Danny was waiting on the bench across from the counseling center.

Joy filled her as she rushed toward him. "What are you doing here?"

Danny took her hand to pull her closer, and he kissed her gently. "I remembered you talking about this today and my last class just finished."

She kissed him back and smiled. "This is a wonderful surprise."

They walked toward her dorm, chatting about their

day. Finally, Michelle said, "There's something I need to talk to you about."

"Baby, you can tell me anything." Danny said, squeezing her hand in his.

Michelle sighed, and she tightened her other hand into a fist. "Last night, I called my brother Jeff. I've told you how difficult he has made it for me and how I never dated in high school."

Danny nodded. "I remember."

"I tried to tell him about you and how I am so happy to have met you," Michelle glanced at the ground before continuing. Danny pulled her to a stop.

"What did he say?" he asked.

"I hate to tell you this, but he was a total jerk about it. I've been talking about his control over me with Angela and she suggested I talk to him, but Jeff shut that down immediately." Michelle took a deep breath. "Angela was proud of me for hanging up on him. She thinks it will get his attention. She also suggested I try talking to my mom and dad about everything. If that doesn't work, she mentioned writing a letter to him."

Danny pulled her into a hug. "I'm glad you're telling me about this. I know it couldn't have been easy to stand up to him." Pulling back, he smiled into her eyes.

"You're not mad?" Michelle asked.

Danny's brow dipped in bewilderment. "Why would I be mad?"

Shaking her head, Michelle said, "I don't know. I was afraid how he reacted would hurt your feelings and you wouldn't want to date me anymore. I just felt like you needed to know."

"I'm not mad at you. Like I said, I'm proud that you talked to him about what you really feel. I don't plan to let his attitude stop me from seeing you." Danny pulled her even tighter against him.

Michelle enjoyed his comforting embrace, and she breathed a sigh of relief. She pulled back and gazed into his eyes. "Thank you for listening. Do you know how wonderful you are?"

Danny's answer was to kiss her. His kiss deepened as his free arm wrapped around her waist while his other hand held her hand against his chest as if she was a treasured gift.

When he pulled back, Michelle whispered, "I love you."

"I never tire of hearing you say that. I love you, too." Danny's lips captured hers in another gentle kiss before he walked her back to the dorm. He had to study while she called and talked to her parents. They planned to meet at dinner and she would update him on their conversation.

Michelle was happy to see that neither Hannah nor Jackie were in the room as she dialed the number to her home.

"Hey, Dad," Michelle said when her father answered.

"Michelle!" he exclaimed in a jovial tone of voice. "How are things going?"

Michelle enjoyed catching her dad up on how things

were going at school. She asked to speak with her mom since she was another female and would understand better than her crazy brother did.

"Hi, sweetie!" Her mother sounded excited to hear from her and it gave Michelle hope.

She filled her mom in on what she shared with her dad before she paused. "Mom..." she said, "there's something I want to talk to you about. Is this a good time?"

"I just finished my work for the day, so this is a perfect time," her mother said. Michelle's mom was an editor for a large company and she went into her office three times a week. The rest of the time, she completed her work from home.

Michelle took a deep breath. "Mom, I've been going out with a guy and he is so wonderful. I called Jeff, and he wasn't happy with me about it. Then I tried to talk to him and tell him how much of a gentleman Danny is. I also tried to reason with him by telling him that I'm older now.."

Her mom sighed on the phone before she spoke. "I knew this day was coming. We allowed your brother to have too much authority over you. It brought us comfort. We were grateful he was so involved because we knew you were always safe. Your father and I should have spoken up about it sooner in your teenage life."

"You know how much I love Jeff," Michelle told her mom. "I appreciate how much he cares about me, but I'm not fourteen or fifteen anymore. I'm almost twenty, and I feel like I am old enough to decide for myself."

Her mom answered her, "Yes, you are. It's time for us,

and him, to let you go. You're old enough now that if you get hurt, you need to learn how to pick up your own pieces and not rely on us."

"Thank you for the support, Mom," Michelle said. "Can you talk to him? I also wanted to tell you that Danny's family invited me to their home this weekend. His parents live about an hour away."

"I'm happy for you," her mom said. "Tell me more about his family." Michelle filled her in with details that she had learned from their conversations. Her mom said, "I will speak with your brother and see if I can't calm him down."

"Thanks, Mom! And, please tell him not to come here! I love you!" Michelle blinked away the silly tears that were filling her eyes. She really was going crazy if the blessing from her mother to date Danny was making her get all weepy about it.

***

That night, outside of the dining hall, Michelle pulled Danny to the side and shared what her mother said before they ate dinner with their friends. Danny's face lit up, and he was beaming from ear to ear as Michelle shared about her mom's support and willingness to help. He pulled Michelle close and kissed her soundly. Michelle felt lightheaded when he released her, and he placed another gentle kiss on her forehead.

She beamed up at him and said, "I'm so excited about meeting your family this weekend."

"Me too!" he replied as he took her hand and led her into the dining room.

Later that night, she updated her roommates on what was going on with her and Danny. It had been a week since the three of them sat down and talked, so she was happy when Hannah suggested they get an ice cream to catch up. She also reminded them she was going to Danny's home over the weekend.

"Ooh!" Hannah teased. "You're meeting his parents! This sounds like it's getting serious!"

Jackie chuckled and said, "It won't be long until you have a ring on your finger, just like Hannah."

Frowning at them, Michelle said, "It's way too soon for that! I need to make sure Jeff won't kill him first!"

***

Thursday afternoon, Michelle was walking out of the dorm to go to the library when she noticed Brandi coming her way. She nonchalantly looked ahead to make it look like she didn't recognize her. Michelle darted behind a tree in the front yard as soon as she passed and watched Brandi walk inside of the dorm.

She had asked Jennifer if she knew anyone who lived in the other old homes that had been converted into apartments on Wednesday. This was before she knew that Jennifer and Jackie were interested in each other. The building friendship helped Jennifer tell her truthful facts of what she knew.

Jennifer mentioned the name of a girl that came from a wealthy family. She also mentioned two cheerleaders and that they also shared one of the apartments.

Michelle turned the opposite way to follow Brandi back inside, hoping to see where she was going. Brandi walked down the old hallway where she and Jackie had lived their freshman year. It was the hall where they lived beside Hannah and her crazy roommate, Rhonda. Michelle darted around another girl who was walking toward her and she noticed Brandi take the next hallway on the left. Trying to stay inconspicuous, Michelle stopped and peered around the corner. Her heart started pounding when she saw Brandi pull something out of her pocket and jiggle one doorknob.

However, she yelped and covered her mouth when she felt a tap on her shoulder. Michelle turned and Jackie stood behind her.

"I've been calling your name, but you didn't hear me," Jackie said with a slight frown on her face.

"You scared me to death!" Michelle exclaimed.

The frown dipped lower on Jackie's forehead. "What are you doing?"

"What? Oh, nothing." Michelle looked past her best friend, trying to think of an excuse to be in this hallway. "I was going to one of my classmate's rooms to ask for some research they found for a project we are working on."

Jackie continued staring at Michelle. "Okay, so what room is she in?"

"I got turned around!" Michelle said. "I actually needed

to go down the other side. Silly me!"

Shaking her head, Jackie said, "I hope you aren't following anyone and trying to see what they're doing."

Michelle rolled her eyes. "I told you and Hannah that I wouldn't."

When Jackie narrowed her eyes, Michelle felt a pain in her chest. Jackie said, "You better be telling me the truth about this."

"Come on." Michelle said. "Let's go back to the room and I will call her to see if she is there."

Chapter 12

Danny looked forward to his therapy session with Mark. He believed he was getting a handle on his life, but his future was still a question mark for him.

Mark shook his hand enthusiastically when he entered the center. After walking to his office, Danny handed over the journal he had been writing in. "Before I take time to read this, how has everything else been going?" Mark asked.

"Great! I've been eating healthy and I've started running two days a week on the days I don't play basketball. I'm keeping the log you gave me about monitoring my sleep." Danny said.

"Wonderful. Let me glance over at it." Mark was quiet for a few moments as he perused through Danny's entries and studied the sleep log. When he glanced up, he said, "Danny, I'm really proud of you. You went from being in total denial to learning how to take care of yourself. It's something you will be grateful for thirty years from now."

"Thank you," Danny smiled.

After a long silence, Mark said, "It seems like your sleep is slightly erratic. Have you considered why?"

Danny sighed. "I have a hard time when I contemplate school."

"What do you mean?" Mark frowned.

"I told you when I first started coming to you, I am not sure if I am on the right path with my major." Danny said. "The work on my anxiety has been good, but I want to determine what I'm supposed to do with my life and my future." Danny's voice rose in volume and he leaned forward, shoving his hands through his hair.

"I remember you telling me that. But I felt that getting a handle on your anxiety would be a great first step. Tell me why you aren't sure." Mark said.

"I always imagined I would become a coach like my dad. But the more I try to focus on it, the more I don't want to do it." Danny complained.

Mark remained silent for a moment. Then he said, "What are things you really care about other than basketball and school now that you've started your college path?"

Danny pondered. "I care about getting good grades. And I have deep feelings for Michelle, the girl that I'm dating." Mark smiled and nodded in encouragement. "I like my class focusing on the development of children's minds."

Mark nodded again and his gaze was intense. "That's an impressive list. I'm glad you're dating, my friend. I believe this will also help reduce your anxieties, unless you concentrate on those worries about being perfect for her."

Danny's face turned red. He looked at his hands. "Those thoughts have crossed my mind."

Mark chuckled. "We can definitely strive toward overcoming that as well." Mark paused again. "I'm going to veer away from your major for another session. I understand you want a clear answer of what you are supposed to do, but working to manage your anxiety will help make that path clear."

"What do you suggest now?"

"I want to introduce you to mindfulness. I realize it might sound like crazy mumbo jumbo, but I like the results when my clients learn to use it correctly." Mark handed Danny a small book and another cassette tape. "Listen to this and read two chapters from this book. Write your thoughts in your journal."

"Okay." Danny studied the book, reading the blurb on the back.

"Next. I want you to list, *struggle with my major* at the top of a blank page in your notebook. Then I want you to write about why you perceive it as a problem. After that, brainstorm as many solutions as you can."

Danny nodded in agreement. Mark continued. "I'm going to write these down so that you don't forget. We will talk about all of it when you come next week."

As usual, the session flew by and the hour ended. Frustration filled Danny because he felt as if there was so much to work on. As if he sensed his thoughts, Mark said, "I promise all of this will lead you in the right direction. I need you to trust me on this."

Danny thanked Mark, and he set up another appointment when they walked out to the lobby. His mind felt like scrambled eggs when he exited the counseling center. He shoved the tape in a pocket of his backpack and flipped to the table of contents of the book on mindfulness.

***

Friday afternoon arrived, and Michelle paced with excitement. She planned to spend the entire weekend with Danny at his home! She considered herself as someone who did not get emotional over events, but she couldn't stop fidgeting in anticipation.

"You're going to wear a hole in the carpet," Jackie said.

"Yep, I say this is serious if you can't sit still! I remember feeling the same way when I went with Michael to his home!" Hannah laughed as Michelle glared her way in exasperation.

Her mom called the evening before to tell her she talked to her brother. She honestly stated that she hoped he would back off, but she couldn't guarantee it. Then her mom let her know he wouldn't be coming to visit. She suggested Michelle call him when she came back from Danny's home and introduce them over the phone.

"Keep talking to him," her mom encouraged. "He will eventually come around."

Michelle huffed out a breath. "Thanks, Mom." When she hung up, the ideas were turning as she sat on her bed, hoping her mom was right. As she considered her mom's suggestion to introduce Danny by phone, Michelle was uncertain why that hadn't occurred to her. Deep down, she realized her intention was to protect Danny from Jeff and his ridiculous safeguarding of her. She also remembered Angela's suggestion to write a letter. She would pick one of those when she returned from meeting Danny's family.

The phone rang, and it roused her from her thoughts. Hannah stood nearby, so she answered it and teased, "Your man is here, so you better meet him in the lobby!"

With her sarcastic manner, Michelle said, "Get ready for some teasing from me with you and Michael." She shouldered her bag as her friends were still giggling.

"Have a great time. See you Sunday!" They both spoke to her at the same time as she waved and walked out of the room.

Danny's smile spread across his face as she walked toward him. He kissed her cheek and took her bag from her. "Are you ready?"

"Yes," Michelle smiled back.

"I'm so excited you're coming home with me!" He took her hand and kissed it softly before entwining their fingers and leading her out to his truck.

"I hope they like me," Michelle mumbled.

After he opened her door and got into the driver's seat,

Danny said, "They will love you! They already love the things I've told them about you. And I know you and my sister will get along well!"

The drive didn't take long at all. Michelle was aware of it, but she still couldn't believe how short the trip actually was. The trip to her Beaumont home, southeast of Houston, took five hours. The two stop lights in the tiny town differed from the traffic she and Jackie usually encountered.

When Danny pulled down a long drive, she noticed a lovely ranch-style house among rolling hills. "Wow! I love this!" Michelle exclaimed as she gazed around. Cattle grazed near the fence as they drove down the long driveway. "Are these your parents' cattle?"

"My dad helps my grandfather with managing the herd. My grandfather was a rancher, and he's semi-retired now." Danny squeezed her hand, which he had been holding most of the drive.

"This is so beautiful," she said with shining eyes, as he slowed down and parked to the side of a two-car garage.

With a wide smile, Michelle jumped out before he came around to open her door. "Sorry," she said. "I was excited about looking around."

Danny took her bag and touched her cheek. He gazed at her tenderly. "No problem," he said. "Make yourself at home."

However, nerves rushed over her as they walked through the spacious garage where Danny opened the door. "Hey, we're home!" he called.

A tall and willowy blond haired lady walked into

the kitchen and hugged Danny. "I'm so glad you're home! How was the drive?" Michelle recognized the resemblance as she immediately considered her beauty. She had shoulder length feathered hair, and she wore high-waisted polyester pants and a blouse with a bow tied at the neck. It represented typical fashion for women in the eighties. Michelle's mother wore similar attire.

"The drive was great! But you're strangling me!" Danny choked as his mother didn't let go of his neck. Finally, she pulled back as Michelle laughed at him, rubbing his throat.

Danny put an arm around Michelle's waist as he drew her closer. "Mom, this is Michelle Walters."

"Michelle," Danny's mom smiled at her as she took her hand in hers. "Danny has told us so many wonderful things about you! We're so glad you came for a visit."

Michelle smiled as she couldn't help but notice the strong Texas accent in Barbara's voice. "Thank you for having me, Mrs. Peterson. I'm glad to meet you as well!"

"Please call me Barbara," Danny's mom said. "Danny, take her to the guest room."

"Already on it, Mom." Danny said. "What time is the game tonight?"

"It starts at seven thirty, so we will get pizza before the game. Your dad can meet us for a few minutes at the restaurant before he has to go back to the football field. Does that sound okay?" Barbara Peterson followed as they walked down the long and spacious hallway.

"That sounds great. Thank you." Both Danny and Michelle answered at the same time.

Danny led the way into a lovely room with a window facing the direction they drove in. "Here you go," he commented as he set her bag on a chair sitting close to the window. A love seat sat beside it in a small sitting area.

Michelle gazed around at the lovely room, decorated in blues and yellows. She was surprised to find a bathroom connected to the room. "This is so beautiful!" she commented and she repeated, "Thank you so much for having me!" She observed a TV on a small stand across from the bed.

Barbara pulled the blinds up to let in more light as she said, "You are so welcome. When my grandmother couldn't live independently anymore, she used this room and bathroom. We had it built to provide her personal space away from all of us when she needed it."

"I love it," Michelle exclaimed as she walked to the window to gaze at the lovely view. "This is all so lovely!"

"Danny can give you a tour when you're ready. Tom's parents live a little further up the lane you drove in to get to our house. They're coming for supper tomorrow night, so you can meet them." Danny's mother joined her at the window. "Well, I will let you get settled in. There are fresh towels in the bathroom, but please let us know if you need anything." Barbara walked out after Michelle thanked her again.

"I love your mom!" she said with fervent emotion.

Danny pulled her into his arms. "She liked you, too!" Then he leaned down and kissed her softly until Michelle pushed back.

"I don't want her seeing us kissing!" she whispered.

Danny didn't let her move too far away as he gave her another gentle kiss. With teasing in his eyes, he said, "This room is a long way from the rest of the house. So we are safe for a few kisses."

Michelle didn't argue anymore as he kissed down the side of her neck causing bumps to raise on her arms and she lost all train of thought. Every time Danny touched her, it felt like she lived a fairytale.

Danny pushed her up against a wall, and he continued kissing her thoroughly. He paused and ran his fingers through her hair and said, "We need to postpone this for now. I agree with you. I don't want my mom walking in to see me doing more to you than kissing." He whispered in her ear. "I plan to pick this up again tonight when everyone has gone to bed." His mouth grazed it and Michelle began shivering with delight. After one last kiss, Danny stepped away and said, "We have time if you want a tour around the property."

"I would like that," Michelle whispered, shaking her head to get her senses back. Danny's kisses always wiped all coherent thoughts away.

The gleam in Danny's eyes showed his pride as he noticed her flushed neck. He repeated the sentence from earlier. "Later..."

He gestured for her to leave the room before him and then his hands grasped her waist from behind, where they trailed down her hips and her butt, causing her to squeal. "Stop it," she hissed as his teasing gaze darkened with desire.

He caught up to her and wrapped an arm around her

waist. "I'm so glad we have all weekend where I can touch you."

Michelle gazed at him, "Me too, but there will be no touching around your family." But she leaned against him as they continued down the hallway.

Danny's mom relaxed on the couch with a book in her hands. She changed into blue jeans and a t-shirt with the school mascot on it. She had reading glasses perched on the end of her nose as she glanced up.

"Mom, I'm going to drive Michelle around the property," Danny said as he leaned down and kissed the top of his mom's head. "What time do we need to be ready to go to dinner?"

"We will go around six thirty," his mom said as her eyes returned to her book.

It was only three o'clock, so they had several hours to kill before dinner.

***

After driving her around the expansive ranch property, Danny gave her a tour of the rest of the house. He was right in saying that the remaining rooms lay opposite the expansive living area.

For the millionth time, Michelle repeated her original statement. "It is so beautiful here!"

"Thank you." Danny opened the door to his own room, where he placed his bag on his bed. In all of his showing Michelle around, he hadn't brought her into his bedroom. Michelle gazed around at the eighties hair band posters along with pictures of famous country singers.

Michelle smirked at Danny. "This room definitely looks like you!"

The teasing in Danny's eyes returned, "Oh, you presume you know me?" Danny made a move to pull her to him again, but she skirted away from him with a flirtatious look. Michelle heard Danny groan in frustration and it made her chuckle as she peeked into the room across the hall from his room.

She could tell it was Beth's room, with the door slightly ajar. Michelle caught purple and pink coloring. Not wanting to intrude, Michelle didn't go any further into her room.

Beth would be home in half an hour to rest before getting ready to go back to the school where her dance team would perform at the football game.

She walked back into Danny's room. He had a queen-sized bed that looked extremely comfortable. "So, is there anything you would like to do?" As he asked, a beautiful Australian shepherd wandered into his room. "Hey Luna," he murmured as he reached down to hug her, petting her face and ears.

"What a gorgeous dog!" Michelle squealed as she said, "Hi girl! Her name is Luna?"

"Yep," Danny replied as he knelt beside her and wrapped his arms around her.

"I love her! I love all dogs!" Michelle said as she sat down beside her and she stroked her head, face, and neck. Luna leaned in, relishing the attention of someone new.

"Are you sure there isn't anything you want to do?" Danny repeated his question.

Michelle smiled, petting Luna who leaned against her legs. "I wouldn't mind some water; afterward, we can do anything you wish." The time there had been wonderful so far.

"Sure, I could use a snack," Danny said. He led the way down the hallway, back through the living room, and to the kitchen. A large table sat at one end of the spacious kitchen. Luna followed behind, sniffing for find food on the floor. Danny walked to one cabinet to get out two glasses, and then he opened the fridge. "Are you sure you just want water? I see a pitcher of sweet tea in here."

"Oh, that sounds good! Thanks, but can I help?" Michelle joined him where he stood in front of a large island. Danny poured tea for both of them.

"Can you carry these to the table while I look and see what snacks are in the pantry?" Danny asked.

Michelle happily offered her assistance. "Is there a special place where I shouldn't sit? I don't want to sit in anyone's spot."

"My parents sit on either end, but you can sit any-where," Danny said as he kissed the top of her head before joining her at the table with a bag of chips and a package of cookies.

As they enjoyed their snack, the garage door opened and a beautiful blond girl walked in. She looked like her mother. However, her blond hair fell longer down her back and across her shoulders. Beth wore a stylish blouse that was tucked into Guess jeans. Her shoes matched her blouse.

"Bethy!" Danny said, as he stood to wrap his sister in a hug.

Beth giggled in his tight grip. "You're smothering me!"

When Danny pulled back, he took Michelle's hand and drew her into his side. "This is Michelle Walters, my girl-friend."

When he called her that word, Michelle's heart always beat faster, bringing a smile to her face. "I'm so glad to meet you. I've heard wonderful things about you!"

With a teasing glance at Danny, Beth said, "I've heard him gushing and mooning over you as well. When he last came home, he talked of nothing else!"

"Hey! I did not!" Danny argued, and Michelle laughed at the blush that stole over his face.

"Finally, the tables have turned on the blushing!" Michelle teased sarcastically. Then she asked, "Do you want a snack with us?"

Beth put her bookbag in her room and joined them at the table. Danny had poured her a glass of sweet tea. Just as Danny predicted, she and Beth hit it off famously. She reminded her of Hannah due to her sweetness. Michelle observed a gentle heart in Beth.

Every person Michelle encountered in Danny's family turned out to be absolutely wonderful! She was so glad she came home with him. She understood his bragging about their wonderful nature.

***

When they arrived at the pizza restaurant, a tall man climbed out of a large truck and Michelle understood, without introductions, that it was Danny's father. The two of them looked exactly alike. He dressed in sports pants with a polo shirt and he looked very much like a football coach.

"Hey Dad," Danny said as he walked to his dad, and they embraced.

"Good to have you home, son!" He said. Seeing their embrace filled Michelle's heart with warmth.

Danny proudly pulled Michelle to his side and said, "This is Michelle Walters."

"I'm so glad to meet you!" Michelle said, her hand held in Tom's large hands.

Danny's dad winked at her. "I can see why my son likes you so much! It's wonderful to meet you. You are a beautiful young lady!" As soon as he said it, he turned and pulled Barbara close, planting a kiss on her lips. Michelle couldn't control her blush. However, she enjoyed seeing the intimacy between the two of them.

They placed their order at the counter before sitting so that their food would be ready sooner because Danny's dad and sister had to get back to the football field.

Michelle had a wonderful time at the meal, enjoying Danny's family together. Each of them did all that they could to include her in the conversation. At one point,

Danny reached under the table for her hand and he rested both of their hands on his knee. Uncomfortable at first, Michelle's heart twittered at the love among all of them.

***

After they found their seats beside his mom at the football stadium, Danny and Michelle walked to the snack bar for a drink. She felt quite satisfied with the pizza supper, but she happily strolled with him. On the way there, many who recognized Danny and welcomed him home stopped them. She knew he had been the former high school football star, but it amazed her to see the king-like treatment he received.

Danny clasped her hand in his as they stood in line. He asked, "So, what do you think of my family? They haven't scared you away, have they?"

She smiled as Danny used his free hand to brush a stray hair away from her face. "You have a great family! Your dad is a complete charmer, so I see where you get it from!"

"Oh, I'm a charmer now, am I?" Danny teased as he wrapped his arms around her waist and pulled her in for a gentle kiss. "First, you know what my room should look like, and now you say that I am a charmer." He rubbed his nose against hers before kissing her one more time. "I believe you are getting to understand too much about me."

"Mmm..." Michelle breathed out. "You just proved my point."

Danny gazed into her eyes as he whispered, "Maybe I am a charmer, but you're the only one that I have any desire to entice."

Up at the front of the line, they almost lost their spot because of being wrapped up in each other. After they received their drinks and Danny paid for his candy, they walked back to join his mom.

Danny's arm remained wrapped around Michelle's waist as they walked back. A woman's voice announced, "Hello, Danny Peterson."

Not releasing Michelle, he turned them and noticed a beautiful blonde glaring at Michelle. She shot daggers in her direction. Her hair had been curled and styled in the latest eighties fashion, with bangs.

"Hey, Rachel," Danny said. "How are you?" Friendliness characterized his tone. Danny tightened his hold on Michelle's waist. "This is my girlfriend, Michelle."

Michelle couldn't help but compare her lack of beauty with this beautiful creature standing before them. However, she made herself smile. "Nice to meet you."

With a look of judgement, Rachel said, "Nice to meet you, too." Her voice lacked any conviction in it. Then she had the audacity to step up to Danny and run her hand across his free arm. "I broke up with David. He's such a moron!"

Danny gently removed Rachel's hand from his arm. "I'm sorry to hear that, Rachel."

"Maybe we can get together while you're home and

talk." Rachel's lips pouted as she batted her lashes flir- tatiously at Danny. She tried pushing closer to him, com- pletely ignoring Michelle.

Danny pulled himself, and Michelle, a step away from Rachel. "I'm only here for the weekend, Rachel, and all of my time will be spent with my family and Michelle. Like I said, she and I are dating. Great to see you!" Entwining their fingers, he pulled Michelle back around to walk back to their seats.

"Wow! It seems to me she still likes you! I take it you two dated," Michelle blurted out as they walked away and jealousy shot through her. She glanced back and watched Rachel glaring after them with a disappointed look in her eyes.

Danny appeared nonchalant saying, "We only went on a couple of dates, so it wasn't serious or anything."

Not meaning to say it aloud, Michelle murmured, "She's beautiful," before putting a hand over her mouth.

Danny stopped them and pulled her into a dark cor- ner behind the bleachers. He placed his hands on her shoulders. "You're beautiful, and so much more than her because you are beautiful on the inside and the outside."

Michelle felt uneasy with his words and she attempted to look down. However, Danny held her gaze with his hand on her chin. "Michelle, please tell me you believe me."

"I realize I look nothing like her, so I'm unsure if I believe that," Michelle murmured as he embraced her and she rested against him.

"Baby, we've had this conversation. Can you hear my

heart racing in my chest? You are the only one who does that for me." Danny kissed the top of her head before he pulled back.

Overwhelmed, as always, by his attraction and his choice of her as his girlfriend, Michelle's gaze held vulnerability as she said, "I hear it, but I'm always afraid something is going to happen and you won't want to be with me anymore."

"That will never happen," Danny said, as he shook his head adamantly. "You have so much more than Rachel can ever offer because you are warm, kind and you have a beautiful heart!"

The desire to trust him filled Michelle. "Thank you. I really do want to accept that."

"I can prove it." Danny leaned down and captured Michelle's lips in a kiss. As she leaned into it, he deepened it.. By the time he pulled back, his hands cradled her head as he ran his fingers through her hair.

A few moments later, they joined his mom again just as the band and drill team marched out for their pregame show. Not having gone to any of her high school games, Michelle enjoyed it immensely. She got drawn into the competition of the game. At one point, Danny pulled out a blanket to cover the two of them because it had gotten cold as the sun set. Michelle snuggled up against him as he put his arm around her to pull her closer.

Chapter 13

When the game ended, Danny and Michelle rode back with Danny's mom. When they got to the house, Barbara hugged both of them and said good night before getting a glass of water. She disappeared down the hallway to her room.

Thinking she and Danny would do the same thing, Michelle took a shower. As she pulled back the covers on the bed, Michelle heard a knock on the door. Walking to it, she was surprised to see Danny smiling at her. His hair was damp from a shower and he was wearing sweatpants and a form-fitting T-shirt.

"What are you doing?" she exclaimed as he pushed her inside and shut the door before planting a steamy kiss on her lips.

"Don't you remember I told you we would pick things up later?" He mumbled the words against her lips before deepening it to where Michelle became breathless.

Feeling woozy, she whispered, "I don't want your parents to find out you are in here!"

Danny touched her face. "Don't worry. This is so far

away from the rest of the house that they won't hear a thing. I shut my door to look like I had gone to sleep, so nobody will know."

Michelle knew deep down that she wanted to be with him again, so she said nothing else as he picked her up and placed her on the bed. Then he locked the door before joining her. She was wearing a robe with a tie over a tank top and shorts.

Danny leaned down and kissed her again as his fingers trailed over her robe and he untied the sash. As it fell open, he gazed at Michelle's creamy skin showing under her tank top and shorts. He murmured softly. "I love your skin." His hands ran up and down her arms before caressing her shoulders and neck.

Danny's touch was so intense that goosebumps appeared all over Michelle's skin, following the path of his fingers. He pushed down one strap of her tank top and leaned down to pebble kisses on her shoulder and neck.

Meanwhile, her hands found their way under his shirt as she nudged it up to where he finally pulled it over his head. Michelle inhaled sharply as she gazed at his muscled chest and arms that tapered down to a slim waist. "You are so hot!" she whispered before his lips captured hers again in a deep kiss where their tongues tangled with desire.

His lips went back to her shoulder, neck and he began kissing his way down her chest while one hand went under the hem of her top and caressed its way up to right below her breasts. Tracing under her breast, he took his own sharp breath as he realized she wasn't wearing a bra.

Impatiently, Michelle took his hand and placed it on her breast. His hand traced around it and then moved to the other breast. Seeing her hardened nipples through her tank top nearly sent him over the edge. He leaned down to lick them through the top, causing Michelle to moan.

Danny quickly pulled her tank top over her head and he threw it on the floor as he gazed at her in wonder. "You're so beautiful," he whispered, and he leaned down to take a breast in his mouth. Michelle moaned loudly.

Michelle's hands traveled down his stomach. She caressed him through his sweatpants. Danny groaned as her hands dipped inside the waistband to grip him. He followed her lead as his own hand went inside of her shorts, dipping into her panties to find her warmth. It pleased him she was wet and ready for him. Sliding his fingers deeper into her underwear, her moan became louder.

"All clothes need to come off now!" she demanded as she slid out of the rest of her clothes while he did the same. Before throwing his pants on the floor, he fished a condom out of his pocket and set it on the nightstand.

One hand fondled her breast as the other slipped between her legs to caress before he slid a finger inside of her. Michelle moaned and thrashed. His mouth closed over a breast as his fingers pumped in and out of her. "Danny...oh!" she cried against his neck, which was totally hot to him.

After her orgasm finished, Danny sheathed himself in a condom before he moved inside of her. Michelle had learned quickly how to move her body with his to increase the pleasure as he kissed her again. Michelle's gaze widened as their movements brought them to their climax simultaneously. Danny fell on top of her before removing the condom, moving to the side, and pulling her into his embrace.

Exhausted and completely comfortable, Michelle fell asleep wrapped in his arms. A while later, she felt his lips kiss her forehead before he whispered, "Good night. I love you." She missed him when he left to go back to his own bed.

The rest of the weekend flew by as Michelle thoroughly enjoyed her time at Danny's home. Saturday night was a wonderful time of meeting his grandparents, eating Texas brisket with all the fixings. If Michelle wasn't in love with Danny before, this would have been the weekend where she would have declared it to him after seeing him with his family. His dad was just as kind as Danny was and he spent Sunday afternoon teaching Michelle the basics of riding a horse. As Danny predicted, she and Beth hit it off. The two of them were quickly becoming friends.

Sunday morning, she joined Danny's family at their church and the people who went there welcomed her with kindness. It was already past lunch, and Danny told his parents it was time to start their hour-long drive back to school. His family had completely fallen in love with

Michelle and she received warm hugs from his dad, his mother, and Beth. The two girls had grown close in the short time and Beth promised to come and stay with her, Jackie, and Hannah soon.

Michelle stared out the window in bliss as Danny drove. She was pulled out of her daydream when she felt a warm hand touch her cheek.

Danny said, "What's on your mind?"

Michelle gazed at him with a smile. "Thank you for inviting me to meet your family. You should be proud of all of them! They are wonderful people."

Reluctantly pulling his gaze away to watch the road, Danny said, "I'm proud of you. They complimented you several times."

Intensity filled Michelle's stare as she murmured, "I love you, Danny Peterson."

Her hand was already in his, so he squeezed it. "Baby, I love you, too."

Ten minutes later, he pulled his truck into a parking space outside of her dorm and parked. They both got out, and he walked around the car, pulling her into his embrace.

They stared at each other for a few seconds before Danny broke the silence. "Man, I'm going to miss you!"

"Me too." Michelle said, "but I will see you in the morning." Spending the entire weekend together sparked the idea of being together all the time instead of when they could manage their busy schedules. Michelle mentally shook her head, thinking that she was not anywhere near a point of living with a guy. That thought brought back all the worries about Jeff. It was time for her to work out a plan to get him on board.

Danny kissed her, and then he whispered his love, which she repeated back to him.

***

The next morning, Michelle was hurrying from her first class to her next one when her gaze landed on Brandi walking in her direction. Her gaze appeared sullen as she spied Michelle in her path.

"What's your name?" she demanded in a harsh tone.

"Excuse me?" Michelle blurted out.

"Look bitch, I saw you try to follow me a week ago." Brandi sneered.

"I don't know what you're talking about," Michelle answered as she was filled with alarm. She thought she had been subtle in following Brandi.

Brandi snorted. "Don't be stupid with me. I saw you in the dorm."

"I live in that dorm," Michelle retorted, trying not to hide the trembling in her legs from this confrontation.

Brandi took a threatening step toward Michelle when they heard her name called. Instinctively, Michelle took a step back. To her relief, Hannah and Jackie walked quickly in her direction.

Brandi jabbed a finger toward Michelle as she backed away. "Stay the hell out of my way!" Brandi darted off before Hannah or Jackie reached the two of them.

Michelle had never been happier to see her room-mates than she was at that moment. As Hannah walked up to her, she said, "Who on earth was that? She doesn't look like someone in the business school."

"I've seen her in the counseling center," Michelle hedged, and she refused to look at Jackie.

"Somehow I don't see her getting counseling," Jackie said as she caught Michelle's gaze and Michelle could see the speculation in her eyes.

She was not normally a liar and didn't know what overcame her at the moment, but she said, "She has to go as part of her community service from getting in trouble last year."

"Michelle, is there something wrong?" Hannah asked with concern in her eyes.

"No. Everything is fine." Michelle replied lightly. She hanged the subject. "Where are you both going?"

"We saw each other coming out of the education building and Jackie asked me to come to get a coffee with her before our next class, since we have a few minutes." Hannah explained as she gestured toward the cafe.

"I'll join you. A coffee sounds good," Michelle said, pleased with her diversion tactic.

Michelle spoke to Danny about getting on a call with her to meet her brother. She hoped to convince Jeff to release his ridiculous control over Michelle's dating life, or lack thereof. She asked him about it on the way drive from visiting his family, and Danny was completely supportive. That evening, she planned to write him a letter, as Angela had suggested.

That afternoon, Michelle drove over to Danny's apartment and she quickly parked the car, smirking as she saw Hannah's vehicle already parked in the shared driveway. There were several nights a week when Hannah stayed with Michael.

Not quite ready for that kind of step, Michelle was deep in thought as she knocked on Danny's door. Surprise raced through her as Danny's roommate, James, opened the door with a grin.

"Hey, Michelle," he commented as he opened the door wider so she could step inside before he stepped out. Michelle noticed the bookbag on his shoulder.

Michelle looked at him, feeling guilty. "Don't let me push you out the door."

"Nah," James said. "I'm on my way to the library, so it's not a problem."

Michelle knew James was in pre-law classes and would eventually need to transfer to a different school to complete his law degree. This was closer to home, so he spent these first two years without having to drive as far.

"See you later," she mused as Danny was walking into the small kitchen, distracting her from all thought. She couldn't help but admire how wonderful he always looked.

Danny grasped her shoulders when he stopped in front of her. He whispered, "Hey baby." Then he planted a sensual kiss on her lips and Michelle forgot why she was even there. Her hands moved up his chest and around to the back of his neck as she returned his kiss for a few more seconds.

She pushed him back and shook her head. "We need to focus. This is not helping."

Danny chuckled, "Why not?" His mouth was nuzzling her neck and his arms had not released her yet.

"Danny!" she said, but her voice was not as firm as a moment ago. Michelle's eyes were closing despite her argument that they needed to stop.

"Okay, okay," he said. Danny reluctantly released her, pulling her into the living room.

Michelle sat down and faced him with her hand clasped in his. "Let's talk about how we need to approach Jeff."

"I will follow your lead," Danny said as he stroked her cheek with his free hand.

"We can't give him any idea of how intimate we are, got it?" Michelle was firm again as she spoke.

"I don't really want him knowing about our sex life," Danny answered, and he laughed when she smacked his shoulder playfully.

Michelle looked at him and she said, "I want him to hear how wonderful and thoughtful you are, so anything we can tell him regarding that would be great."

"That will be easy," Danny said, "because I love being thoughtful with you." He leaned in and kissed her softly.

She smiled at him. "I know. It's why I love you so much! Are you ready?"

"Absolutely," he answered as he kissed her nose before standing to get the cordless phone that was plugged in at their side table.

Michelle dialed her brother's number and tapped her leg impatiently as she waited for him to answer.

To comfort her, Danny covered her hand with his and squeezed, causing her to look into his eyes and smile.

"Hello." Jeff answered the phone.

"Hey," Michelle said.

"Muppet!" Jeff said with happiness in his voice. "I'm sorry for how I reacted the last time we talked. I know I upset you and Mom helped me to see that you are older now and not a little girl anymore."

"Thanks." Michelle said, "I actually called because I want you to meet Danny over the phone so that you can get to know him. I'm hoping to bring him home sometime soon."

Silence filled the phone line, and then Jeff spoke. "Alright." Michelle could sense his reluctance.

Danny turned on the speaker button on his cordless phone. "Hey, Jeff. It's nice to meet you! Michelle has told me so many great things about you."

"Hello," Jeff answered. "I've heard a little about you as well."

"We just got back from seeing Danny's family," Michelle piped in. "And..."

"You went home with him?" Jeff asked, interrupting what Michelle was going to say next.

She pushed down her irritation. "I went home with him to meet his parents and sister."

"Where are you from, Danny?" Jeff's forced politeness was annoying to Michelle.

Danny was kind as he spoke. "I'm from Groverton, which is about an hour from here. My parents have a house on land with my grandparents outside of town."

Jeff replied, "Uh-huh, so you live out in the country."

Michelle rolled her eyes but let Danny talk as he filled Jeff in on details about his family.

"What does your dad do?" Jeff was continuing to be polite, but wary of his questions. Michelle knew him so well that she could see right through his questioning, which was becoming more of an interrogation.

Danny smiled over at Michelle, squeezed her hand and said, "He's the football coach at the high school. My mom works in the school board office and my sister, Beth, is sixteen. She will graduate in two years." Michelle wanted to giggle as Danny answered the twenty questions that he knew were coming from Jeff.

"Uh-huh," Jeff answered again, and that was all he said.

Her headache returned with a vengeance as Michelle said, "Jeff, he just shared with you about how wonderful his family is."

"Michelle, can you take us off speaker so that I can talk to you alone?" Jeff asked.

"You know, I have tried to include you in my life choices since I've moved to college. But you are unwilling to listen or be happy for me." Michelle said as her voice started quivering, "I'm really disappointed in you, Jeff. We are trying to include you and you are acting so rude toward Danny."

"Michelle..." Jeff tried interrupting, but she wouldn't allow him to interject. "Goodbye, Jeff," she said as she hung up the phone.

When she covered her face with her hands, she began crying softly. Danny pulled her into his gentle embrace. "Michelle, it's okay. It may take him a while longer to come around to the idea of me in your life."

With tears rolling down her cheeks, Michelle looked up at him and said, "I love Jeff, but he refuses to change or even let me grow up. It hurts that we have this enormous gap in between us, but you are too important to me! I refuse to let his negative attitude ruin what we have!"

Danny kissed the tears rolling down her face, tasting their salty flavor. "I'm so sorry," he whispered. "If I need to back away for a while, I will do that. I don't like to see you cry and I don't want to come between you and your brother."

"No!" Michelle cried. "I want to be with you and I want to move ahead in our relationship!" She wrapped her arms around his waist and laid her head on his chest. Danny held her close like that for a while longer.

Chapter 14

When Michelle arrived back at the dorm, she filled Jackie in on what had happened with her brother.

"I agree with Danny," Jackie answered. "Jeff may need more time to get used to you dating someone seriously." She shook her head. "I don't understand why he is so against you and dating. It's something I haven't ever understood."

Michelle cried silently as she prepared for bed, unable to sleep. Wiping tears away, she stood up and walked to her desk to find paper and a pen. When she was settled in her bed, she began writing the letter to Jeff as Angela suggested. It was tough as she put everything on the page bringing on more tears. But she felt better once she was finished. It was as if she had expunged all of her feelings to the page and a peace settled over her as she laid down and fell asleep. The normal uncertain feelings were nowhere to be found. Michelle was confident that she had done the right thing for herself by writing the letter.

Dear Jefferson,

I am writing to you to tell you again how disappointed I am with you. Twice, I've tried talking with you about how important Danny is becoming to me and you refuse to listen. And I don't understand why you believe you need to keep such a tight hold on me. When you spoke with him on the phone, you came across as a total jerk. I'm sure deep down that he doesn't care for you because of how you treated him.

I want to communicate to you again, Jeff, that I am old enough to make choices for myself. You refuse to acknowledge that I've actually grown up into a mature human being.

I told you on the phone that if you cannot accept this relationship, you will no longer be a part of my life. It hurts me so badly to say that. I wish more than anything that you would open up your heart, and your ridiculously closed mind, to see what an exceptional person Danny is.

If you get in my way of being with him, I will have a difficult time ever forgiving you. I hope that writing this in a letter might get your attention.

I love you, but I will choose Danny over you if you refuse to change.

Sincerely,

Your almost twenty-year-old sister, Michelle

***

As Danny got ready for bed that night, he reviewed the conversation with Michelle's brother. He was an older brother, so he understood the desire to protect his younger sister. Danny would go to the ends of the earth for his sister, Beth. But Jeff took his protection to a new level. Jeff's meddling in Michelle's dating life throughout high school made him realize he wouldn't give in easily. Danny found the sentiment uncomfortable, something he'd never experienced before. He never faced anyone who disliked him in that way. Danny was unable to stand it when Michelle broke down into tears. But even though her brother remained a problem, he had never loved Michelle more. It was difficult to face rejection of this kind. Danny was familiar with everyone in his childhood town, and he lacked enemies. Uncertain about what to do, he needed to talk to Michael and Alex. They had basketball practice the next evening, so he would present the issue to them.

He also had a scheduled session with Mark, but their time was spent dealing with his own issues, as well as what his focus concerning his future. As always, his desire to be completely perfect for others had him searching for a solution. It took a while before he could fall asleep. Danny hadn't really begun the mindfulness exercises, so other than focusing on eating healthy and exercising, not much had been done to keep his anxiety at bay. He didn't even recognize that his worry about being perfect was filling his mind as he tried to sleep. The weekend at his home had also gotten him off track from tracking his sleep habits, and he didn't even ponder it as he tossed and turned.

***

"How are you, Danny?" Mark asked after he closed the door to his office.

"Okay," Danny said.

"What did you do this weekend?" Mark kept the conversation light.

Danny smiled. "Michelle went home with me and met my family."

"I guess it went well from the smile on your face."

Danny's smile deepened. "Yes, it was wonderful. My family loved her and she fell in love with them, just as I expected."

"Great!" Mark smiled encouragingly. He waited a few moments. "Have you listened to the tape or read any of the mindfulness book?"

Danny averted his gaze, tightening his fingers into fists. "Not really."

"No problem," Mark said, completely surprising Danny.

"You're not upset?" Danny asked.

"Danny, you are in control of the progress you make. It has nothing to do with me. I'm just here to guide you in the direction you wish to go. You don't need to worry about pleasing me."

Danny let out a breath of relief. "Okay, thanks. I was afraid you would be mad."

"Your life is going to be busy. You spent time with your girlfriend and your family this weekend. That's totally understandable."

Danny's gaze was troubled. Mark could sense that it had nothing to do with himself. "Did something happen?"

Danny explained the situation with Michelle's brother. Mark nodded to show he was listening, but his face remained impassive. "What should I do?"

"Nothing," Mark said.

"What?" Danny asked. "Nothing?"

Mark leaned forward. "Danny, you don't control Jeff and his feelings toward you. Neither does Michelle. You can't make him like you."

"So what do I do?" Danny rubbed his forehead.

"Keep doing what you are doing. If you and Michelle are still comfortable moving forward with your relationship, continue growing together. You said she's coming here for sessions too, correct?"

Danny nodded.

Mark touched his chin. "Let's plan a session for her and Angela to join you and me. We can work through it as a group."

Hope filled Danny's expression. "Okay, I would like that." His brow dipped before he continued. "We talked little about me and my anxiety today. I'm sorry about that."

"Danny, there isn't a timeline. You don't have a due date to work through your issues. To be honest, it will probably be something you deal with throughout your life." Mark had honesty on his face.

"Great," Danny said sarcastically before the two of them laughed together. "I promise I will listen to the tape and begin reading."

Mark nodded as they walked out together, and Danny scheduled his next session. "I will talk to Michelle about all of us meeting together. Thanks, Mark."

***

Vicki knocked on Brandi's door while glancing around. Not knowing if people realized this was Brandi's room, she wanted to do all she could to keep others from connecting them to each other.

Brandi's usual irritated expression greeted Vicki as she opened the door, a look that Vicki was growing weary of.

"Get in here!" Brandi demanded, pulling Vicki's arm into her room.

"Calm down," Vicki said, and then she regretted it when Brandi twisted her arm behind her. Vicki did all that she could not to show she was in pain, knowing it would only make things worse.

Brandi said, "What did you just say to me?"

Grimacing, Vicki backtracked, saying, "I'm sorry, I'm sorry. I just feel we need to work together on this."

Brandi leaned close to Vicki's face and she sneered, "I could easily find someone else to help me and they would get the money we steal."

Vicki glanced down. "Like I said, I'm sorry."

Brandi released Vicki's wrist. She rubbed it as she walked into her room, which was a colossal mess. Alternative rock band posters were all over the walls. She remembered that, like herself, Brandi was in her own room because of the school's fear of her harming someone. She had her own history of legal entanglements including the one involving her and Vicki. Both of them served in community service.

"Sit down," Brandi gestured to her desk chair, and Vicki realized it wasn't a request as she walked over while continuing to rub her sore wrist. Brandi continued by saying, "That stupid girl needs to be stopped from following us. I need you to handle it."

"Michelle?" Vicki asked. "What do you want me to do?"

With a sour expression, Brandi looked at Vicki. "I don't care what you do. Just get rid of her."

"Like kill her?" Vicki's voice was filled with horror, her eyes wide. Shaking her head in refusal, she said, "I don't do that."

Brandi advanced toward her threateningly and said, "You are going to do what I say. And if I tell you to kill her, then you will do it."

"Brandi, I don't want murder on my rap sheet with the cops." Vicki's voice was filled with apprehension.

Brandi's face changed as she looked at Vicki. She tilted her head to glean the response from Vicki from what she would say next. She glowered before she spoke again. "I would hate for something to happen to your precious Colin."

Vicki's mouth fell open at Brandi's mention of Colin. How did she even know about him? She shouldn't be surprised that Brandi dug into her past.

"What do you mean by that?" Vicki asked Brandi.

Brandi said, "I mean accidents happen. I have friends all over the place and they can easily get to him."

Vicki tried not to show panic as she swallowed convulsively and looked at Brandi. "What do you suggest I do?"

"I want you to take her someplace where she can't escape so that we can pull off our plan. If she tries anything funny, then you can kill her." Brandi's face did not show any emotion after those words.

"What makes you certain you can reach Colin?" Vicki asked suspiciously, which she soon regretted because Brandi slapped her shoulder before walking to pick up a folder on the desk. She pulled out a snapshot of Colin walking down the street near his house in the Dallas area where they both were from. She looked at Brandi. "I'll figure something out."

"Good. Once you have a plan, we will meet back here. You will go over it step by step with me to ensure that it is foolproof. Once she's out of the way, we will go back to our original plan." Brandi walked to her door and opened it, giving the message to Vicki that it was time for her to leave.

Vicki walked out and she gripped her head in her hands while murmuring, "What have I done?" As much as she detested Michelle, she had no desire to kill the girl. Worried about Colin's safety, she quickly retreated to her room to brainstorm a solution. This situation was larger than anything she had ever handled before.

***

As Michelle hurried back from her last class to go meet Danny on the following day, she glanced in the parking lot and noticed there was a black truck that looked just like Jeff's. When she got closer, Jeff was getting out of the truck and walking toward her. Rage filled her at the idea of him invading her life in this way.

She rushed toward him and yelled, "Jefferson, what are you doing here? You need to leave!"

Eyes filled with remorse, Jeff held up his hands. "Michelle, I'm sorry for how things ended on the phone last night. I read your letter, and I realized I was wrong." He held up the letter she had written to him.

"Unless you are willing meet Danny and talk to him, you've wasted a trip. I need to go put my bag in my room." Michelle stalked away toward the front door of the dorm.

"Muppet, I said I'm sorry. Please, can we talk?" Jeff pleaded as he rushed to keep up with her.

Michelle turned and looked at him. No matter how much she tried to fight him, he was still her older brother. "Give me five minutes to put this away and then we can go to the diner down the road." She stalked a few steps away before turning around. "Also, I've asked you to stop calling me that name."

Jeff lifted his hands in surrender. "Okay, okay..." Then he asked, "Is Danny available to come with us?"

"He has class until four today." Michelle answered, but

her gaze was on the ground, refusing to look at him. Jeff could hear the defensiveness in her voice.

"I'm willing to meet him," Jeff said, "Can we go get dinner? I will buy it for all of us."

Michelle's took a step back and her eyebrows rose. "I need to see if he is available. He has basketball practice several nights because games start next week. I don't remember if he has practice tonight or not. I'll be right back." Michelle walked to her room and set her backpack on the chair in front of her desk. She pulled out the homework she needed to complete later, she set it out to remind her when she came back later.

When she came out, she walked toward Jeff's truck where they got in and she directed him to the diner down the road.

Once they ordered coffee, which Jeff's eyebrows rose when she placed her order, but he didn't comment. It was her hope he was slowly accepting her as an adult and he would finally let go. Michelle's hopes rose slightly.

Jeff said, "I promised Mom that I would work this out with you. She was pretty mad at me for being so rude to Danny on the phone."

"Good." Michelle said. "You owe him an apology as well."

Jeff was contrite as he placed a hand on top of hers. "Michelle, I only want what is best for you. My only question to you is this. Are you sure that you and Danny should be so serious? He's the only guy you've ever dated, and it seems awful fast."

"Whose fault is that?" Michelle retorted with fire in her

eyes. "You're the one who wouldn't let me get any dating experience when I lived at home. If I had experience, I would understand how to work through things with him."

"I know, I know," Jeff said. "But don't you think you need to go on other dates with other guys before deciding Danny is the one?"

Deep down, Michelle really hadn't considered it. It made her stop and question herself about committing to Danny so quickly. Even though she was angry with Jeff, his question made her pause.

Jeff continued by saying, "I realize I was wrong in keeping you from seeing guys. But I want you to be wise in making choices, even though you are over eighteen. Yes, you met his family, but you've only been dating him for a few months. You need to take some time and decide if he's the only one you want to go out with."

Michelle remained quiet as she considered Jeff's words. She didn't have any idea how she felt about the matter. So far, Danny was the only guy ever interested enough in her to ask her on a date. She really didn't have an answer to Jeff's question. Michelle wasn't about to admit it, but the question made her stop and wonder if she jumped in too quickly. Her worry headache was back in a flourish and she rubbed her forehead.

"Let's put a pause on this conversation and you can catch me up on everything else with you." Jeff suggested. "I've missed you, Muppet... er, Michelle. Tell me how things are going."

Eyes clouded with self-doubt, Michelle updated Jeff on school and her friendships with Jackie and Michelle. The thought didn't cross her mind that Jeff might be purposefully planting fears in her mind. She just knew that confusion was warring with her thoughts.

An hour later, Jeff drove her back so that she could call Danny and see about him joining them for dinner.

When Michelle walked into the room, Jackie and Hannah were lounging on their beds with textbooks in front of them.

"Hey," Jackie said as she caught Michelle's expression. "Where have you been?"

Michelle filled her friends in on Jeff's surprise visit and their conversation over coffee. "I'm calling to see if Danny can go out with us to dinner."

"Michelle," Jackie said. "I am sure he is still trying to watch out for you, but don't take those suggestions to heart. To me, it sounds like another way for him to brainwash you from going out with Danny or anyone else."

Michelle rubbed her aching head. Her eyes were still troubled. "I've never thought about those questions before. What if I just fell for Danny because he's the only guy who's ever been interested in me before?" She walked into the bathroom to find the aspirin.

Hannah piped in. "Perhaps he is the one, and you were just waiting to meet him."

"That could be true." She swallowed the aspirin by scooping water from the sink into her mouth. Michelle walked back into her room, sitting down gingerly as a million thoughts were racing through her mind. Reaching for the phone, she dialed Danny's number. When he answered, he sounded so excited to hear from her.

After asking him out to dinner with her and Jeff, Danny appeared overwhelmed with excitement as Michelle told him they were on their way to pick him up.

While they were at dinner, Jeff was cordial and spent the entire time talking with Danny, making it seem like he had finally accepted him. He and Danny found some things to talk about and even laughed together over specific things they found similarly funny. The two of them had a shared love for football and they talked about various teams, a topic Michelle had no interest in at the moment. Michelle said little because the uncertainty in her mind grew to be larger than ever. She kept tossing Jeff's question around in her mind.

Again, what she didn't surmise was if Jackie was right. Was it that Jeff manipulated the entire situation by placing the concerns in his sister's head? Michelle couldn't imagine him doing something so cruel. She pushed the idea down, hoping that her brother would never stoop to such a level.

Jeff gave Michelle a hug and told her he was staying at a hotel in town. When he drove off, she watched his truck until it disappeared from sight. Her head seemed to roar with dismal thoughts.

***

Danny was standing by Michelle in front of the dorm, and he reached for her hand. "You've been quiet this entire time. Is everything alright?"

In her blunt nature, she blurted out, "Danny, do you suppose we have been moving too fast with our relationship?"

Danny's gaze became cloudy, and he opened his mouth as if to speak before he shut it again. "What are you talking about? I think things are wonderful with us." He squeezed her hand as he tried to step closer. If he could pull her into a hug, it might help reassure her of his feelings for her.

However, Michelle stepped back. She hunched her shoulders and shoved her hands into her back pockets. "You are the only guy I've ever dated, and I'm not sure if we should be so serious. It's possible I need more experience dating other guys before committing to you." Danny's heart dropped from the expression on her face.

"Michelle, please don't talk like this. Where is this coming from?" Danny pleaded as he took her other hand in his.

Michelle refused to gaze into his eyes; instead she stared at the ground. "Jeff mentioned you are the only guy that I've ever dated and he talked about how I need more experience going out with other people before committing to you."

Danny's face drained of color. He shuttered his eyes. "Is that what you want?"

Michelle fought back tears as she whispered, "I don't know. I'm really mixed up right now."

Danny's voice was soft as he said, "I think you let Jeff influence what you and I have together. Could it be possible that he wanted you to doubt us?"

Michelle's gaze was defensive as she said, "He is my older brother and I know he's only trying to look out for me because he cares. Danny, I realize this isn't what you want to hear, but I need some time to process these thoughts and figure things out. I'm sorry, but I hope you will respect my wishes." Michelle pulled her hands from his as she rushed inside. She was thankful Danny didn't see the tears as they began falling down her cheeks.

Danny stood there, wondering what had just happened. Inwardly, he sensed this was another method for Jeff to prevent her from dating. He trudged back to his apartment with heavy steps, his heart breaking. He clenched his fingers and began breathing heavier, wanting to rage against Michelle's brother.

Michael was coming out of his door when he said, "Hey man!"

Danny didn't reply, and Michael noticed his facial expression. "Are you okay? What's wrong?"

With a heavy-hearted sigh, Danny explained the conversation he just had with Michelle along with the dinner with Jeff.

"Man, that's tough! I'm so sorry, Danny! I think you might be right about her brother. If he's here for another day or so, you can talk to him one on one and see if you're right." Michael clapped Danny on the shoulder.

"Thanks," Danny answered. "I appreciate you letting me vent to you." Danny found that he really felt better about the situation. He knew deep down he wouldn't abandon Michelle. Part of him blamed himself for not being the man that she needed and already standing up to Jeff. That would soon be corrected. With the knowledge of where Jeff was staying, he would call him as soon as he completed some homework that was due.

***

As Danny dialed Jeff's number, his gut burned with more anger at the interference.

"Hello," Jeff answered quickly.

"Jeff," Danny barked. "What the hell, man?"

Jeff was quiet for a few minutes. "What are you talking about?"

"Jeff," Danny answered. "I have a younger sister and I get your desire to protect her. But this is taking it too far. Michelle just broke up with me and I think you had something to do with that!"

Jeff's voice became cold and hard. "This is not personal against you. My sister is inexperienced, and she doesn't need to start her dating career with a former quarterback."

The line was quiet until Danny repeated Jeff's question. "What are you talking about?"

"Dude!" Jeff bellowed. "You probably dated a different girl every month because you were the football star and they probably did anything you wanted them to do. I don't want my sister to be a part of your list of women."

"Are you serious?" Danny asked in bewilderment. "You're judging me without even knowing me! Yes, I dated a lot of girls, but Michelle is the first one who has meant anything to me. I wouldn't hurt her! I can promise you that!"

Jeff was quiet until he said, "It sounds like she's decided. If the two of you are supposed to be together, she'll come back to you. Take some time for yourself and to carefully consider everything. Good night, Danny."

Danny grabbed the first thing he saw, a textbook, and threw it against the wall in frustration. He was thankful James wasn't home as he grabbed his head and growled.

Chapter 15

After being chewed out by both Jackie and Hannah, Michelle was more mixed up than ever. She was surprised that she'd actually broken up with Danny. She kept pinching her upper lip between her thumb and forefinger. Michelle wondered if her head was going to explode from another headache. Her own heart had broken when she walked away from him, and he didn't notice the stream of tears running down her cheeks. Deep down, she was miserable. And she realized she only had herself to blame.

She went through the motions of going to class and completing assignments. Her heart was bleeding from what she had done and she constantly questioned herself. Was she allowing Jeff to control her, as usual? Because of what she did, Michelle avoided meals with all of her friends, knowing Danny would be there. She used her meal card to buy items at the snack bar to avoid running into him. Hannah and Jackie told her she was making a huge mistake, but they left her to decide what she needed to do.

Michelle was more thankful than ever for her planned session with Angela that afternoon as she hoped Angela would help her untangle her emotions and the never ending thoughts that would not stop running through her mind. She hid in a study room in the library until it was time for her to walk to the counseling center. Relieved that the time had finally arrived, she breathed out a sigh of relief. "Hopefully, I can get some answers," she muttered to herself as she shoved her textbooks and notebooks into her backpack. She shouldered it to start her trek across campus and her heart felt just as heavy.

Lost in her own world, she bumped into what seemed like a brick wall without realizing her surroundings. She didn't realize she had walked all the way across campus without paying attention to her surroundings. Startled, she realized it was Danny as he kept a firm hold on her upper arms until she was steady on her feet again. A sad smile was on his face as he said, "Hey."

"Hi," she whispered back and then she stepped back. Michelle looked at the ground because she found herself unable to glance into Danny's beautiful eyes. "I have a counseling session and I don't want to be late."

With hands in his jeans pockets, Danny asked, "Can I walk with you?" I'm headed there to meet with Mark and I really would like to talk." Longing filled her and even though she wanted to say no, she nodded her head. Danny moved beside her as they started walking toward the counseling center.

After a few moments of silence, he said, "Michelle, what's going through your mind right now? What made you decide we didn't need to be together anymore?" He didn't dare mention his phone call to Jeff because he was afraid it would make her angry.

Tears sprang to her eyes, and she looked the opposite direction so Danny wouldn't see her blinking furiously to dismiss them. "M-m-My brain is so m-muddled right n-n-now." Her eyes widened at her stuttering and her hand rubbed her mouth as if to rub the stammering away.

"What are you confused about?" Danny probed her gently with his question. Her heart broke when she recognized the pain and torment in his eyes. "Two days ago, you and I were in a wonderful place. I don't understand where these doubts came from."

Michelle stopped to gaze at him. "When we first started going out, I t-t-told you I had no experience with any kind of r-r-relationship. I fear I j-jumped in too quickly with y-you."

Danny placed his hands on her shoulders before he caught her gaze. He waited until she stared back at him. "I doubt that's your honest opinion. Michelle, I wonder if you are struggling with guilt and the desire to please your big brother. I certainly don't want to cause a rift in your relationship, but I believe he said something that caused you to doubt this wonderful thing that you and I have together." Danny continued, "I wasn't taking advantage of you. Since I was aware you were new to dating, I checked with you and asked you about every step we made in this relationship. You didn't start having any doubts until Jeff showed up."

Michelle took a shaky breath, and she realized Danny was right. However, she looked at him with tears shining in her eyes. "I-I know you d-did, and I did t-trust you." With a pleading look in her gaze, she continued, "Will you be p-patient and give me some time to figure things out? I n-need time to think."

Danny pulled away. He shoved his hands back into his pockets as he said, "I want to say yes, but my heart is breaking right now. I love you so much, Michelle, and I will try to give you time. But if it's truly over and you date other guys, I won't be able to stand seeing that."

Michelle's shoulders were shaking with silent sobs. "I u-understand. I am going to talk to Angela and g-g-get advice from her. I promise not to keep you waiting, Danny." Danny wanted to pull her tightly against his chest because her stammers and tears were breaking his heart. Deep down, he wondered what he had done to fail Michelle.

"Will you be willing to go out tomorrow night so that we can sit and talk? Are you still coming to my game tonight?" Unable to help it, his hand reached up and softly stroked her cheek. His nature of wanting to fix things rose with ferocity, and he continued by saying, "When we talk, I'm confident we can work out everything. I don't really believe it's over in your mind anymore than it is in mine." He didn't say anymore, even though he wanted to declare that he would go to the ends of the earth to ease her doubts so that they could continue forward in their relationship.

With a sad smile, Michelle said, "I w-wouldn't miss it for

the w-world. And, I would like to go somewhere to t-talk tomorrow night. Jeff will be b-back home and I will have some feedback from Angela by then."

Danny nodded and smiled. "Okay, I look forward to tomorrow night."

"Bye," Michelle murmured to herself while staring longingly after him. He shook Mark's hand and walked to the other side of the office with him.

Angela glanced at Michelle's face and remained silent. Angela placed her arm around Michelle's shoulders, and she guided her back to her office.

Once both of them were seated, Angela said, "Talk to me and tell me what's wrong."

Michelle gazed down at her hands. "I broke things off with Danny and I'm not even sure why I did it." She explained Jeff's unexpected arrival, along with his words of advice. "I'm not sure if I let him g-get into my h-head. What if I just ended things w-w-with the love of my l-life?" The ever present tears rolled down Michelle's cheeks. Ever since starting things with Danny, she had become an emotional wreck. Michelle always thought of herself as calm and collected.

Angela nodded quite a bit, but she listened objectively without asking questions. For the first time, Michelle sensed slight irritation toward Angela because she wanted her to interject more. With impatience, she finally asked, "What should I do?"

Angela was quiet as she took a long time to close her pen. Her face was impassive as she placed it on top of the notebook before turning back to stare Michelle squarely in the face. She took a breath. "I predict I'm going to hurt your feelings when I say this, but I guess I'm the best one to do it." She paused again, and it seemed like her eyes were drilling holes into Michelle.

Michelle leaned forward, wringing her hands in agitation, before she finally said, "W-What are you going to say?"

Without preamble, Angela said, "Michelle, you are simply scared. A moment ago, you were wondering if you let him get into your head. I'm of the opinion that you did. I suspect you are avoiding confronting your feelings for Danny because his impact on you has frightened you. Therefore, when Jeff mentioned you should date other people, you allowed his words to take root in you and you accepted them as the truth."

As Angela projected, her heart was bruised. "I-Is that all y-you think?"

Angela leaned forward. "No, it's not all. I am proud of you for putting yourself out there in a relationship and learning how to navigate through it. You allowed yourself to take a tremendous leap into what I consider is a special love. But you blindsided Danny by breaking things off. And I don't think you were fair to him with how you brought your time together to a halt. So what if you've not dated much? Why are you allowing that to cloud your moral judgment?"

Tears were streaming down Michelle's face as she sarcastically muttered, "Thanks for being completely h-honest with me."

"I realize this isn't what you wanted to hear. Most of our time together has been to help you get past your own traumas. Today we are focusing on you, and what you need to work on in order to live a complete and full life." Angela leaned and touched Michelle's hand in comfort. She grabbed the tissue box and handed it to her.

Grabbing several to mop the tears on her face, Michelle said, "S-So you're saying that I don't h-have a complete life as it is?"

Angela sighed. "That's not what I'm saying at all. You were allowing yourself to experience a deeper kind of richness until your brother planted those seeds of doubts within you. Right now, these tears are a result of your heart reacting to your emotions. That is a good thing, but you are scared because you've not dealt with similar emotions in the past. Confronting Jeff showed great courage, but it backfired when you needed to please him again instead of yourself. I'm also understanding that it was easier for you to stand up to him over the phone because you caved as soon as he arrived here in person. I think when you are face to face with him, it's harder for you to fight for what you want."

"I know, I know..." Michelle mumbled. "When he f-f-first got here, I was strong in standing up to him. But when he began talking, I c-crumbled and allowed him control over my life again." As she opened up the crumpled tissue, Michelle used it to wipe her eyes and then she kept them covered for a few seconds. When she removed her hand with the tissue, she looked at Angela and said, "What do I need to do?"

Angela was absolute in saying, "You need to talk to Jeff and establish boundaries with him again. I agree with Danny that you are still in love with him and that the two of you have something very special. You need to decide if he's important enough to stand up to your brother once and for all. I can't tell you what to decide, but I think it would be sad for you to throw away something so special. You can certainly date other people to get a better sense of yourself, but it may serve to only confuse you more."

"So I should continue dating Danny?" Michelle asked with hope in her voice.

"I can't answer that for you. I can tell you that you need to sit and talk with Danny. The two of you both need time to better understand who you are before committing any deeper to your relationship. The nice thing is that you are both young and you have time to learn those things. I'm not sure if that will mean together or apart." Angela's eyes and smile were gentle as she squeezed Michelle's hand. "You will get through this. Trust me."

When the session was over, Michelle was actually relieved because she felt drained from hearing Angela's observations. However, she realized that meeting with her helped, so she set up another session for the following week. Angela gave her a gentle hug before Michelle walked out.

As Michelle walked back to her room, lost in thought, she was suddenly grabbed from behind by someone who had jumped out of the bushes.

A sinister voice commanded, "Do not make a sound," and Michelle yelped in fear. You're coming with me."

***

Danny said nothing as he and Mark walked to his office. The look of raw pain on Danny's face had Mark speechless. He gently clapped him on the shoulder, but the only thing he said was, "I'm here when you're ready to talk."

Danny nodded, but he still remained silent.

"Danny, I'm here for you. It looks like you are dealing with something heavy at the moment." Mark didn't even reach for his notebook or pen. He sat forward on his knees to give Danny his full and undivided attention.

"Thanks." Danny mumbled.

Mark reached to squeeze his shoulder. "You don't have to tell me anything if you aren't ready. We can just sit here and I will be whatever you need."

"Michelle dumped me." Tears dripped out of Danny's eyes and onto his blue jeans. "Her brother visited, and I suspect he planted doubts in her head about us."

"What makes you say that?" Mark probed gently.

Danny grabbed a tissue, mopped his eyes, and wadded it up. He tossed it across the room. "We were fine when I last talked to you. I met him on the phone when we came back from visiting my family. She also wrote him a letter to tell him how she hoped for his support in our relationship. Then, he showed up yesterday. As soon as we all got back from dinner, she told me she's confused and needs time." Silent sobs shook Danny's shoulders. He wasn't one to cry easily. In fact, he only saw his dad cry when his great grandmother passed away. Other than that, the man was stoic about his emotions.

Mark sat there, rubbing his shoulder, not saying anything.

"I'm not sure what to think. Deep down, I suspect she's scared and confused. I think her love for me is still there. But how can I fight against a man who has practically raised her?" Anguish was in Danny's face when he looked at Mark.

"You can't at the moment." Mark said.

Danny flinched at Mark's words, and his eyes became hard. "That doesn't sound very supportive, man."

Mark sighed. "I'm sorry to hurt you. It seems you should give her some space and honor her wishes at present. In my opinion, your assumptions are right. The two of you have a deep connection and you have developed a sixth sense in knowing her inner heart."

"That's likely why it's so painful. I think she's the one for me and I'm not sure if I can actually let her go." Danny's eyes were downcast again and his hand rubbed up his neck and through his hair.

Mark squeezed Danny's shoulder. "Don't view it as letting go completely. This is just a pause in the relationship. Everyone goes through bumps and hurdles when they build a relationship." Mark smiled. "And the hardships are just beginning. Unfortunately, it will get tougher, even if you get married. Love and commitment are hard."

"Tell me about it," Danny murmured. "She agreed to talk with me tomorrow. The two of us are going out for dinner."

"That means the door isn't completely closed." Mark smiled encouragingly. "Sorry, we haven't talked about any of the other stuff today."

"Danny, it isn't a problem. I've said before that life is not a planned road map. Things will happen and there will be detours." Mark said.

"I listened to the tape, and I started the preface of the book. It's good, man. More so than I originally considered," Danny said.

The two of them talked briefly before Mark encouraged him. "Don't let this stop the good work you've already done."

"I haven't done much."

"I disagree," Mark said. "You've been watching your diet and monitoring your sleep and exercise. Those are steps in the right direction."

"Thank you," Danny whispered.

"Your homework is to write these feelings in your journal."

Danny opened his mouth when Mark raised his hand. "I realize you haven't been taught to focus on emotions. I wasn't either when I was growing up. But your feelings are genuine. You will learn through the mindfulness training that you need to sit with your emotions. I want you to write until your hand feels like it will fall off. Just let it all out on the page. I promise it will bring you some peace." Mark reluctantly stood. "I'm sorry. I have another patient after you."

"Thanks, Mark," Danny said, and his heart felt a little lighter. He understood Mark was right. It helped to express his feelings.

***

Michelle tamped down panic as she recognized Vicki's voice. When she glanced down, she noticed a small gun pointed at her side. Vicki was holding it in an obscure location where others couldn't see.

"What do you want?" Michelle asked, suppressing her rising fear. Her knees began shaking as she looked wildly around. The absence of familiar faces filled her with dread. She wished more than anything that Danny was still with her. However, he was still inside in his session.

Vicki jammed the gun harder into her side. "You're coming with me. Your nosiness needs to stop and I'm taking care of it."

"I'm sorry," Michelle retorted as she raised her hands in surrender. "My involvement in what you're doing was unintentional. Don't worry, I'll leave you and Brandi alone and pretend this never happened."

Vicki sneered, "Walk." As she began nudging Michelle forward, she continued, "You're too late to back out of this. You've heard too much and we can't trust that you won't stay quiet."

"Who's *we*?" The words tumbled out before Michelle realized what she was asking because it was clear to her that Brandi was the other person involved.

"Shut up and walk." Vicki said as she jabbed the gun harder into Michelle's side. "Because you stuck your nose where it doesn't belong. And now I have to take care of you and this problem. So this is completely your fault!"

They were walking toward the apartments where Michelle followed Vicki a few weeks before. However, she glanced over and saw Danny walking out of the counseling center. He was looking their way. Danny squinted as he recognized Michelle. He walked in their direction and Michelle tried to give a subtle shake of her head for him to stay where he was. Panic filled her as she realized he didn't know what was happening. He jogged toward her, shouting her name, "Michelle!".

Michelle sensed a bruise forming as the gun was jabbed even harder into her side. Vicki snarled in her ear, "Don't say a word to him. Do you hear me?"

Michelle nodded her head, shaking in fear, and she tried to ignore that Danny was continuing to call her name. The corners of her mouth were tense and her heart was pounding as Michelle said, "He will follow me if I don't tell him something. I can make him go away."

"Okay, fine. Get rid of him," Vicki growled as she pushed the gun into her pocket, but it was still against Michelle's side. Michelle stopped to face Danny, and she tried to paste a natural smile on her face. Michelle widened her eyes to appear normal. She knew that they looked awkward with Vicki standing behind her.

"Hey," she replied to Danny. "I doubt you've met Vicki, have you? She has a class with me and we are walking to her apartment so that I can give her some notes for our next test. She was absent from class this morning." Michelle tried disguising the distress in her voice.

Danny walked closer and looked into her eyes. He remained quiet until he said, "Are you okay? Vicki, can I speak with her in private for a moment?"

Vicki quickly spoke up and her voice was rushed. "I'm sorry. I need to get these notes from Michelle right now. You can speak with her later." Vicki's eyes darted around them.

With forced brightness in her tone, Michelle said, "I will call you later and we can plan a time for our date tomorrow night, okay?"

With suspicion in his voice, Danny said, "That will be fine." And he let them walk on toward the apartments.

Chapter 16

Danny had a strange feeling that something wasn't right as he watched Vicki and Michelle. Michelle's movements were extremely stiff. His original plan of studying changed as he followed them. Danny had never noticed Vicki near the business building. He remembered her from her involvement in Hannah's abduction. Vicki's poor reputation followed her, and he recalled other incidents involving the police.

Danny quickened his pace until he caught up with them, but he made sure that he remained a distance behind. He narrowed his eyes as he observed Vicki holding an object against Michelle's side. Danny mumbled to himself, "I need to get closer to examine what that is." When he noticed Vicki glance behind them, Danny quickly ducked behind a large tree.

Once the two of them began moving again, he watched Michelle stumble slightly, and he realized something was terribly wrong with this situation. His hero complex kicked in as he closed in the distance between them. As Danny squinted at Vicki's hand on Michelle's side, he realized the object was a gun. His heart began pounding as he wondered what on earth Michelle had done to be taken hostage by Vicki. "What is going on?" he whispered.

Danny remembered her interest in Vicki a few weeks back during dinner, and he came to the conclusion that Michelle inserted herself into something extremely dangerous. The gun held against Michelle's side was certainly evidence of that!

Danny was intelligent enough to understand that overtaking either of them was impossible while Vicki threatened Michelle with a gun. As he crept carefully out of sight, he saw Vicki push Michelle toward one of the apartments. His heart skipped when Michelle tripped and fell. After grabbing her roughly by the arm, Vicki forced Michelle back to her feet. When she saw an opportunity to escape, Michelle scrambled to her feet. She tried to run in the other direction. Chasing her, Vicki pulled the gun out and used the butt of it to whack her in the face. Michelle's pained cry nearly made Danny drop to his knees, but he was determined to continue toward their destination.

Vicki and Michelle disappeared between one breezeway in the apartment complex. He jogged to find out their direction. As he peered around the corner of the outside corridor, he observed Vicki pounding on a door. Danny nearly had a heart attack when he recognized another girl, who had an even worse reputation. The other girl opened the door wider, and Vicki shoved Michelle inside. Michelle stumbled and fell a second time, but this time the other girl yanked her to her feet.

"Damn," he exclaimed to himself. Danny knew he needed to inform the authorities, but leaving Michelle with those two lunatics was unbearable to him. He was consumed by indecision for the first time in his life.

Michelle made herself take a deep breath as Vicki rapped three times on the door to an apartment. Her heart sank even more when Brandi opened the door.

"Well, well, well, look who we have here," Brandi taunted, and she opened the door wider. "Come on in."

"What do you want with me?" Michelle asked, and she stumbled over the threshold of the doorway. "I haven't done or said anything to anyone." As she dropped to her knees, she felt the skin tear on one of her kneecaps.

Pain ripped through her upper arm and shoulder as Brandi yanked her back up to her feet. Michelle felt the blood soaking through her jeans. "Yeah, but you know way too much because you didn't stay out of our business, am I right?" Brandi leaned closer to Michelle's face with a menacing smile. Not seeing it coming, Brandi slapped Michelle across the cheek. It was enough to make her eyes sting, but Michelle swallowed the tears. The other cheek throbbed from being hit in the face with the gun earlier and she realized she skinned her knees when she fell the first time. "Tie her up." Brandi ordered. At the moment, the wildness in Brandi's face reminded her of Rhonda and how she looked when she was angry.

Michelle shook her head at her irrational thought as she tried inhaling and exhaling deep, steady breaths.

Vicki stayed where she was. "Look Brandi, this is going too far. Neither you nor I have ever kidnapped anyone before, and we've never threatened to kill them. If we get caught, we will serve a lifetime sentence if not worse. Why can't we just rough her up a little and then let her go?"

The same hand that slapped Michelle reached up to slap Vicki. Vicki's head snapped back as Brandi said, "Shut up! I told you never to question me, especially in front of someone else. Now tie her up."

Vicki muttered under her breath as she nudged Michelle to walk to the lone table. One chair sat beside it.

Brandi sneered, "Shut up! If you keep muttering, the first person to receive a bullet will be you. Or do I need to say Colin's name? That seemed to quiet you before." Brandi stalked away into one of the two bedrooms.

She forced Michelle into a chair and murmured, "Why couldn't you just stay out of this?'"

"Vicki," Michelle whispered. "You can do the right thing and let me go. I promise I will tell no one and you won't get into any more trouble. I suspect you want to do the right thing because deep down, I think you care more than you let anyone know. This might be a chance to turn your life around."

"It's too late," Vicki replied, and she picked up two strands of rope and tied one strand tightly around Michelle's ankles. Yanking Michelle's arms behind her,

Vicki tied her hands.

"Who's Colin," Michelle asked.

"Just don't talk anymore and don't say his name, got it?" Vicki jammed the gun into Michelle's cheek. "I'm already in too deep and it won't hurt me if I use this on you."

"I've been so stupid," Michelle whispered to herself. She whispered it for the past fifteen minutes. It was clear to her that Brandi intended to kill or otherwise harm her. Michelle wished with all of her heart that she had listened to Hannah and Jackie as they warned her not to get involved. Deep down, she sensed she wanted to prove her ability to manage tough situations. She murmured to herself, "Who am I trying to convince?" Now she might never see her family, friends, or Danny again. She heard Brandi and Vicki talking in the bedroom, but their voices were low and Michelle was unable to distinguish the words. If only she had gone to tell the police the first time she heard the two of them talking in the conference room. She might have told Angela, and she knew that Angela would have listened to her. Now it was too late.

Tears slipped out of her eyes and rolled down her cheeks. With her hands tied, Michelle wasn't able to wipe them away as they dripped onto the table. As Michelle sat there, she realized that she was wrong about trusting Jeff over Danny. She had allowed confusion to muddle her mind. Because of that, she wasn't sure she would ever talk to Danny again to tell him how much she loved him.

"I've been so stupid." Michelle chanted the words as the bruises on her face throbbed. The tears fell harder and her shoulders shook from her sobs. Her neck and shoulders ached from her hands tied behind her back. "Danny, I'm so sorry." Michelle tried to move her wrists to determine if she might loosen the rope. It was up to her to escape and get out of this mess.

***

An hour passed, and Danny waited. He crawled to the window of the apartment that he had seen them go into. At first, he saw nothing as he peeked over the ledge. The only thing in his line of sight was a couch and the front door. When he shifted to the side, his heart nearly stopped at the sight of Michelle tied to a chair. Rope secured both her hands and feet. Her head was down; Danny wasn't sure if she was awake. His hands clenched into fists as he considered what he wanted to do to these two bitches for putting their hands on her.

Vicki and the other girl walked into the room. Afraid of being seen, Danny ducked down. He crawled out into the trees before standing up and walking a short distance. Danny paced back and forth, racking his brain for a few seconds, hoping to come up with a plan.

He glanced around and saw a couple of students he recognized from around campus. With a whistle directed at one, he gestured the guy closer.

The guy stared at Danny for a few minutes, a strange expression on his face, as if he wondered if Danny was crazy. Danny saw the doubt in the other man's gaze, yet surprisingly, he still walked toward him.

"Hey man," Danny whispered. "I've seen you around. My name is Danny Peterson."

"Jeremiah," the other guy whispered back as he gestured behind him, "I need to get going."

Danny swallowed, hoping the guy would believe his words. He whispered, "Look, man. I'm aware we are strangers, but I just saw my girlfriend pushed into that building with someone pointing a gun at her. "She's inside there and they've tied her to a chair. I'm afraid they are going to hurt her or kill her. I need to get help, but I don't want to leave her."

The corners of Jeremiah's mouth tensed and his eyes became wider as he asked, "What do you want me to do about it? I really don't want to get involved." He was speaking in a normal tone, forgetting to whisper until Danny put his finger to his mouth for him to lower his voice.

"Do you notice those old houses down this block?" Danny pointed toward his apartment. "I need you to knock on either of the doors of the first house. My roommate, myself, and two other friends live in those apartments. My roommate's name is James. Michael and Alex are in the second apartment. Will you go tell them I'm here and ask one of them to call for the campus police?"

Jeremiah's eyes darted away from Danny and he squinted before he nodded. "Sure, I'll go ask."

"Thanks man, please knock on both doors and update them all," Danny whispered as Jeremiah walked away from his view. He glanced back at the apartment building but didn't notice Jeremiah shake his head and go the other way toward the campus.

***

Danny looked at his watch and he realized it had been two hours. His heart sank as he realized Jeremiah had no intention of actually helping him. He began pacing back and forth, trying to decide what he should do. There weren't any other students coming or going at the moment.

Danny crept closer, hoping to peek into the window again. He leaned up to where only his eyes were showing. There was no sight of Brandi or Vicki. When he crawled to the left of the window, he observed Michelle in the same position she'd been in a few hours earlier. Danny touched his fingers to the windowpane, wishing that she had an idea that he was here. Tears welled in his eyes as he continued observing her sitting there with her head down.

Danny sat down under the window. He leaned against the brick wall with his head in his hands. "What should I do?" he whispered. It was possible he might have the element of surprise. Neither of them would expect it. He was the quarterback of his football team. He was trained on how to tackle someone on the ground. Desperate to do something, Danny crawled on his hands and knees until he was out from under the window. He stood up. Then he walked closer to the door of the apartment. Indecision swept over him. He paced back closer to the window. The second time he approached the door, it opened. The other girl stepped out. He saw a gun being shoved in his face. A terror Danny had never experienced before filled his gut as he stared down the barrel of the pistol. He swallowed convulsively while raising his hands in front of him.

Chapter 17

"Who are you?" The other girl opened the door, and she was holding the gun.

"I don't mean any harm," Danny began, while holding up his hands. "I saw my girlfriend, Michelle, walking in this direction with Vicki. I followed her to make sure everything was alright."

The girl sneered at him. "You shouldn't have done that. Now you're a part of this." The girl gestured toward the door. "Get in here."

Danny didn't move. "If you can just let her go, we won't go to the police or anything. I don't know what's going on. I just wanted to make sure she's okay."

"Too late," the girl said. "She's not going anywhere and neither are you. I will shoot you if you don't get inside right now!"

"Okay, I'm coming." Danny's voice was calmer than he felt, and he raised his hands higher. He found the apartment empty, with a sagging couch and a small table in the eating area. Michelle was tied to one of the two chairs. Upon seeing Michelle's face, his heart dropped as he entered the room. A nasty bruise marred the right side of her face, and a red handprint marred the opposite cheek. She sat bound to the chair, her hands and feet secured by ropes. Her eyes widened in panic at the sight of Danny.

"Danny," she whispered. "What are you doing? You should have stayed away."

"It seemed like something was wrong." Danny said, as he tried stepping toward Michelle.

However, the girl with the gun stepped in his way. "I don't think so. Move over there." She motioned to the sagging couch in the tiny living room.

Danny didn't move as he asked Michelle, "Are you okay?"

"I said move!" the girl shouted as she pulled back the hammer on the pistol.

Michelle yelped with an ashen face. "I'm fine, but please do what she says." A couple of tears leaked out of her eyes and down her tear-stained face.

Danny walked to the couch, and the girl glared at Vicki, "Tie him up." Danny watched Vicki's eyes fill with slight irritation at the order, but she didn't argue as she grabbed another rope to tie his hands around his back. Vicki secured another rope for his feet.

"Please, let Michelle go," Danny urged, trying again. "You can keep me here if you need to hold someone."

"Shut up!" the mean girl said, as she slammed the barrel of the pistol against Danny's head, causing his ears to ring and stars came into his eyes.

Michelle cried out as she watched. The girl stalked

across the small room and she pointed the gun at her face. "You shut up too or I will do worse to him and you."

"Brandi...this is becoming too involved. We have two hostages now and we are looking at serious prison time." Vicki's eyes filled with dread as she realized she just said Brandi's name out loud.

Brandi stalked over to Vicki and she used her free hand to slap her face. She growled, "Why did you say my name, you stupid bitch?"

Vicki's face mirrored the pain, but she said nothing else. "I'm sorry! It just came out, but I'm afraid we are in over our heads now."

Brandi leaned closer to Vicki's face. "Remember Colin? That should keep you in check as well." Danny wondered who Colin was and what connection he had with Vicki.

"Look, Brandi," Danny tried to speak to her diplomatically. "I don't understand what's going on here. Since I don't have any idea, you can let us go. I promise you we won't say anything to anyone."

Brandi shouted at Danny as she waved the gun wildly with it still in her hand. "If you speak to me again, I will make sure that you won't ever talk again! Do you understand?"

Michelle's whimper made her whirl on her as she continued, "And I will do the same thing to you!" Then she looked at Vicki and said, "I need to deal with a few things. Keep an eye on these two and do whatever you need to shut them up if they give you any problems. If you don't handle them, then I will handle you!"

The fear in Vicki's eyes showed Brandi had some sort

of control over Vicki and that it involved someone named Colin. Danny needed to learn who that person was to Vicki. It might be a way out of the situation.

"They will stay right here," Vicki promised.

Brandi handed the gun to Vickie, grabbed a backpack, and she said, "Lock the door behind me. Got it?"

Vicki nodded, and she followed behind Brandi. She set the deadbolt and the chain before turning back. Mumbling to Michelle, she repeated her words from earlier, "Why couldn't you just leave things alone? It's because of you we're in this mess."

"Vicki," Danny tried to reason with her. Even though she was crazy, he observed a meager amount of remorse in her eyes. "Don't do this. Please do the right thing and let us go."

Vicki glared at him before she turned and followed Brandi into the bedroom.

***

When Vicki strolled into the other room, Danny frantically whispered to Michelle, "Are you okay?"

Michelle nodded, tears welling in her eyes. "I'm so sorry. I didn't mean to draw you into this. This is all my fault!"

Danny gave Michelle a steady look. "Michelle, I still love you despite all that's happened. I wasn't able to leave you to face something terrible like this alone."

Michelle sighed and whispered. "Danny, I still love you, too. I'm sorry I've been so confused. But I can't stand the thought of you being hurt because of me."

"We're both in this now and I am fine." Vicki didn't do a great job of tying his feet together, so Danny worked his feet out of the rope. He forced himself to stand, and he crept nearer to Michelle while keeping an eye out for Vicki. He tried to sound reassuring. "Can you please fill me in on what's going on with them so that I can try to help?"

Michelle nodded her head again, and she kept her voice at a whisper as she filled Danny in on what she overheard in the library. She told him about her ridiculous plan of finding out what Vicki and Brandi were doing. She shook her head. "This is my fault. I shouldn't have tried to follow them or solve it myself."

Danny knelt beside Michelle, hating his bound hands and his inability to touch her. "Your heart was in the right place, but you should have told me and we could have figured this out together. And you should have alerted the authorities."

With eyes full of love for him, Michelle said, "I know. I've thought about all that I should have done while I've been sitting here. I'm so sorry!" Tears leaked out of the corner of her eyes and rolled down her cheeks.

Before Danny spoke again, they heard Vicki yell, "What the hell are you doing?! Why are you over there?!" Vicki rushed toward him and she used the handle of the gun to hit Danny on the back of his head, causing him to fall on the floor unconscious. Michelle screamed, fighting for breath. She began shaking uncontrollably. "Vicki, please stop!" Michelle ducked her head, and the tears continued to stream down her face as she sobbed. Her crying was so heavy that she began having the hiccups.

Vicki forced Danny to his feet and shoved him back over to the couch. "Shut up!" Vicki yelled at Michelle as she pushed Danny back to the couch. "Apparently, I need to tie the rope much tighter."

Michelle pushed down the sobs, but she had to breathe for several moments.

"I told you to shut up!" Vicki snarled.

"I-I-I'm trying..." Michelle continued to breathe in and out.

***

Danny's grimaced as he opened his eyes. Gingerly lifting his head, he didn't see Brandi or Vicki. Danny remembered Vicki forcing him to his feet and shoving him back onto the couch. He must have passed out right after.

He felt panic roll through him and he breathed a sigh of relief that Michelle was still there. She was quietly watching him. Michelle let out a soft breath as she noticed that he was awake. Her face was streaked with tears and she was trying to control tremors in her hands and feet. Michelle didn't make a sound as she mouthed, "Thank goodness you're okay."

Danny tried to wink at her, and he winced in pain. "I'm going to get us out of here." His martyr complex was rising inside of him. He hoped more than anything that Jeremiah had gotten to James, Alex, or Michael. If so, Michael would have called Jackie and Michelle. Danny hoped they alerted the police, and they were aware of what was happening.

With wild eyes, Michelle shook her head. Her lips and chin were trembling. "Don't let them hurt you anymore than you are!" She lifted her hands slightly. Danny noticed she had been trying to work her way free from the restraints. Her wrists were red, raw and bleeding from trying to free herself. Nodding his head, he began working on the rope, tying his hands together. When he heard Brandi and Vicki coming out of one of the other rooms, he stilled his hands. Danny leveled a warning glance at Michelle, hoping she would do the same. Thankfully, she did.

Brandi walked to Michelle, and with hatred in her eyes, said, "Get up."

"Where are we going?" Michelle asked without thinking. Brandi slapped her. "Shut up and don't talk."

Danny noticed stars from the rage rushing through him as he saw another handprint on Michelle's right temple.

Brandi leaned toward Michelle. "We're about to take a drive to a place where you won't be able to talk or squeal about us anymore."

"Brandi, don't do this," Danny pleaded. "Think about how much trouble you will get into if you do this. It sounds like you're talking about murder."

Brandi stalked over to Danny and she punched him in his face, causing it to snap back. Michelle cried out as she saw blood spurt from either his mouth or his nose. She continued to whimper in a shrill voice. "You don't know when to shut up, do you? We're going to take care of you as well."

Vicki was pushing Michelle toward the door with the gun pointed at her back when they heard a noise outside.

***

"This is the police," a voice announced. "We don't want anyone to get hurt. We are asking you to release the people you have in there with you, and then we can talk."

"You did this, didn't you?" Brandi screamed in rage, and she rushed toward Danny while pulling the trigger of the gun. The shot echoed around the empty room, causing Michelle to cover her eyes. She screamed, and she began shaking all over again. Her heart was in fragments as she watched Danny writhing on the floor.

Danny's cry of pain had Michelle wailing, "Please stop! He didn't do this. Our friends must have figured out we were missing." Watching their violent treatment of him was killing her. Her heart ached from the pain of having to witness it.

As Brandi pointed her gun at Michelle, they heard an officer outside. "We know a gunshot just sounded. Please put the gun down. Let Michelle and Danny go. We don't want anyone else to get hurt. If you don't surrender, we will have no choice but to force our way inside." The officer repeated, " Put down the gun and open the door so that we can talk."

Brandi shrieked in anger again as she looked toward Vicki, noticing the fear in her eyes. "What are you doing? Don't just stand there. We need to get them in one of the back rooms now!"

Michelle watched as if in slow motion as Vicki shook her head in denial and she rushed toward Brandi. With the element of surprise, Vicki tackled Brandi to the floor. They were wrestling and each trying to get the gun.

Danny crawled over to her, leaving a trail of blood. He whispered, "Get down," gesturing for them to crawl under the table. Neither of the girls were paying attention to them as they shrieked and screamed bloody murder.

"That's enough!" Vicki roared. "If you keep shooting, we are both going to get killed."

Vicki twisted Brandi's arm holding the gun, as Brandi howled, "You stupid chicken shit! Now, I'm going to kill you!"

However, Vicki continued grappling with Brandi's arm as the gun went off again. Crying out in pain, Vicki clutched her side as she knocked the gun out of Brandi's hand. Once the gun fell from Brandi's hand, Danny crawled to reach it before she could recover it. Meanwhile, Vicki was holding her side in pain and attempting to fight against Brandi. Danny clutched his injured arm as he picked up the gun as Michelle screamed, "Danny, be careful!"

Due to the commotion, the officer's warning about their arrival went unnoticed by them. The door splintered as it was kicked open. Danny pointed the gun at Brandi, who was sprawled on top of Vicki with her hands at her throat. Blood was spurting out of Vicki's side as she grew weaker, and she was faltering at pulling Brandi's hands away from her neck. It took two officers to pull Brandi from Vicki. One officer forced Brandi onto her stomach to detain her. The entire time, Brandi bellowed in rage. Vicki curled into a ball, gasping for breath.

"Thank goodness!" Michelle breathed a sigh of relief as Danny handed the gun over to a third police officer before he collapsed on the floor. "Help him!" Michelle cried when she watched him fall to the floor. A fourth officer was cutting the ropes on Michelle's hands and feet as she rocked herself back and forth, shivering and moaning at seeing Danny on the ground.

An officer noticed the blood pouring from Danny's shoulder. He noticed the puddle of blood before he realized it was gushing from Vicki's side. "We need medical help! We have two people injured."

"Paramedics are on the way," the voice on the outside echoed into the radio. By that point, they had Brandi on her feet as she continued screaming in rage. They turned her around and pulled her hands behind her back to force handcuffs on her wrists. Michelle witnessed her insanity as she spit on the officer. "You just assaulted an officer of the law. Something else we will add to your list of charges," the officer said calmly as he shoved her out the door. As the paramedics arrived, another officer was using a cloth to help control Vicki's bleeding.

Michelle rushed next to Danny, asking if he was okay. With his arms still behind his back and grimacing in pain, he was trying to reassure her as another officer came to cut the ropes off of him. Once the officers removed the ropes, he doubled over in pain from the wound on his shoulder. The officer laid him down on the floor so that she could place a cloth on his bleeding wound.

One medic came in and was stabilizing Vicki, and another one made a beeline for Danny. Once they packed his wound, they loaded Danny onto a stretcher to wheel him outside.

Watching what they were doing was causing Michelle to hyperventilate from the fear of Danny's injuries being worse than she realized. The officer guided Michelle outside and away from the chaos to the second ambulance that was waiting in the parking lot. Michelle kept sobbing over and over. Her hiccups started again, making it hard to understand what she was pleading. "Please help him. Someone shot him in the shoulder. Please make sure he's alright." Another paramedic put an arm around her and she tried to calm Michelle in a soothing tone.

The medic who was working on Michelle had her sit on the back of the ambulance so that they could work on her raw wrists and bruised face, but her sobbing increased into brief spurts of trying to catch her breath. "W-w-where is h-he?" she kept wheezing because she couldn't see Danny anymore. The medic who was working on her spoke in a calm voice, asking her to take deep breaths.

Suddenly, their friends came running toward the ambulance. Jackie, Hannah, Michael, Alex, Suzanne, Jeff, and James were yelling and running toward them. The medic who was treating her placed an oxygen mask over

Michelle's face as she continued to instruct her to slow her breathing. Michelle felt dizziness as she tried to follow the medic's instructions.

With wild eyes, Jeff reached her as tears were rolling down his cheeks. "Michelle, thank goodness!" He moved to pull her into a hug when he realized she was trying to catch her breath. Turning toward the EMT, he asked, "Why is she wearing oxygen?" It was impossible for Michelle to talk at the moment and she watched with wide eyes as the medic explained Michelle was experiencing a panic attack because of the trauma she had been through. Calmly, they guided Jeff to sit beside her on the tailgate of the ambulance beside her. When her breathing was under control, he immediately pulled her against his chest. "Thank God you are okay!!"

"How did you find us?" Michelle fumbled with her hands as she continued to hiccup from her panic attack.

"Alex and Michael somehow knew. I'm not sure of the entire story. I just know that Jackie called me to come to Michael's apartment." Jeff pulled Michelle tightly against him. "I'm so grateful you're okay. I was scared to death!"

In the meantime, Jackie, Hannah, and Suzanne had also reached Michelle while Alex, Michael, and James moved beside Danny. She overheard Michael asking about Danny's condition.

Michelle looked at her friends. "How did you find out that this happened?"

"Danny talked to some guy. His name was Jeremiah. He asked him to alert Michael and Alex. Michael called me and I knew you had gotten caught up with Vicki and

Brandi." Tearstains were on Hannah's cheeks.

Jackie paced back and forth. "I've never been so scared. I was so crazy with worry that I called Jeff and told him. In my right mind, I would never have done that!"

"Michelle, what were you thinking? We told you to stay out of what they were doing." Hannah's voice raised in volume and her nostrils flared. Tension was on her shoulders.

"I didn't follow them or anything. Vicki just grabbed me as I was coming out of my counseling session. Danny was there with Mark and he watched us walking together. He thought it was suspicious and he followed me." Michelle felt herself get upset again as she thought of all Danny went through to help her. She bent over, sobbing as Hannah, Suzanne and Jackie surrounded her. Jeff rubbed her back as he said, "Stop upsetting her more!"

The medic stepped in, asking the girls to step back. It caused the two girls to back off with their lecture when they realized they were only making things worse. The paramedic placed the oxygen back over Michelle's mouth and nose.

Finally able to breathe again, Michelle pulled the oxygen mask off and looked at Jeff. "I need to go see Danny. Jeff, he was shot, and it's all my fault!" Two tears leaked out of the corners of her eyes.

Jeff kissed the top of Michelle's head. "I'll get an update for you, Muppet. Please stay here and try to keep calm." Her face was pale, and her mouth turned downward as she continued to cry.

Her roommates surrounded her on each side as soon

as Jeff walked to check on Danny. Jackie and Hannah were both talking at the same time. "We're so sorry we upset you. Thank God you are alright." "We were so worried." Michelle collapsed against Jackie's shoulder as Hannah rubbed her other shoulder and arm. Every area of her body felt limp.

Michelle said, "Thank you for helping to look for me. I'm sorry I didn't listen to you." Shaking her head, she continued, "I was so stupid. I'm so sorry." The volume of her voice began rising as her tears increased. Hiccups made it difficult for her to speak.

Both girls reassured her. "Michelle, it's alright. We are just glad you're safe now." Jackie said, "You need to calm down. Just breathe and don't worry anymore about it." Hannah perched on her other side and put her arm around her, squeezing her closer, hoping to provide comfort.

It took several minutes for Michelle to get her breathing back under control.

Jackie said, "James called Danny's parents and they are on their way to the hospital."

Michelle hung her head as her hiccups turned into quick breaths. Michelle stuttered, "This-s is all m-m-my fault that D-Danny got h-h-hurt. I told him n-not to follow me, but he didn't l-l-listen. His p-parents are going to hate m-me. And so is Beth."

With gentleness in her eyes, Hannah said, "Because he loves you, he would do anything he could to protect you. You still love him, too, or you wouldn't be so worried."

Jackie said, "From what you've shared about Danny's

family, I don't think they will blame you. They will defi-nitely have questions, but it sounds like they love you. I'm sure they will be concerned about you."

Jeff walked back. "They're about to load Danny into the ambulance." As he finished, the two paramedics lifted the stretcher and walked their direction.

"I'm going with them." Michelle announced, trying to stand. Her breathing was normal again. Jackie and Hannah tried to detain her, and she could tell Jeff was about to protest. She held up a hand as she looked at him. "Danny got hurt trying to protect me. I love him and you will not stop me from feeling this way about him. If you really love me, you need to stay quiet because I am not leaving his side. Either you support me or you don't. If you don't, you can go back home."

Resignation was in Jeff's expression as he nodded his head. "I will follow the ambulance to the hospital." Jeff looked at Jackie and the others. "Some of you can ride with me if you like."

Right before Michelle climbed into the ambulance, an officer approached her, asking questions about the event. Michelle was also blunt with them. "You can talk with me at the hospital because I am riding with my boyfriend."

The officer realized that Michelle wasn't going to change her mind. Therefore, he agreed to come and interview her at the hospital. He said, "We need to interview the other girl about what happened as soon as she's stable, so we will be there soon."

Chapter 18

Michelle followed the EMTs as they rolled Danny into the emergency room. As she noticed Danny's family, she collapsed in tears again. Since Jeff had followed behind the ambulance, he reached for her and pulled her into his arms as Michelle kept wailing, "I'm so sorry," repeatedly.

With a soothing voice, Jeff murmured, "Muppet, calm down or they will make you sit with the oxygen mask again." He was stroking Michelle's back.

Danny's mom and dad approached. Jeff stepped back to give them space. His mom said, "Michelle, honey. It's okay, we aren't angry with you. We're concerned about both of you." She pulled Michelle into a gentle hug and her hands were massaging her upper back, hoping to calm her. When Barbara stepped back, Danny's dad pulled her into a gentle hug as well. He whispered, "Honey, it's okay."

Michelle wiped her face with the tissues that Jeff was holding for her. "I don't blame you if you are angry." Danny's mom and dad continued surrounding her in a circle of comfort, and it took Michelle a moment to realize that Beth had not joined them. She was standing back with an angry look on her face.

Michelle walked around Danny's parents and moved toward her. "Beth? I'm so very sorry!"

Beth backed away, eyes filled with bitterness as she said, "I really liked you. Danny loved you. How could you lead him into this horrible situation? What were you thinking?"

All Michelle could repeat was "I'm sorry," because hiccups were taking over her breathing. Beth turned and walked out of the waiting room. Michelle doubled over in sobs once again.

As Jeff guided Michelle over to a chair, a nurse approached with a wheelchair. "Young lady, I was told you were a part of the abduction. Is that correct? The paramedics told me to come and have you checked out."

Michelle shook her head, and she waved her hand in refusal. "I'm f-f-fine," she said as the nurse guided her to sit in the chair. Jeff whispered. "Michelle, they need to check you out before they release you." The tone in Jeff's voice was pleading. Because exhaustion was setting in, Michelle didn't argue.

After being given an examination, the only thing the nurse treated Michelle for was dehydration from her panic attack and all the intense crying she had done. The nurse advised her to calm down so that she wouldn't require the oxygen mask again. He also used a warm cloth to clean Michelle's face. It was difficult with the welts and bruises.

Michelle kept asking, "How is Danny? Can someone update me?" Jeff kept trying to reassure her, but Michelle continued asking. "I'm sure someone will speak to you about it soon. Please sit back and rest."

Michelle pleaded with Jeff. "I need to know how he is." Jeff realized she was beyond reason, and he stepped out to see if he could speak with someone about Danny's progress. A police officer was talking to Danny's parents, so Jeff approached them a few feet away. "I don't want to intrude, but Michelle is working herself into another panic attack because she wants to know how Danny is doing."

Danny's mom said, "Call me Barbara and you're her brother, Jeff, right?"

Jeff shook both of their hands and Michelle noticed his guilty expression. He probably felt bad because of how kindly Danny's parents were treating him. He gestured behind him and said, "Do you want to come back and see Michelle? She might like to hear the update from you."

While the nurse was working on rehydrating Michelle, the officer who tried to interview her on the scene stepped into her cubicle. Jeff walked in as he was writing Michelle's statement of what had happened. Jackie explained what had happened, but hearing it straight from Michelle's mouth made it more real. Michelle watched him as he collapsed into a chair because his legs gave out on him. She saw him squeeze his eyes shut and shake his head in denial when he heard Michelle say that Vicki had come up behind her when she was walking out of the counseling center. Then he made a strangling noise when he heard the part about how Vicki put a gun against Michelle's side.

Once the officer left, Barbara walked over and took Michelle's hand in hers. "We were just given an update that they removed the bullet from Danny, and the doctor told us he is going to be fine. He will wear a sling for two weeks until they remove the stitches. We requested they bring him to the cubicle beside you in a few minutes so that you can see him."

"Oh, I'm so relieved!" Michelle answered as more tears filled her eyes.

Danny's mom patted her hand and said, "You need to stay calm, sweetheart, and get some rest."

More tears rolled down Michelle's face. "Beth is so mad at me. I don't blame her."

Barbara gently cupped Michelle's cheek. "It might take her a little longer, but she will eventually forgive you. Please don't worry about her and get some rest."

Danny's parents were distracted when they caught sight of movement. They noticed a nurse pulling a gurney with Danny laying on it.

"Danny," Michelle breathed. He didn't reply because he was still sleeping from the anesthesia the doctor administered to him.

Danny's mom and dad rushed to his side. Even though his mom reassured Michelle, she could see the anxiety in her eyes as she clung to her husband. Colton Peterson wrapped his arm around his wife, and he kissed the top of her head as they watched the nurse check Danny's vital signs. Michelle could see the distressed look on his dad's face upon seeing his son for the first time since the altercation happened. Their family crowded around him, holding his hand, and saying words to him.

Michelle's nurse wheeled a chair into her room. "I understand you are eager to see him, so I will wheel you over if you promise to stay seated in this chair."

"She'll stay," Jeff confirmed. Michelle nodded her head in agreement, and the nurse helped her get into the wheelchair before he pushed her next door.

Danny's family walked out. "He's awake and asking to see you, but the doctor said only a few minutes."

Unable to speak, Michelle nodded silently as the nurse pushed her closer to Danny's bed. She was relieved to see his eyes open as she took his hand. "I'm so glad you're okay." Jeff surprised her by stepping out of the room with Danny's family. The thought of Jeff giving them privacy made Michelle sag back into her chair, and her heart skipped.

Danny tried to smile and grimaced in pain. "Hey, baby," he said, "How are you?" He weakly squeezed her hand.

One of his hands was hooked to a machine. Michelle shook her head. "You don't need to be worrying about me. You're the one who was shot."

Danny squeezed her hand a second time. "I would do it all over again if it meant keeping you safe."

Michelle gazed at him with eyes full of remorse. "Danny, I'm so sorry about everything. And I'm sorry for telling you we needed to see other people. I apologize for not telling you what I knew about Vicki and Brandi. I still love you with all of my heart. I allowed Jeff to put doubts in my head and it wasn't fair to you. I'm so sorry that it took almost getting killed for me to realize it." Michelle glanced down as she continued by murmuring. "I don't blame you if you decide you want nothing to do with me."

"Michelle, look at me," Danny said weakly, and he said nothing else until he had her attention. "I know you're sorry, and I forgive you. I will never stop loving you. I know we haven't been dating long, and we might still have some things to work through, but I believe you are the one for me."

Michelle's gaze was filled with yearning, and her stomach fluttered. "Really? I feel the same way about you." Her smile was tremulous. "Will it hurt you if I kiss you?"

"It will hurt more if you don't," Danny answered.

Michelle gently touched her lips to his, being careful of the tubes and wires attached to him. Danny increased the pressure, bringing his uninjured hand up to hold her head as he returned her kiss.

When she pulled back, Michelle whispered, "I love you so much!"

Danny had just enough time to whisper, "I love you," before the nurse appeared again. "We have a room for you now, so we're going to take you upstairs. The doctor wants to monitor your condition overnight. Miss Walters, you can follow him upstairs and then say goodnight because he will need his rest as soon as we get him settled."

Michelle nodded, and Jeff appeared at her side. Danny's parents also walked into the area. All of them followed behind as the nurse pushed Danny's gurney out of that small area. Jeff was pushing Michelle's wheelchair.

As they passed the waiting room, Michelle noticed all of their friends waiting, slumped in chairs or pacing.

Michelle nodded toward them. "I'll be back in a few minutes. I want to see Danny before visiting hours are over."

Jackie walked up to her. "Are you okay?" Hannah joined her. Michelle shivered and gave a shaky laugh. "I'm fine now that I know Danny is going to be alright. I will see you in a little while." The three of them hugged in a tight circle.

Hannah and Jackie waved at her. "We will be right here waiting for you."

Michelle couldn't stop the tears from welling up again as she realized how lucky she was to have such wonderful friends. She smiled until she caught sight of Beth walking beside her parents, and her heart skipped again. She rubbed her chest from the pain inside of her heart because Beth wouldn't even look at her. Michelle was determined to find time to talk to her, just the two of them. Hopefully, she could repair the damage she had done to that relationship because she adored Beth. The thought of losing her was unbearable to think about.

Jeff ended up staying another night, and he convinced Michelle to come back to his hotel room so that he could monitor her. Michelle agreed with the stipulation that Jeff drive her to the hospital as soon as visiting hours began in the morning. Since Michelle was fine, Jeff persuaded their parents not to make the long drive. Their mom was not willing to stay put until Michelle spoke to them, reassuring them she was okay. She also promised to come home soon. Michelle heard the tears in both of their voices, and she felt even more guilty for her foolish decision.

Michelle was flabbergasted when she noticed Jeff's eyes filled with repentance. She had never seen humility in him before. He said, "Muppet, I was wrong. It took seeing Danny risk his life for you. His bravery showed me he truly loves you. He's the real deal because he is willing to sacrifice himself for your safety. As soon as he is better, I owe him an apology." Jefferson Walters actually had tears in his eyes by the end of his speech.

Michelle thought her tears were dried until her brother apologized for his interference in her relationship with Danny. They started up again, and she blubbered all over him, telling him thank you for believing in her.

Michelle tried to control her sobs, but she failed miserably. She grasped Jeff's hand and said, "Thank you. I love you, big brother!"

Jeff wrapped her in his arms, and the two of them cried together for a few minutes. Finally, he pulled back and smiled at her. "I'm going to trust you in the decisions you make. Just no more heroic efforts to stop two psychopaths, okay? I'm proud of you, Michelle. You have grown up and you are learning to make choices for yourself. If I hadn't been so overbearing, maybe you would have not gotten involved in this abduction."

After hearing his confession and apology, Michelle was beyond exhausted. Both she and Jeff took turns in the shower. The room had two double beds, so after preparing for bed, they crawled under the sheets and passed out until morning.

Chapter 19

As promised, Jeff drove Michelle back to the hospital after they stopped for breakfast. Though lacking an appetite, Michelle pretended to eat to avoid her brother's fussing.

Jeff parked his truck, and he had to run to keep up with Michelle. Her eyebrows were drawn together as she rushed down the hallways toward the elevator. After a few minutes, they stepped off the elevator and walked a few steps to Danny's room. Jeff murmured, "I will wait out here."

Michelle smiled at him before she knocked on the door. Her eyes widened when Beth opened it. Her gaze didn't come across as livid as she had the night before. However, her eyes remained cold and hard.

"Hi," Michelle whispered. "How's Danny this morning?"

Beth pulled the door all the way open, and stepped back. "Come in and see for yourself."

Michelle remained quiet until the two of them could talk together. She walked in to see both of Danny's parents sitting in chairs beside his bed. Danny sat up with a tray of food in front of him. He smiled at Michelle, held out his hand. "Good morning. How are you? Michelle rejoiced at seeing him in good spirits. Danny's next words changed the thought as she touched his hand. "I'm fine. How was your night?"

"I'm ready to get out of here. They don't let you get any rest at all," Danny grumbled, but light remained in his eyes and the corners of his lips curved upward as he gazed at Michelle.

Danny's mom stood. "Finally, a smile came out of him this morning! We will give you some time together." Danny's mom gave her a gentle hug before she shouldered her purse and followed her husband and daughter out of the room.

Michelle sat down when she noticed a scowl on Danny's face. "What's wrong? Are you alright? Should I get a nurse?" She fumbled with her purse as fear raced through her of a complication.

"Don't I get a good morning kiss?" he asked her as his eyes narrowed and he clenched his fingers together.

Michelle turned her head to hide her smile and then she leaned down and gently touched her lips to his. Moaning, Danny ran his good hand through Michelle's hair and deepened his kiss. Michelle felt dizzy as she pulled back. "You need to be careful," she chided. "You probably shouldn't have done that. We don't want to set off your heart monitor." She glanced at it as she spoke.

"Everyone keeps telling me to take it easy and be careful. I just want to go home to my apartment." Danny complained as he scowled. "And I want to kiss you now that we are back together."

Michelle wanted to laugh, but she worried about his reaction. Instead, she turned and pretended to look at his heart monitor again. "Has the doctor been in to see you yet? I'm sure it won't be much longer."

As soon as she finished saying those words, a knock sounded at the door and a doctor walked inside.

Michelle begged for him to wait because Danny's family needed to be in the room to hear an update. Michelle rushed out to find them. Jeff waited outside, so Michelle sent him to find them. Jeff hurried down the hall in the direction that they went.

***

A few minutes later, Danny's family walked into the room. Danny asked, "Are you going to let me out of here soon?" He furrowed his brow at the doctor as he asked.

The doctor smiled at Danny's impatience. "You did well overnight. Your blood pressure and heart rate are normal again." The doctor's expression became stern before he continued, "However, you will need to take it easy for the next several weeks. You lost a lot of blood and you don't want to do anything to cause strain on that shoulder. No contact sports or horseplay of any kind, do you understand? I think you need a week to recover before you resume any normal activities, and that includes attending classes."

Hope burned in his eyes as Danny nodded in agreement. The doctor studied him and he continued, "With that being said, I believe you will heal better at home. I will sign off and get the paperwork started for your release."

Familiar with shoulder injuries as a coach, Danny's father stepped forward. "Will he require any physical therapy for that shoulder?"

"Yes," the doctor answered. "The nurse will go over everything with the papers you will sign. A referral for a physical therapist will be included in those. We will have them call you and set up your first visit. How does that sound?"

Danny sighed in frustration, but he nodded again. "I guess it's fine. As long as I can get out of here, I will agree to anything."

His mom agreed he could stay at his apartment to heal because the physical therapist was in town. His parents would drive home, get a good night's rest, and Barbara would drive back the following day to stay with him.

Before she was released from the hospital the night before, the nurse encouraged Michelle to take a couple days off of classes as well. She volunteered to help with Danny's recovery, but she didn't want to be in his mom's way.

✶✶✶

Before Danny's family began their drive home, Michelle told Danny, "I need a few minutes with Beth, but I'll be right back." Danny reluctantly released her hand. "Okay, hurry back soon."

He was unaware that Beth was angry, but Michelle wanted a chance to speak with her. It was important to talk to her one on one so that Beth's resentment toward her wouldn't fester any longer.

After asking Beth to walk with her to the cafeteria, Michelle said, "Thank you for meeting with me. Will you let me buy you something to drink and a snack?"

Beth nodded, not commenting. After purchasing both of them a hot chocolate, they sat at a table. Both of them remained quiet. Michelle's insides twisted with anxiety, but she was determined to make amends.

Michelle played with her cup for an extended amount of time before she looked up at Beth. "Beth, I am so sorry about Danny getting hurt. I take full responsibility and I realize my actions were unbelievably crazy now that I look back on the entire situation." She swallowed the tears in the back of her throat, and Michelle refused to cry because she didn't want to look like a victim. She wished for Beth to see her owning up to her mistake. She also shook her head as she recognized how true her words were.

Beth studied the table when she said, "My brother is one of the best people that I know. He's always been there for me and I couldn't stand the thought of him being hurt. I believe you didn't purposely put him in that dangerous situation. And I understand him well and I'm sure he felt like he needed to protect you and save you, just as he's always done with me."

Michelle pushed down more tears. "I've learned how

wonderful he is and I believe he wanted to save me. However, I shouldn't have put myself or him in that situation. I realize that is my fault." Michelle shook her head again as she looked down at her coffee mug. Her frown deepened as she studied the design of the cup. "My friends tried to get me to tell the authorities, and I was stubborn. It's a mystery to me why I felt I could do it alone. Danny had no idea about any of it until it happened."

Beth surprised Michelle when she leaned across the table and touched her hand. "I think that's why I felt such anger toward you. If I were you, I might have done the same thing. I realize you and I have had little time to get to know each other, but you are beginning to feel like a sister to me." Tears filled Beth's eyes as she continued, "I want to tell you I forgive you, but it may take me a while to get past my anger."

Michelle nodded. "I understand. I'm going to give you the time you need and I promise to respect your wishes. I don't plan to be apart from Danny anymore. If he still wants me."

Beth's lips curved slightly as she murmured, "Danny is head over heels for you. I've never seen him like this with any other girl. This morning he was a total grump until you showed up. You brought that smile to his face. Believe me, he still wants you."

With a grateful smile, Michelle whispered, "Thank you."

They were finishing up their beverages when Beth's dad walked into the cafeteria. "They're about to release Danny. He's signing the final paperwork."

Michelle and Beth stowed their cups in a bin for dirty

dishes, and they followed Danny's father back upstairs.

***

An hour later, Danny's family hugged him gently before leaving to go back home. Michelle gave them their privacy, and she waited in the living room for them to say their goodbyes. Tears filled her eyes at the sight of their tight family hug as she walked to the couch.

Jeff, needing to start his long drive home, had already said goodbye to Michelle with a hug. He had to be at work the next day.

Danny looked exhausted when he came back into the living room. He wanted to walk his family to the door, but they insisted he stay in his room.

He attempted to sit by Michelle, but she said, "No, you heard the doctor. You are going to bed and rest." Her hands urged him to turn back around.

Danny smiled at her in amusement, and he saluted. "Yes, ma'am." Michelle placed her hands on his back as she followed behind him to his bedroom. She pulled back the covers for him to climb in and she tucked the covers around him. Danny's eyes closed as soon as his head hit the pillow. Michelle kissed him on the forehead, whispering that she loved him. She sat on the couch and leaning her head back against it in extreme fatigue when she heard knocking at the door.

James had been in his room, giving Danny and his family space. He walked out and motioned for Michelle to stay seated. "I'll get it."

Jackie and Hannah walked into the apartment with grocery sacks and some takeout bags. Michael and Alex filed in behind them.

"What are you doing here?" Michelle asked in surprise. She had told her roommates that she would stay at Danny's for most of the day and she would come back to the dorm to sleep that night.

"You need food," Jackie insisted. "I'm guessing you have eaten very little since before all this started."

"And we went shopping for Danny to have plenty for his recovery," Hannah said as she began unloading the bags, placing items on shelves and in the refrigerator. After the groceries were put away, she and Jackie unloaded sub sandwiches, chips, and pickle spears.

Michelle found herself overwhelmed by how wonderful her friends were as another knock sounded at the door. When James opened it, Suzanne walked inside with several kinds of drinks. She smiled as she walked in. "Is this where the party is?" Along with the beverages, she produced a container of chocolate chip cookies.

Jackie motioned toward James and she said, "Come on. We have plenty for everyone. And don't worry, we have something for Danny because he will also be hungry after having to eat nasty hospital food."

The seven of them filled plates, poured drinks for themselves, and moved to the living room so that they could all sit together. Jackie, Hannah, and Michael sat on the floor in front of the coffee table as Alex, Michelle, and Suzanne sat on the couch. James sat in the lumpy chair beside them. As they sat there, Hannah, Jackie, and Michael relayed what happened and how they came to find out. When she understood the extent of her friends' efforts, Michelle's eyes widened, and fear surged again. She made herself take deep breaths so that she wouldn't lead herself into another panic attack. It was tough to listen to the retelling of it..

"That guy, Jeremiah, came and knocked on our door," Alex said. "He inquired about my identity, whether I was Michael or Alex."

"Once I returned to the apartment and Alex delivered the message, I contacted Hannah to find out what happened," Michael said. "When Hannah screamed for Jackie, I knew something was wrong."

Hannah had tears in her eyes. She shook her head. "I've never felt so scared and helpless. Jackie even called Jeff because we had no idea what to do."

Michelle's heart began pounding as Michael talked about stalking close to the window of where she and Danny were being held. He talked about recognizing Vicki when she opened the door for Brandi. "I understood it time to call the police," Michael said. Michelle felt overwhelmed by the love and acceptance from this group of friends. They proved to be a group who would do anything for each other. Tears dripped down her face. Jackie and Hannah moved beside her, and the three of them cried softly together.

The group talked about the police arriving and how an officer chided Michael for going over to the apartments. Michael honestly told the officer of the decision he made and that he had no regrets. "I would do it again in a heartbeat for Hannah, as well as you and Danny."

Hearing the story only highlighted Michelle's immature actions. Michael risked his life to help her and Danny get free. Otherwise, they might be dead somewhere.

Her friends stayed for an hour, helped clean up, and then they hugged Michelle before saying they needed to complete homework or study. Jackie and Hannah handed Michelle her backpack. It was filled with extra clothes and toiletries. They had also included her textbooks and notebooks so that she could study. The three of them hugged tightly again.

James left saying he needed to go to the library to work on a research paper. Michelle felt surprised when he gave her a quick side hug. James never had much to say, and this was the first time Michelle had observed him hugging anyone.

Michelle walked quietly into Danny's room to check on him before settling back on the couch, hoping to get some homework done. However, her eyes became extremely heavy. Still exhausted from the ordeal, she laid down on her side and fell asleep.

A kiss on the nose startled Michelle as she woke up completely disoriented to see Danny sitting beside her with a smile.

Quickly sitting up, she said, "You should be in bed."

"I'm fine," he commented as he leaned close to give Michelle a gentle kiss.

Michelle stood up. "Are you hungry? Jackie and Hannah brought food, and we saved some for you."

Danny followed behind as she walked to the refrigerator to pull out the sub sandwich they saved for him.

"What do you want to drink? There's lemonade, coke and sprite." Michelle tried to walk over to the counter when Danny reached and pulled her close with his good hand. He reached down and kissed her thoroughly until Michelle pushed him back.

"You are supposed to be resting," Michelle chided him.

With a sinful smile, Danny kissed her again. "This is restful."

Unable to stop her giggle, Michelle kissed him back. Then she stepped back and said, "Okay, that's enough. You need to sit down and eat something."

When Danny finished eating, Michelle rejoiced to see his appetite. Then he convinced her to let him lie on the living room couch to rest.

"Please don't overdo it," she pleaded as she followed him. She grabbed a blanket on the back of the couch and covered him, gasping in surprise when he yanked her down beside him. "Danny, what are you doing?"

Danny snuggled Michelle under his good arm and he tucked her against his side, adjusting the blanket. He whispered, "This will definitely help me get better." It was a miracle that they were together after all that happened. Shivers covered his body at the thought of Brandi shooting her with that gun.

Michelle laughed at his words, but she settled herself against him where they both fell asleep again. Upon waking, Michelle was startled to find she had slept next to Danny for two hours. She tried not to wake him and she gently stood. Then she went to the restroom before settling into the chair beside him so that she could study.

That night, Danny convinced Michelle to stay the night and sleep beside him in his bed. Michelle realized her friends packed essentials for her in case she wound up staying. She didn't argue with him. Instead, she made grilled cheese sandwiches to eat with the chips and leftover pickles from lunch. James ate in the dining hall, so she made nothing for him.

Michelle helped Danny into the shower because the doctor told him to keep his bandage dry for another twenty-four hours. She tilted the shower head down as far as it would go so that he could wash the rest of his body without the water getting on his left shoulder. Once she assisted him and dressed him, his face showed the gray of exhaustion. She made him lay against his pillows before she prepared for bed.

Danny suggested they watch television in his room for a while before going to sleep. The two of them drifted off, so she took the remote from Danny's hand and placed it on the table beside his bed. Michelle shifted to lie beside him where they faced one another. Danny intertwined their fingers together with his good hand.

Chapter 20

Danny spent the week resting in his apartment. His mom stayed with him for two nights. When she left, Michelle insisted on staying the rest of the week. Danny was grateful to have Michelle there with him, and he didn't complain. He felt his heart sink at the thought of losing her. The trial they endured deepened their connection.

Danny grew weary of his one-armed routine. But he felt extremely thankful that he and Michelle were back together. Danny didn't want to do anything to mess that up.

The police officers involved in the situation stopped by to update them. Her effort to prevent Brandi's actions resulted in Vicki facing lighter penalties compared to Brandi. The police took Vicki's heroics into account and lightened her charges. She would spend a few years in prison for kidnapping Michelle, and she would serve time for possession of a firearm. Vicki's time at their small university was finished. The school officials had officially kicked her out.

Brandi was being charged with kidnapping, assault, and illegal use of a firearm. They couldn't charge her with attempted burglary because she never committed the act, even though Michelle included it in the statement. The police didn't recover any solid evidence of Brandi's plan to commit any theft. But Brandi would go to prison for at least twenty years.

Michelle and Danny visited Vicki to thank her for protecting them from Brandi.

With tears in her eyes, Michelle said, "Thank you for what you did. You saved Danny's life and I appreciate you taking that risk."

Danny smiled. "You also prevented her from shooting Michelle or anyone else. We owe our lives to you."

Vicki shared her feelings, but she didn't apologize or ask for their forgiveness. "I knew we were going too far. I should have never listened to that crazy bitch." Michelle actually found peace after their conversation with her.

Nightmares came to both Michelle and Danny. The two of them spent many therapy sessions helping them learn to work through everything. Both Angela and Mark insisted on meeting with their group of friends again to gauge everyone's reaction to another traumatic event. Danny had not heard the retelling of what had happened. He clutched his head and turned pale as their friends talked about it within the group session. Michelle wept silently, with tears streaming down her face. Danny gazed at her, realizing how fortunate they were to be gifted with such wonderful friends.

"Thank you," he whispered to Michael. "You put yourself in danger when you came to check things out. Brandi may have added you as a hostage, or even worse, she might have shot you. I know I asked for your help, but it means so much to me."

Overwhelmed with emotion, Michelle could only nod in agreement with Danny's words.

"That leads me to a topic of discussion," Mark said. He looked each member of the group in the eye. "This is the second time you inserted yourselves into a volatile situation. I have some thoughts to share concerning it." Mark glanced at Angela and she nodded in agreement.

"My concern involves your safety, which should be your priority. Twice, you became involved in situations that are above all of you." Mark looked around at each member before he continued. "All of you need to learn to walk away and alert authorities in times like these."

Michael said, "I agree, but this time, the police wouldn't do anything until we had further proof. What were we supposed to do about that? Danny and Michelle could have been killed before they would have even investigated."

"I agree with Mark," Michelle said. The group looked at her with widened eyes or open mouths. "As I sat tied to the chair, I realized that I should have alerted someone. I could have come to him or Angela. The police might have listened if an adult were involved."

Mark smiled in thanks at Michelle. "Michael, you raise a valid point. It sounded like the situation was escalating from the moment it started. However, it seems you should have alerted a university official, as well as calling the police. Brandi and Vicki were being watched because of concerns about their threatening behavior. Like Michelle said, the police might have responded sooner."

Angela piped in. "All of you are bright and intelligent. It is a privilege to work with every one of you. But we can't do that if you aren't with us anymore." She gave a pointed look at each person. "Does that make sense? We want more time to get to know all of you and see you reach your dreams. So from now on, I will share my personal number with you for emergencies. We hope situations like this won't happen again. But if you are in danger, please call one of us day or night." Mark nodded his head in agreement.

"Okay." "We will." The group answered at the same time.

Mark and Angela insisted that Michelle and Danny meet in a couples session. Michelle intended to ask, yet she was thankful when Angela suggested it.

During a session together, Michelle learned about Danny's anxiety. The guilt over what she did increased once she learned about it. Michelle shared her people-pleasing inferiority complex with Jeff. It didn't surprise Danny, but he felt gratitude for her sharing it with him. Even though it was tough, the two of them took the safe space to openly talk about their weaknesses.

The following day, Danny had a one-on-one session with Mark. Mark looked at Danny. "Why did you feel you needed to follow Michelle? Why didn't you go to the authorities right away?"

Danny looked at his hands, clasped in his lap. "I was scared to death when I saw Michelle being pushed by Vicki. It terrified me to see her pointing that gun at her side." He continued clasping and unclasping his fingers nervously.

Leaning forward, Mark's expression showed intensity. "What possessed you to wonder if you could have stopped it? You didn't even possess a weapon or any type of defense."

"I'm not sure," Danny answered as he continued anxiously playing with his fingers. Without realizing it, his shoulders hunched tighter from the tension. This line of questioning made him uncomfortable. "I just didn't want to let Michelle get out of my sight."

"Danny, look at me," Mark commented, and Danny raised his gaze. "We've addressed your desire to solve every problem for every person you love. This is a large response to your anxiety. Why did you suppose you could rescue Michelle?"

Danny was shocked when the tears sprang to his eyes. "I'm not sure. I don't want to let anyone down. It matters to me that people I care about know that they can always count on me." A tear escaped and trailed down his cheek.

Mark crossed one leg over the other before he said, "Danny, nobody expects you to be perfect. They know they can count on you. You don't have to achieve perfection to prove yourself. Let me ask you a question. Why do you pressure yourself to live to perfect standards?"

Danny shook his head. "I'm not sure. I've always considered it a duty to meet the needs of others, and I still fulfill that expectation. Keeping my word is really important to me. I have a guilty conscience if I can't complete it immediately."

"Can I share some thoughts with you I've been considering?" Mark asked gently. Danny's eyes were troubled. Mark continued, "We've already talked about how being the oldest, you had double the pressure. The oldest child wants to be the best at everything they do. I doubt your parents intended it, but they may have told you that you needed to protect your little sister."

Danny nodded his head, and his eyes widened. "Yes! They did that!" Then he shook his head. "They didn't mean to put that kind of pressure on me."

Mark said, "You are from a small town and your family is viewed as its heroes because of the role your father has as the high school football coach. He has led the team to many state championships in his years of coaching. You were also expected to be the 'star' because of your dad, right?"

"Yes!" Danny exclaimed a second time. Light reached his eyes, and it seemed his eyebrows might lift off his face. These were ideas deep within him, but he had never completely processed them.

This time, Mark shook his head. "Danny, that's a lot of pressure on one human being. You've allowed these circumstances to pile burden after burden upon your shoulders. It's too much for one person! From what you've told me of your parents, you need to talk to them and tell them how you feel about this. I think they will be supportive of you and want you to stop expecting so much from yourself. Otherwise, you are going to lead yourself to health problems too early in your life! You will also always deal with tremendous amounts of anxiety, which would essentially lead to depression when you sense you've failed. The good news is that you are still young and you are learning how to cope with all of this." Mark paused. "But I want to repeat what I said to the group the other day. Don't allow yourself to be pulled into a dangerous situation like that again. You have my number, so call me. I can help call authorities."

Danny stared into space. "I've never considered any of that and how much it affected me!" He looked at Mark. "This week has given me time to read about mindfulness. I'm not sure I believe all of it, but I've been working on the breathing exercises that the book teaches." He shook his head. "I know I was in over my head when Vicki had that gun. I promise to call you if something like that ever happens again."

"Danny, that's great that you're practicing breathing techniques. You needn't accept all of mindfulness, but I find its teachings beneficial for the overly anxious. I can testify that it has helped me in my life." Mark smiled easily and gave Danny time to process what he just said. "Your homework this week is to call and talk to your parents. Tell them how you feel. I have faith in their ability to handle it. I suggest you write it down and share it with them after you've recorded your thoughts." Mark gestured to the notebook beside Danny before he stood and opened his door, ending their session.

"Thank you," Danny said, and he shook Mark's hand vigorously. As he walked out, he wondered if he could take a quick trip home this weekend. Of course, he wanted Michelle to come home with him as well. He pulled the journal to his chest and he whispered, "First, I need to write about it."

Walking from the counseling center, Danny found Michelle waiting and his heart beat faster at her beauty. She sat on the bench across from the center and the light shone beautifully on her hair as her face glowed in the sun.

He walked up to her and pulled her into a tight hug. "Hey, baby." He kissed her softly.

Michelle hugged him back before pulling away to gaze at him. "How are you?"

"Much better now." Danny said, and he explained how the session had gone with Mark. Michelle learned Danny was not a person who held back from sharing about himself. Unlike herself, he didn't have problems opening up with her.

As if he read her thoughts, Danny said, "When I first started counseling, I didn't know how to talk or open up." He smiled down at Michelle while lacing their fingers together. "I know I've been pouring my heart out to you.

What can I say? You bring out the best in me."

Michelle smiled up at Danny. "I'm glad you are learning how to talk about your thoughts and feelings. It's a wonderful thing that I am the person who gets to hear you talk about them." She nodded her head in agreement with Mark. "I need you to stay strong and healthy! Please let go of the pressure you feel! Okay?" She paused for a minute. Then she said, "I love when Angela has me write things down. It is much clearer on paper. If you want, I will listen if you need an ear."

Danny leaned down and he kissed Michelle softly. "Thank you. I love you so much!"

The next day, Michelle had a private session with Angela. Upon seeing Michelle, Angela hugged her warmly. "Thank goodness you both are alright. Girl, you need to learn how to stay out of trouble for a while." The two of them had not had time to speak one on one. The group sessions had filled up the past few days. Michelle chuckled, happy for her own time to share. "I agree with you on that, and I promise not to be a detective by myself ever again. It is definitely a lesson learned!"

Once Angela led the way to her office, Michelle talked about all that had transpired. She unloaded all the ongoing challenges she faced regarding it. Angela listened the entire time. Michelle was tired of the constant tears that ran down her face.

There was a brief pause before Angela spoke up. "Michelle, today I want you to work on learning not to be such a people-pleaser with your brother. I am happy that he apologized. But part of me wonders if you got into this entire investigative mindset with Vicki because of trying to do something you knew Jeff would never approve."

"I thought about that as I was strapped to that chair," Michelle sighed. "It was as stupid idea."

Angela reached to touch Michelle's hand. "Don't beat yourself up about it. I believe you attempted to show that you possessed strength and decision-making capabilities. It seems deep down, you took a risk as an act of rebellion toward Jeff's stronghold on you. You tried rebellion in high school and the plan was foiled. Now that you recognize it, allow this to teach you a huge lesson regarding you and your brother."

"Okay, so I recognize I tried to free myself from Jeff. How do I change in this area?" Michelle's gaze was open and earnest.

"I think you need to start with minor changes in your life. Look deeply at the choices you are making. Are these things that will truly make you happy or are you deciding to do them because of Jeff, your parents, or anybody else?" Angela said.

Michelle was quiet for a few minutes before looking at Angela. "How do I do that?" She wanted to become more independent and learn to make wise decisions for herself. The idea occurred to her that it included taking things slowly with Danny.

"First, you're coming to counseling. So that's a good

thing. Second, you need to listen to the self-help tapes that I gave you. Did you listen to any of them?" Angela asked.

With a guilty expression, Michelle shook her head *no*

"Michelle," Angela continued. "What you take out of these counseling sessions is entirely up to you. You don't even have to do these things in order to please me. I will not get angry if you didn't listen to the tapes. This is what I want you to consider. I want you to realize that what you do is not meant to always please others around you. I want you to focus on yourself for the next few months."

"How do I do that?" Michelle asked for the second time.

Angela reached over and placed her hand over Michelle's. "You have the notebook I gave you, right?"

Michelle nodded as Angela continued, "Make a list of things you truly want in your life. Are you happy with your major? Do you need to slow things down a bit with Danny? Do you need an actual break from him? How do you spend your free time? Do you choose activities that you truly enjoy? Your next homework assignment from me is to write ideas about you."

Michelle continued nodding. She was in a daze at the thoughts running through her head. "I can do those things."

"Fill up as many pages as you can with thoughts focusing on *you* and what matters most to *you*," Angela suggested. "We will talk about them at our next session."

Michelle nodded in agreement. The first thing she realized about as she walked out was that she wanted to sit down with Danny and talk through all they had gone through. There had been little time to work out their differences after she put the brakes on their relationship. Deep down, the first thing she really wanted was to resolve things with him. She didn't need to write it down to determine it as a priority.

***

When she got back to her room, her roommates were both out. She dialed Danny's number, and her heart quickened when his deep voice answered. Michelle hoped she would always feel this way.

"Hi," she said. "How are you feeling?"

"Better now that you called." Danny complained. "I'm actually climbing the walls from being cooped up in here all week. My only destinations have been therapy for my shoulder and therapy for my mind."

Michelle chuckled at his joke and she said, "I can help you with that. Do you want to go somewhere tonight instead of staying there like we've been...?"

She couldn't even finish her sentence before he yelled, "Yes, yes, yes!" Michelle had to lower the phone from how loud he was. She laughed out loud as she did.

"You name the place," Michelle suggested. "Do you want to eat dinner or do you just want something like ice cream?"

"Let's go out longer than it takes to eat ice cream!" Danny said fervently.

"How about the diner down the road? The Mexican

restaurant is usually too noisy, and I want to sit and talk together." Michelle said.

"Anything is better than here!" Danny declared.

Michelle grinned at his tone of voice and she said, "I will come around five. That way, I can complete a couple of homework assignments."

This time Danny's voice softened. "Thank you, Michelle."

Michelle smiled into the phone. "You're welcome."

Michelle arrived at Danny's apartment right at five o'clock. It took a few minutes to drive down the road to the small diner that served wonderful food. She found she had an appetite for comfort food and she imagined it would also go over well with Danny.

Michelle requested a booth and the host led them to a secluded one. Danny nudged Michelle to scoot over in the booth. Danny placed his uninjured arm behind her in the booth, and he reached to kiss her softly again before looking at the menu.

Chapter 21

After the server took their drink and food orders, Michelle turned toward Danny. "Danny, I want you and I to talk about what happened with Jeff. Things have been so crazy that I don't think we've really talked about what happened before Vicki and Brandi took us hostage. I want us to share our feelings and work things out."

Danny stroked her hair gently. "You understand that I've forgiven you, right?"

"I know," Michelle replied. "But we never really talked about what I did and why it happened."

Danny pushed the hair behind her shoulder before he whispered, "Those were the hardest days of my life." His eyes fell on her hair. When he raised his gaze, Michelle saw the agony in his eyes.

Michelle's eyes closed as she heard the pain in his voice. She murmured, "I'm sorry that I let Jeff's words sway my feelings about you. It's just that I am so inexperienced with dating and I had no idea what I was doing. Jeff's words confused me more than ever."

The server delivered their drinks, and Danny hesitated

before continuing until she walked away. "I never intend-ed for you to feel like I took advantage of you. I look back now and see that maybe I pushed for things to go faster than I should have." He unwrapped his straw and placed it in his glass of soda.

Michelle touched his hand. When Danny turned to-ward her, she grasped his face in both of her smaller hands. "I realize you weren't trying to pressure me. I'm the one who kept agreeing for things to continue moving forward."

Turning his face to kiss her palm, Danny whispered. "My heart broke into tiny pieces when you told me you wanted some space." His eyes were the deepest shade of blue she had ever seen.

Blinking back tears, Michelle whispered, "I am so sorry. I didn't mean to hurt you so badly."

Danny leaned and kissed Michelle softly before he pulled away "I guess I need to know where we stand now in our relationship."

Michelle swallowed convulsively, and her throat was tight with her own tears. "I only want to be with you, Danny. But I have some things I need to work on that have to do with me. Angela is bringing up difficult topics to work through, and one of them is learning to put limits on pleasing others around me."

Hesitation filled Danny's face as he simply replied, "Okay."

"I'm not totally breaking things off. I want to be with you as much as I can. However, I need you to be patient as I work through these issues inside of myself. Also, I want to pause our intimate moments together." Michelle wanted Danny to see nothing but honesty in her eyes.

Danny breathed a sigh of relief. "I don't care about that part. I only want to be with you and you can set limits on how far you want to go, in kissing and other stuff. I understand I can come across strong, but it's only because I care about you so much. It's a weakness in me you will have to accept."

Michelle smiled into Danny's eyes. "I can think of worse weaknesses than that."

The server brought out their food and the two of them stayed quiet for a few minutes as they began eating. Danny had removed his arm from behind Michelle in order to eat with his good hand. His other shoulder was still in a sling. "Oh my word," he moaned. He ordered chicken and dumplings, and Michelle could see how much he enjoyed them. She felt happy she had recommended this place.

Finally, he looked over at Michelle and asked, "What does this mean for us?"

She swallowed the bite of food in her mouth. "It means we are dating. I realize we can't go all the way back to the beginning, but I would like to slow everything down with good old-fashioned dates with you. I think it will help us to truly get to know each other and it will teach me what dating is really like."

Relief swept over Danny's face, and his shoulders relaxed. "I can live with that." He nudged her shoulder. "Prepare for me to sweep you off your feet, beautiful lady!"

Michelle experienced a breathlessness at his words.

The way he gazed at her gave her a heady sensation. It took several seconds for her to inhale. "Okay," she whispered.

Once they finished their meal, Danny suggested they order dessert. Then he said, "I know you need to slow things down, but I would like to sit and talk more if you are comfortable with that."

"I'd like that." Michelle's smile was filled with pure contentment.

The two of them sat and talked for another hour in the restaurant. They didn't notice any of the people who came and left because they were completely absorbed with each other. So that the server wouldn't become angry, they ordered another beverage. Danny's arm stayed behind Michelle, and he pulled her closer to his side.

When they left and Michelle drove them back, Danny asked, "Can you come inside?"

Apology showed in Michelle's eyes. "I can't tonight. I have an exam tomorrow and I have homework for Angela." She got out of the car so that she could hug Danny goodnight.

"Is it too much for me to say 'I love you?' Danny whispered as she wrapped her arms around his waist.

"Absolutely not!" Michelle exclaimed. "I would be disappointed if you didn't."

Danny leaned down and he gently kissed Michelle. He deepened it. Danny moved back, his gaze filled with ardor as he breathed, "I love you, Michelle."

"I love you, too," she whispered, and she leaned up and kissed him a final time.

***

In their thanks for his heroic attempt to protect Michelle, their parents invited Danny to come to her home for Thanksgiving along with his parents and Beth.

Michelle spent another weekend with Danny's family on their ranch so that he could take the time to talk with his parents about what Mark had revealed to him in counseling. Just as Mark predicted, Danny's parents showed more concern than anger. Some parents didn't handle their children going to therapy very well. Danny's mom and dad supported his thoughts, and they listened to everything he wrote in his journal. Michelle stayed in the guest room, giving them privacy to talk things out.

After the time with his parents, Danny shared how his dad pulled him into a tight hug and apologized for making him feel like he had to be perfect. His dad said, "I've always struggled in the same way about myself. I'm glad you're getting help and learning to not let it ruin your life!" He talked about how his heart turned over from the tears his mom had in her eyes from hearing her husband confess those feelings to Danny.

Their family possessed a closeness that Michelle had never seen before, and she found herself envious of their relationship. She loved her parents and brother, but the family dynamic in which she grew up differed from what she observed with the Peterson family.

Michelle and Beth found their way back to being

friends again. One way of doing that was for Michelle to be completely open and honest with Beth about her weaknesses and her plan to improve her outlook on life. It gave Beth the utmost respect for Michelle when she revealed her innermost feelings. Michelle loved becoming the 'older sister' once again.

"I'm so sorry that I sensed a need to prove something because my brother was so protective," Michelle said with tears in her eyes, thankful it was just the two of them. Danny's mom visited their grandparents while Danny and his dad worked in the barn. "Now that I look back on it, I realize that it's a miracle that we made it out alive." She shook her head in derision at herself.

Beth's eyes shone brightly with tears. "I understand, because Danny has always been protective of me. Maybe not to the same extent." Beth placed a hand on Michelle's and continued, "I apologize for being so hard on you. It wasn't fair how I treated you."

"You're forgiven!" Michelle exclaimed as she pulled Beth into a hug.

Beth leaned back before she looked into Michelle's eyes. "Now you need to forgive yourself. Don't keep apologizing to please me. Let it go and we can move on!"

Michelle's sob sounded like a laugh as she said, "Okay, I'd like that!"

Their relationship improved so much that Beth came and spent the weekend with Michelle, Jackie, and Hannah. Michelle instructed Danny to allow them to have a 'girls' weekend. He, Michael, Alex and James traveled to Alex's home. The four of them relaxed and enjoyed some time fishing.

***

Michelle stopped Danny one morning before they walked into breakfast. "Hey, I need to talk to you about something."

Danny's eyes widened, and his eyebrows raised from curiosity. "What is it?"

"I want us to go out with Jackie and Jennifer." Michelle studied his eyes before she continued. "Would you be open to that?"

"Michelle," Danny placed his hands on her arms. "Jackie is your best friend. Of course, I'm open to going out with her and Jennifer."

She watched him. "You understand they are a couple, right?"

Danny rolled his eyes at her. "Yes, I know that. I'm fine with it."

Unexpectedly, Michelle threw herself into his arms and whispered, "Thank you."

That weekend, Michelle, Danny, Jackie, Jennifer, Hannah and Michael went on a triple date to their favorite bar over the state line. They invited Alex and Suzanne, but the two of them had gone to Suzanne's home for the weekend.

The six of them crowded around a table and they split wings and fries. At one point, Jackie and Jennifer clasped hands on the table. Nobody in their group blinked an eye when they did it. However, there were other patrons who gawked at them.

"Jennifer, do you want to be a coach like Jackie?" Hannah asked.

"Actually, I want to be a science teacher. I love physical science and experiments. I know it makes me seem like a nerd!" Jennifer chuckled, and the group laughed with her.

"I would not have guessed that you are a science nerd," Michelle said. "But I applaud you for doing something you're totally passionate about!"

Jackie beamed at Michelle as Jennifer mumbled, "Thank you."

The rest of the conversation remained natural and relaxed. Michelle experienced joy when she saw Jennifer grow into an important part of their group of friends. The idea of Jackie sensing any kind of awkwardness around all of them was unacceptable and Michelle wanted to do all that she could to support her friend.

The four of them took a restroom break and when they were at the sinks washing their hands, a lady passed by them with a frown before hurrying out the door.

"Okay, that was strange," Michelle commented. Before she could say anything else, another lady exited a stall. As she washed her hands, she scowled their direction just as the first lady had done. "What is wrong with everyone?"

Jackie sounded disheartened. "Not everyone is as accepting as all of you are."

The two girls had danced together and held hands at the table during the meal.

Hannah spoke with compassion. "It doesn't matter

what they think or say. We love you both and you will always be accepted by us!"

Michelle nodded as Hannah pulled everyone into a group hug.

Thanksgiving break arrived, and the school time proved extremely busy. Students studied for finals and completed research for term papers due at the end of the semester. These things would take place when they came back from Thanksgiving break. Michelle and Danny were thankful for a week away from the chaos and stress of school.

The Sunday before Thanksgiving arrived. The two of them stayed at school a few extra days so that they could squeeze in a date.

Time had been short between studying and basketball, and Danny aimed to win Michelle's affection in the way she truly wanted. It was beyond romantic. After they talked things out, Danny had never seen such peace on Michelle's face. He was also grateful that his kisses were accepted and he wasn't pushing her too hard.

Danny found a restaurant one town over situated on a lake. Candles burned on the tables and the lighting remained low in the restaurant. Danny made reservations for a table on the terrace overlooking the water. The sunset put on a show as they gazed at the colorful rays that reflected over the water's smooth and still surface.

Once they sat across from each other, Michelle smiled at Danny. "This is so beautiful. Thank you for arranging it."

Danny kissed the back of her hand. "You're welcome. The scene isn't the only thing that is beautiful."

Michelle's face turned crimson red. Danny's joke a few weeks earlier about being ready for him to date her properly was not just a jest. He completely amped up his game, charming Michelle in the most meaningful ways.

Danny squeezed her hand, bringing her out of her daydream. "Would you like to dance?"

"Yes," she whispered as he helped pull out her chair.

Danny pulled her gently against him and she leaned into his solid chest, resting her cheek on it.

When they drove back to Danny's apartment, he had a dozen roses on his table. She cried in response to the lovely gift.

"Thank you," she whispered as he grasped her face and kissed her softly.

"I love you, Michelle," Danny whispered against her forehead.

Her eyes closed, and she said, "I love you, too."

They spent the rest of the night dancing to soft music he had recorded ahead of time.

***

As they drove, Danny asked, "How much longer?" He must have asked her a hundred times.

Michelle laughed at him. "You sound like a little kid. We still have another half hour. I warned you how long this trip would take."

Danny drove, following Michelle's directions as they entered the eastern side of Houston. He glanced over at her; her beauty, beside him, overwhelmed him. He reached up and stroked her soft cheek, so thankful that she chose to be his girlfriend. Honestly, Danny was happy to spend time with Michelle without sex. He looked back and realized he pushed way too fast in that area. Without the pressure of intimacy, he and Michelle became best friends. They relished the time of truly getting to know each other. Their powerful connection created the to struggle resist each other from the start. The two of them still kissed and made out for long stretches of time, but Danny pulled away before Michelle sensed any pressure to give in to him.

After everything they had been through, and meeting with Angela and Mark together, the two of them did not take their relationship for granted. The communication between their counselors had also helped deepen their relationship. Mark and Angela had them working on couples' therapy so that they could work on their individual issues together.

Danny confessed to Michelle his feelings of always trying to be perfect for everyone around him, including her. Mark had helped him to see how those expectations had gradually happened as he grew up and became the football hero of his small town. His complete honesty with her made Michelle express how much more she loved him.

Michelle continued to work through her people-pleasing complex with her brother, Jeff, and her desire to obey him because of the parent figure he was in her life. She learned the importance of freeing herself from his control. Danny was proud of her. However, it remained a work in progress. Danny felt some anxiety because he wasn't sure if Jeff would dissuade Michelle with his words while he was there.

"Take the exit onto this road," Michelle pointed out, and he turned on his signal to take the exit ramp off of the interstate. "Why don't you let me drive the rest of the way since there are some tricky turns to my house?"

"Yes ma'am," Danny teased, knowing it drove Michelle crazy as he pulled into a gas station. After slapping him playfully on the arm, they switched places. Danny detained her before she put the car into gear and she turned toward him in surprise as he leaned toward her and kissed her thoroughly.

"What was that for?" Michelle asked, gasping for a breath.

Danny entwined their fingers together. "Your house is going to be full of both of our families, so we won't have much time to do that. I want to take advantage of it while we can."

Michelle leaned toward him and smiled. "I certainly won't argue with you about that."

Their kiss became deeper, and Danny wrapped her tightly in his arms. She shook her head in wonder. "Wow!"

"Wow," Danny repeated. "I love you, Michelle."

"I love you, too." Michelle replied. Thankfully, Danny knew not to press too far with either of them.

Chapter 22

Ten minutes later, they pulled into the driveway of a lovely two story home. Michelle's parents both stepped out of the front door. Danny had spoken to them over the phone, but this was their first time meeting each other in person.

"We are so glad your family could join us," Michelle's mom said as she wrapped her arms around her daughter.

"Thank you for inviting us, Mrs. Walters," Danny replied as she pulled him in for a hug as soon as she released Michelle.

With a gentle smile, Michelle's mom said, "Please call me Judy."

Danny was thankful not to answer her because the thought of it seemed disrespectful. Michelle's dad shook his hand vigorously, preventing him from forming any kind of reply.

Michelle's dad said, "Thank you for taking care of our girl. It's difficult living so far away and not being able to get there quickly."

Michelle snorted before she said, "The distance surely didn't stop Jeff!"

Both of her parents chuckled in reply. "That is very true. Both of you, come inside," Judy said.

Danny shouldered both of their bags and he followed them into the house.

"We're so excited your family can join us!" Judy continued talking as they walked up the stairs.

"They should be here tomorrow afternoon," Danny answered. The following day happened to be Wednesday. He continued by saying, "Unfortunately, they will need to leave soon after dinner on Thursday because my dad has to drive to Houston to meet the team for the championship game on Friday. My mom and sister will also go with him."

Danny actually felt relieved that he didn't have to attend the game on Friday. He was learning how to let go of specific expectations from his family and the people within his community. Danny shared with them the boundaries he established, and his parents offered support. Both of them shouldered guilt for placing too much pressure on Danny's shoulders throughout his life. Michelle offered to go with him to the game if he really wanted to go, but he told her he was happy to stay there with her family.

Michelle led the way to her room, decorated in pink and yellow with a canopy over the bed. Setting her things down, she said, "Jeff's old room is across the hall."

Danny followed her as he turned on the lights to a room decorated in blues and reds. Jeff would join them on Thursday for the meal, but he would go back to his apartment for the night.

"We'll let you kids get settled in," Michelle's mom said as she began walking back toward the stairs. "Come on down when you are ready and you can have a snack."

"Okay, mom," Michelle said, and she turned to follow behind her mom. Danny reached for her and pulled her into his arms. "What are you doing?" Michelle whispered.

"Kissing you again," Danny said as he pulled her to a corner that couldn't be seen in the hallway. As his lips touched hers, Michelle sighed in contentment as she melted against him and allowed him to kiss her passionately. Danny kissed the side of her face and down her neck as she whispered, "We really should stop."

"Mmm.." he said as his mouth found hers again.

Michelle finally pushed him back and said, "I'm serious. If we don't eventually go down there, my mom will come up here again."

"Okay, okay," Danny groaned, and he kissed her one last time before pulling back and saying, "Lead the way."

As they reached the bottom of the stairs, Danny turned and studied her. He noticed an expression on Michelle's face. Danny paused for a moment. "What's on your mind? Why does your face look like that?"

Michelle wrapped her arms around his neck since they had the entryway to themselves. "It's difficult to be consistent with our deal that we shouldn't make love during this time."

"You're telling me," Danny said as he glanced around before kissing Michelle once more. However, they heard her parents nearby in the den. Both of them pulled back, but Michelle held Danny's hand as they walked in to join her mom and dad. Neither of her parents noticed.

The rest of the afternoon and evening turned out wonderful. Michelle's parents took them out to dinner and Jeff drove straight from work to join them. Danny and Jeff shook hands. Danny remembered Jeff's apology before he left to drive back to his apartment. Danny had been gracious in accepting his apology, and Jeff accepted him as part of their family now. It was a start to a lovely time spent with their families celebrating the holiday.

Sunday arrived, and they began the return trip to school after the week at her family's home.

Michelle's mind continued to turn over and over as she wondered if she and Danny were ready to be more intimate again. Her distraction didn't go unnoticed by him. It was almost as if he could tell she wasn't ready to discuss it. He held her hand, so she squeezed it and smiled at him. Michelle fell deeper in love with him these past weeks, and it was a more solid emotion without the intimacy and sex. She experienced the feeling of being not just loved, but also cherished. His restraint and respect for her wishes deepened Michelle's feelings for him. All she had to do was tell him what she wanted, and he always agreed.

Sometimes Michelle questioned if was he trying to be

perfect. His typical answer became, "I try not to, but I always aim to please you. You're much harder to refuse because I love you so much." Michelle found it hard to continue her request that they abstain from sexual activity. Her love for Danny deepened as he showered her with love and attention on the many dates they had been on. His promise to date her properly had been more than fulfilled.

She recalled one morning when she found a note taped to her dorm room door. It was a lovely note from Danny expressing his love for her. When she attended one of his basketball games, a single red rose occupied the bleachers where she and her friends sat. The tag had her name on it. Of course, Hannah and Jackie rubbed the gesture in her face, giving her a hard time. As Danny raced down the court, his eyes landed on her and he winked at her. She almost swooned on the spot, egging on Hannah and Jackie's glee.

This past week, they spent several nights cuddling close on her parents' couch while watching Christmas movies. Michelle learned that wrapped in his arms became one of her favorite places to be. He made her feel so safe, and twice their kisses grew more passionate. However, Danny remained a gentleman, and he pulled away. Michelle recognized his action as fulfilling his commitment to not pressure her. Michelle felt certain that Danny was the love of her life. She didn't need to date other people to realize it, and she experienced thankfulness that he was the one and only guy she ever dated.

Danny drove at the moment. He glanced over at

Michelle with a question in his eyes. "Are you okay?"

Michelle's eyes softened with love as she saw the genuine concern in his eyes. "I realize I've been preoccupied, but I promise that it's not anything bad."

"Okay," Danny commented, keeping his eyes on the road.

Michelle sighed and whispered, "Danny, I can't wait until we can have sex again. I promise these feelings are all inside of me and that I do not feel any pressure from you."

Danny's eyes darkened, but he said nothing other than, "Go on..."

"I know you are the love of my life, Danny Peterson. The time spent at my family's house helped me to see that. Because of that, my desire for you has deepened and I'm ready to move on to more." Michelle's voice sounded firm, but it tapered off to a whisper again.

Danny swallowed hard. "What are you saying?"

Michelle breathed out, "I want to be with you in that way again. I'm not sure if we should talk to Angela and Mark first to see their thoughts on how we've grown together. But the past few nights, I've not wanted to stop kissing you."

"Michelle..." Danny began. "You're killing me here. I'm driving and I want nothing more than to stop this car and kiss you."

"Okay," Michelle murmured. "Why don't you?"

Thankfully, the next exit had several places for Danny to pull in and park the car. He moved to the back of a fast-food restaurant parking lot in an obscure location.

After he parked the car, he moved as if in slow motion.

Danny turned toward Michelle, took both of her hands in his, and lifted them to his lips, where he kissed each individual finger. He didn't take his eyes off of hers as he did, and Michelle's insides melted into a puddle. Then Danny pulled her closer, and he cradled her face. His hands were so large that his fingers fanned into her hair. He leaned toward her, and his gentle kiss expressed his longing. Want overcame him as he deepened the kiss. As Michelle's mouth opened in invitation, his tongue crept inside. When he pulled back, they were both out of breath with intense expressions on their faces.

"Oh, my!" Michelle gasped. "That's even more intense than before!"

Danny studied her before he whispered, "How was it? I want to know your thoughts before we do anything more."

Michelle reached up and caressed his hair as she exhaled. "It was one of the most wonderful kisses you've ever given me. I believe it felt wonderful since I'm certain of my feelings for you. And I want much more."

She experienced shock at the tears in Danny's eyes, and she wanted to ask what was wrong. He spoke before she could. "I'm thankful for these weeks of abstaining. I have cherished getting to know you and I am certain about my feelings for you as well. I love you, Michelle!"

"Danny, I love you, too!" she whispered back.

After a few more kisses, they went into the restaurant for a break from the car. They stocked up on snacks for the rest of the drive before they got back on the road again.

***

Once they arrived back, Danny couldn't sleep that night. He didn't sense that it had anything to do with anxiety. Michelle's admission of being ready for more intimacy filled him with an emotion he couldn't identify. His heart was beating intently because of it. Danny rejoiced to learn that she was ready because he felt the same way. However, his thoughts took a more permanent turn and he wondered if his feelings related to it. He took the time to speak with both her dad and Jeff while Michelle worked with her mom in the kitchen. Most people thought asking a father's permission to be old-fashioned, but Danny believed that the tradition was warranted with all that happened with Jeff. Danny pondered back over the conversation on Friday afternoon.

At first, Jeff had argued and objected, but his dad stopped at him. Danny's heart swelled even more as he remembered the words of Michelle's dad.

"Jefferson, you've interfered enough in their relationship. Michelle is twenty years old. By the time they get married, she will be twenty-one. This is no longer a decision for either you or I to make." Mr. Walters looked at Danny. "You make my daughter happy. I appreciate you coming to us and talking to us about it. You know we will support you, but the decision needs to be Michelle's and not ours. We've coddled her enough. We want her to decide for herself."

"Thank you, sir," Danny said, shaking his hand.

Danny's heart leapt at the idea of forever with Michelle, and thoughts of proposing were foremost in his mind.

***

The next day, Danny and Michelle walked together to the counseling center. They had one-on-one appointments, but they tried scheduling them at the same time. The two of them enjoyed talking about their sessions as soon as they finished. Mark and Angela had both encouraged them to be open and honest with each other.

The office was a split level, so the two of them went separate directions toward their counselor's office.

Angela inquired, "How did your Thanksgiving go?" Your families celebrated together, right?"

Michelle's eyes turned dreamy and her shoulders relaxed more than Angela had ever seen since she started. "It was wonderful. Our families hit it off. Danny's parents invited my family to come the day after Christmas to visit them."

"Michelle, that's wonderful. How did Jeff behave while you were there?"

"He seemed more relaxed I had ever seen before. He and Danny's dad hit it off, talking about football. Jeff has always been a fan of all levels of football-high school, college, and professional."

Angela smiled. "How did that make you feel?"

"Honestly, I worried about it at first. I questioned

whether the real Jeff lurked below, searching for a time to attack our relationship. But the conversations we've had about trust came to mind and I realized I need to trust Jeff just as much as I trust Danny." Michelle's eyes beamed with pride. She sat taller in her seat with her chin high.

Angela teared up. "I am so proud of you, Michelle. You have come so far in working on yourself. Of all my patients, I feel you have learned more about yourself than any of my others."

Michelle leaned forward. "I can't thank you enough. I believe that your faith in me helped me to strive toward healing my insides." She held up her hands. "I realize I am not done and I have so much further to go."

"We are all a work in progress," Angela said. "How are things with Danny?"

"Fantastic," Michelle smiled. "The weekend with our families only deepened our feelings for each other." Michelle paused hesitantly.

"What's on your mind?" Angela asked.

Michelle exhaled loudly and her shoulders visibly tensed. "I'm not used to talking with someone about this."

"You can talk to me about anything. You should be aware of that by now."

"I know." Michelle smiled. "I'm ready to get back to deeper intimacy with Danny. I talked to him about it on the way home."

Angela smiled. "That's marvelous. But since I am your counselor, I will give you some advice."

"Sure," Michelle said, looking directly at Angela with raised brows.

Angela touched Michelle's hand. "I'm happy for you to grow in your relationship with Danny. The two of you have been doing great work on yourselves and as a couple."

"But..." Michelle said.

Angela said, "It's wonderful to express yourself with someone you love. My advice is not to lose who you are. Sometimes that type of expression makes us lose a part of ourselves if you aren't careful." Angela leaned forward. "Keep being Michelle. Don't change who you are, okay?"

Michelle nodded. "Thank you for speaking so candidly with me. I promise I won't."

At the other end of the hallway, Mark and Danny spoke about mindfulness, breathing exercises and how Danny had grown considerably because of his willingness to work on himself.

"How are things with Michelle?" Mark asked.

"Wonderful," Danny said.

Mark looked at him. "Wonderful, how?"

"The more I learn about her, the deeper I fall in love with her. Seeing her with her family and in her childhood home helped me to learn more about why she is who she is." Danny grinned as he gazed in the distance.

Mark smiled. "So, are you happy about this pause in your relationship?"

Danny nodded. "It's been the best thing for us. I realize

now that I pushed too hard when we first started going out. I'm glad Michelle took this time to learn about herself. Honestly, it made me think about myself."

Mark's smile widened. "What have you learned about yourself?"

"I learned I don't want to become a coach like my dad," Danny said.

Mark's eyes widened. "Go on..."

Danny hooked one leg over the other. "I want to become an elementary teacher. When I worked with younger kids my senior year of high school, I felt a deep passion for it. Don't get me wrong, I want to coach, just not full time. I've concluded that I can coach on the side. I can do that while teaching younger children full time."

Mark laughed. "Congratulations, Danny! I'm so glad you've come to realize where you need to focus."

"I can't thank you enough for all the time with you. I would still be clueless if I didn't make time to come and see you when I did." Danny's voice deepened with emotion at his last words.

"I'm glad I could be here to help." Mark said. He stood, and Danny always felt down when their time concluded.

"Don't get me wrong," Danny said. "I still have a lot of work to do on myself."

Mark clapped him on the shoulder. "We all do. You will work on yourself for the rest of your life!"

When Danny and Michelle walked out, the two of them reached for one another at the same time. The kiss held the promise of long-lasting love.

Epilogue

Christmas was in the air when Michelle and Danny made it back to school after the Thanksgiving weekend with their families. Both Danny and Michelle remained busy with projects and preparing for final exams. They spent as many moments together as they could. Danny also had basketball games to complete for this season. With finals week finally here, they looked forward to a reduced workload once it was over.

Once they came back from Christmas break, Michael proposed to Hannah and they were now engaged. The two of them would begin planning their wedding for next December, which would be in Hannah's hometown. Jackie, Michelle, Jenny, and Suzanne would be bridesmaids while Hannah's sister, Denise, would serve as her maid of honor. Alex, Danny and James would be groomsmen along with Michael's childhood friend, another Michael. From what Michelle gathered, it would be a grand event. Hannah complained often about her mother's desire to make their wedding a tremendous event. Michelle couldn't help but wonder what her own wedding would be like. She stopped, clutching her chest. This was the first time she considered a permanent relationship with Danny. She felt a tingle of excitement at the prospect of being with such a wonderful man for the rest of her life.

***

The Saturday before Christmas break, Danny and Michelle took time out to go on a much needed date. Danny reserved a table at the restaurant at the lake, which had become their favorite place to go.

Michelle sat in Danny's truck, holding his hand as they cruised the thirty-minute drive to the restaurant.

"I'm so glad we can do this tonight," Michelle commented.

Danny squeezed her hand and replied, "We need a night just for the two of us."

"Yes," Michelle agreed. "A night away from the library and textbooks."

"Are you ready for your finals?" Danny said, squeezing her hand again.

Michelle exhaled, and her grip tightened. "I think so. I will definitely cram more this week, but I think I am ready. What about you?"

"I think so," Danny commented. "That class that Hannah, Suzanne and I share involved a gigantic project. I couldn't have gotten it done without their help." He turned the truck into the parking lot of the restaurant and Michelle gasped at the Christmas decorations.

"I forgot how beautiful it is at Christmas," she commented as Danny helped her out of the truck.

"You're beautiful tonight," Danny whispered as he kissed the top of her head. She cuddled against him with his arm wrapped around her waist.

"Thank you. You don't look so bad yourself!" Michelle leaned back and Danny leaned down to kiss her softly. The two of them enjoyed dressing up when the opportunity arose.

They enjoyed a lovely seafood dinner and dessert. Danny and Michelle enjoyed swaying together on the dance floor before they realized how late it was.

As Danny guided Michelle out the door, she noticed a familiar vehicle in the parking lot. "That looks just like Michael's car, doesn't it?" Her brow puckered in bewilderment.

Danny mumbled something, but Michelle didn't understand what he said. He glanced down, and in just a few seconds, she thought his expression looked different. "Are you okay?" She asked as she studied his face.

Finally looking at her, Danny said, "Would you like to take a walk down to the lake?" He stood straight and Michelle wondered at how formal his voice sounded.

It felt chilly, but not bitterly cold. "That sounds wonderful, but is something on your mind?" Michelle repeated.

Danny was definitely hiding something as he spoke without looking at her. "You just look so beautiful tonight. I'm not ready for the night to end."

"It's not because I'm staying at your place, remember?" Michelle was perplexed by his odd behavior.

Danny didn't reply, and they walked, following the path to the lake. The twinkle lights reflecting on the water, made it even more beautiful. Danny tugged on Michelle's hand in front of a lovely bench and gestured for her to sit. She wanted to comment about sitting instead of walking, because his suggestion was a walk. However, she remained silent.

Instead of placing his arm around her, Danny sat forward on the bench. "Michelle," he began. His face was pale and Michelle wondered if he was getting sick.

She started to speak when he turned and placed a finger over her lips.

"I am so thankful that you finally talked to me and gave me a chance two months ago. I'm thankful that you gave us a chance. You are the piece of me that was missing. I always wondered why I never felt satisfied when I dated in high school. Now I know I was waiting for you." Danny's knee bounced, and Michelle noticed a slight sheen of moisture on his upper lips.

She started to question him a second time when Danny suddenly knelt on the ground in front of her. Michelle's jaw dropped and her heart began palpitating. "What are you doing?"

Then Danny smiled up at her and holding a box with a ring inside of it. "Michelle Walters, I love you so much. Will you marry me?"

Gasping, Michelle's hands came to her mouth and her eyes became huge. Tears sprang to her eyes and she couldn't move.

The way Danny gazed up at her would be a memory

that would burn in her mind for the rest of her days. Finally, she put her hands on his shoulders and she said, "Yes. Yes, I will marry you."

Danny pulled her to stand, and he slid the ring out and onto Michelle's finger. Then he pulled her as closely as possible. Danny kissed her like there was no tomorrow.

As they embraced, Michelle heard cheering to the side. When she pulled back, she saw Hannah, Michael, Jackie, Jennifer, Alex and Suzanne rushing toward them, yelling, "Congratulations!"

"I knew that was Michael's car!" Michelle exclaimed as her friends grabbed her in a group hug. "Where on earth have you been that we didn't see you in the restaurant?"

"Oh, we were there," Jackie commented. "The two of you were so caught up in each other that you didn't even notice."

"I would have seen you!" Michelle insisted.

"We sat in the back room," Suzanne answered. "When Danny told us his plan to propose, we didn't want to miss it!"

Michelle and Danny had been separated by the congratulations by their friends. He came and anchored her to his side as Michelle said, "Thank you for being here. You are the best friends in the world!"

The group walked back inside to the back room that their friends had reserved. They ordered hot chocolate and coffee to warm up. Michelle admired the gorgeous ring Danny had chosen for her. His hand did not leave hers even when he talked with Michael and Alex. He had already moved her chair closer to his and when she nestled up against him; he wrapped his arm around her shoulders. The servers were closing the restaurant when they finally realized that they needed to leave to go back to the university.

***

Once they made it back to the campus, Michelle went to Danny's apartment. She remembered James' plan to stay at his girlfriend's house a town over. He and Danny celebrated earlier in the week when Danny shared his plan to propose to Michelle.

"Wait a minute, young lady," Danny said as he moved around to the passenger side of the truck. After he helped Michelle out, he picked her up and carried her to his front door.

"Danny," Michelle chuckled. "This is supposed to happen after we are married."

"I need the practice," he answered as he unlocked the door and carried her into his room. A vase of a dozen roses sat on his bedside table.

"Danny," Michelle breathed with wide eyes as she gazed at the lovely blooms. "Thank you!"

"You're welcome" Danny lowered Michelle to the ground where he kissed her passionately.

"What if I said *no* tonight?" she teased.

Danny nuzzled her neck. "You wouldn't have said *no*."

Michelle tried to sound miffed, however she didn't manage to pull it off. "You're so sure of yourself, aren't you?"

Danny pulled back an inch, gazed into her eyes. "Yes, I am." Then he kissed her passionately and all teasing left Michelle's brain.

Danny kissed her with fervor. He moaned and tugged her even closer. With his hands tight on her hips, he lifted her off the ground, her mouth level with his. Michelle surprised him by kissing him fervently. Danny groaned a second time at her responsiveness. Then Michelle sighed as Danny's hands cradled her face and one hand moved down her neck to her shoulder.

Upon hearing her sigh, his hand plunged under her hair to tickle the back of her neck and he gripped her neck lightly as he angled their mouths to deepen the kiss. He peppered kisses down the side of her face to her neck. Michelle shivered as Danny's tongue joined his kisses, leaving wet trails on the back of her neck.

Danny murmured, "My word, I love your skin." He moved around behind her and he lifted her hair to kiss the back of her neck as one arm wrapped around her waist from behind her. His hand trailed down to the hem of her dress. Danny paused and whispered, "Are you sure you're ready?"

When Michelle nodded impatiently, he lifted her dress up over her head. Throwing it on the floor, his hands reached around for Michelle's breasts from behind as he continued feasting on her neck and her shoulders.

Michelle's pulse felt haywire from the erotic sensations rushing through her. "Danny," she said, unable to speak coherently as his mouth kissed her jumping pulse.

His fingers slipped under her bra strap and he lowered it. Danny inhaled sharply at seeing the curve of her breast in the cup of her bra. "You are so beautiful," he whispered as his fingers rubbed the fullness of her breast as it protruded out of her bra.

Overwhelmed by so many sensations and emotions, Michelle sighed and she whimpered again from his light touch. She tried to reach around and release the clasp on her bra, but Danny's hand stopped her. The hand that was on her stomach drifted down to her pantyhose and his fingers slipped under the material tickling across the lower parts of her stomach.

"One of my favorite things is undressing you," he said against the skin of her neck. His lips continued kissing every part of her neck and her shoulders.

Michelle whimpered a third time since she was unable to touch him. She attempted to turn around to kiss Danny, but he said, "In a minute. I need to love you first," and he continued the slow torture to where Michelle had a hard time remaining on her feet.

His fingers pushed the bra strap all the way down and off of her arm. Again, he reached around and caressed the soft skin of her breast protruding from her bra.

Danny did the same thing with the other bra strap and finally, he turned Michelle into his embrace so that he could touch both breasts while kissing her deeply again. With his tongue plunging into her mouth, his right hand unclasped her bra, unveiling her breasts completely.

"Michelle," Danny breathed as if he had never seen her before.

Impatient with him, Michelle raised his shirt over his head, and she threw it to the floor. Then she pressed her breasts against his chest attempting to get near him, and Danny thought he might die from the sensation of her nipples pressing against his chest. "You feel so good," he whispered as his thumbs rubbed across the hardened peaks.

His hands continued fondling them as his mouth found hers again. "So wonderful," he breathed against her mouth. His thumbs continued to rub each breast.

Danny pulled back, and he began pushing Michelle's pantyhose off of one leg and then the other. Then he removed her panties along with his other clothing.

He gently placed her on his bed before climbing onto it. He gave her another kiss before he lowered his mouth to one breast and he pulled a nipple into his mouth. Then he moved to the other breast, feasting on them equally. Michelle writhed beneath him.

Michelle gasped in ecstasy. She caressed all of Danny that she was able to reach from his back to his chest, down to his stomach and below, causing him to moan softly.

Danny kissed her breasts again and down to her stomach before moving back to her mouth. His fingers found her sensitive place between her legs as he gently touched her, and he felt amazed at her readiness for him.

He moved in between her legs and Danny quickly opened the foil packet of a condom and slid it on before pushing inside of her. "Michelle," he whispered as he took both of her hands and interlaced his fingers with hers.

Danny pulled her hands above her head as he pulled a nipple into his mouth. Michelle was overcome by the sensations raging inside of her as he began to move.

Danny moved in gentle motions, but he created enough friction that both of them gasped in pleasure.

He sensed Michelle's orgasm before moving into his own. Danny collapsed against her, both in exhaustion and exhilaration.

"I love you," they both said at the same time and they laughed softly together. Danny pulled Michelle against him as he kissed the top of her head.

"That felt absolutely exquisite," he commented, still slightly breathless. "It felt like it was our first time together."

Michelle chuckled softly, and she replied, "I have a confession to make."

Danny squeezed her close. "You know you can confess anything to me."

Michelle murmured, "I thought about this all day, too. It was very hard to concentrate on studying and completing that gigantic project that is due next week."

Danny said, "So you didn't feel pressure from me?"

"Absolutely not!" Michelle exclaimed. "I've been wanting this for a couple of weeks now." She leaned up and his attention diverted from her face because he noticed her cleavage as her breasts fell upon his chest. "There have definitely been some deeper emotions."

Danny ran one finger in between the cleavage and he said, "I love you, Michelle."

Michelle leaned in to kiss him and she shivered from

the sensation of his fingers. "I love you, Danny."

After they enjoyed a second time, he held Michelle's hand with the ring, studying it. Her head pillowed on his chest. "This ring was made for your finger."

"I love it so much and I love you," Michelle whispered.

Danny pulled her closer to him, and they fell asleep wrapped around each other for the rest of the night.

***

She woke up to Danny making her breakfast, and then they called their families. Michelle had to move the phone away from her ear when Beth screamed so loudly that all of east Texas must have heard it! The two of them promised to celebrate together when Michelle's family came for Christmas.

When Michelle made it back to her room on Sunday afternoon, her roommates had it decorated with an enormous banner saying, *Congratulations*. She was engulfed in hugs the moment she stepped in the door.

Hannah, Jackie, and Michelle celebrated in their room with sparkling grape juice and delicious snacks. Suzanne had been called along with Jennifer, and the five of them relaxed together. Michelle was extremely grateful for the friends she made in college. These women were truly lifelong friends, and she knew she could always rely on them. She would be there for them as well.

Michelle hadn't really cared before today, but she asked Hannah about her wedding details. Hannah shared books and magazines with her and they spent the rest of the afternoon poring over them. Even though her wedding was a year away, it didn't hurt to look and think about ideas for herself. She had never considered a wedding and how she wanted it to be, even as a little girl. Jeff's hindrance to her dating had her wondering if she ever would get married. Her dreams had far exceeded what she imagined. It all focused on this amazing man she would marry.

About the author

About the Author:

Liz Hamilton lives with her husband in central Georgia. Having spent most of her life growing up in Texas, she was able to use her experience of living there to help in writing this series of books. She has two children, Hannah and Caleb. She has two dogs, Walter and Chloe. Balancing a full time teaching position as a middle school Language Arts teacher, she was able to use her passion for writing to publish her first book and she hopes to make this a second career when she retires from education. Her hobbies include reading, cooking, walking her dogs and traveling with her family.

Thanks

Thank you to my husband and best friend in life. Thank you to my two kids, Hannah and Caleb, for your support in my pursuing this as a dream. There were times I bounced ideas off of all of you and appreciated the feedback you were able to give me. Thank you to All Write Well for your mentorship through this overwhelming but exciting process. I appreciate your guidance throughout all of it. Thank you to Krystal Craiker for your support and feedback. Finally, thank you to all of my readers for supporting my dream.

Connect with me

Connect with Me:

Follow me on my Liz Hamilton Facebook page or lizhamilton0801 on Instagram.

Find my paperback using the QR code.

www.ingramcontent.com/pod-product-compliance
Lightning Source LLC
Chambersburg PA
CBHW030131310726
48970CB00005B/1381